ChangelingPress.com

Renegade/ Wire Duet

Harley Wylde

Renegade/Wire Duet

Harley Wylde

All rights reserved.
Copyright ©2020 Harley Wylde

ISBN: 9798673939420

Publisher:
Changeling Press LLC
315 N. Centre St.
Martinsburg, WV 25404
ChangelingPress.com

Printed in the U.S.A.

Editor: Crystal Esau
Cover Artist: Bryan Keller

The individual stories in this anthology have been previously released in E-Book format.

No part of this publication may be reproduced or shared by any electronic or mechanical means, including but not limited to reprinting, photocopying, or digital reproduction, without prior written permission from Changeling Press LLC.

This book contains sexually explicit scenes and adult language which some may find offensive and which is not appropriate for a young audience. Changeling Press books are for sale to adults, only, as defined by the laws of the country in which you made your purchase.

Table of Contents

Renegade (Devil's Boneyard MC 6)..............................4
   Chapter One..5
   Chapter Two 19
   Chapter Three..33
   Chapter Four..48
   Chapter Five 61
   Chapter Six...73
   Chapter Seven 85
   Chapter Eight...97
   Chapter Nine 106
   Chapter Ten 118
   Chapter Eleven..130
   Epilogue 139
Wire (Dixie Reapers MC 13) 147
   Chapter One...148
   Chapter Two 161
   Chapter Three..175
   Chapter Four..191
   Chapter Five 203
   Chapter Six...214
   Chapter Seven 229
   Chapter Eight...239
   Chapter Nine 249
   Chapter Ten 265
   Epilogue 278
   Harley Wylde 288
Changeling Press E-Books 289

Renegade (Devil's Boneyard MC 6)
Harley Wylde

Darby: At fifteen, I thought I knew everything. Having been in foster care all my life, not much scared me. I'd already faced monsters parading around as upstanding citizens. But life hadn't prepared me for a biker who would lure me in, kidnap me, and abuse me for five years. I got Fawn out of it, my precious girl, and a lot of bad memories. Being tossed into a dumpster and left to die wasn't at the top of my list, but Renegade found me. I've never had a man be kind to me or my daughter before -- especially not a biker -- and I'm not sure what to think. I want to trust him, but I don't want to give him my heart only to have him turn out like every other man I've ever known. It would break me.

Renegade: I lost my family a long time ago, and I vowed I'd never have another. I still have Nikki, my baby sis, and that's enough. My club is a family, but that's different. I trust them, and in my own way I love them, but it's not the same as having a wife and kids. I'll never go down that path. Then I found Fawn and her mother, Darby, thrown away like unwanted trash. Yeah, Fate's laughing her ass off right now. They're in my home, and slowly worming their way under my skin. Hearing their story is enough to make my blood boil and send rage flooding through me. I'll exact revenge for all they've suffered, and then they'll truly be free, able to move on without fear of being taken again. Except... I might not want to let them go.

Chapter One

Renegade

I fucking hated this time of year. The pumpkins and shit didn't bother me, it was more the memories attached to the month of October that got to me. Today especially. My parents and brother had been gone for fourteen years but time didn't make the pain lessen any, which was why I was at the liquor store restocking my beer, rum, and picking up a bottle of vodka. Time didn't heal all wounds, but at least alcohol would numb me enough to make it through to tomorrow. I knew my sister, Nikki, still had trouble with this day as well, but she'd suffer on her own or with friends. I didn't see her as often as I'd like, but I tried to keep her away from the club. She garnered too much interest when she came around, and I didn't want to beat on my brothers.

I set the items on the counter and the woman popped her gum and held out her hand. I took out my wallet and pulled out a few twenties, but she shook her head.

"ID."

"Are you fucking kidding me right now?" I demanded. "I'm forty-four years old and I don't look old enough to buy this shit?"

"Sorry. I don't make the rules." She pointed to the sign behind her. *We have the right to refuse service for any reason. ID will be required for all purchases.*

I growled as I jerked my license from my wallet and threw it on the counter. The last thing I needed right now was someone hassling me over my purchase. It wasn't the first time I'd been carded and wouldn't be the last, I just wasn't in the mood to deal with it right now. While it was the law to card everyone, I'd noticed none of my brothers who actually looked their age ever dealt with this shit.

The woman looked at the ID, scratched at the surface, and gave me one of those disbelieving looks.

"It's not a fake," I said. "Who the fuck fakes the age of forty-four?"

My mother had once said that there would come a time I would like looking younger than my actual years. So far, that hadn't proven true. It was fucking annoying.

She handed the license back and took my money, then rang up the alcohol. By the time I was walking out of the store, I was livid, but I knew it wasn't really the woman's fault. She'd been doing her job and not intentionally hassling me. It was just this shitty day. I'd brought my truck, knowing what I wanted to buy wouldn't fit in the saddlebags on my bike, and stashed the rum, vodka and two cases of beer in the back seat, then pulled a can from one of the boxes. Before I could pop the top, a sound drew my attention. A scuff or scratching noise. I set the beer down and slowly crept toward the side of the building, pausing at the corner. Might just be a stray scrounging for food, or it could be trouble. A liquor store at night had a tendency to draw in the bad elements. Wouldn't be the first time the place had been robbed, or someone had been held up in the parking lot.

There was a shuffle and something kicked a can. Dog? I listened harder and heard what sounded like a human's footsteps. I reached for the gun at the small of my back, pulling it before I edged around the building, my finger on the trigger guard of my Sig. Very little light pierced the darkness, but I saw a small shadow moving. It wasn't very big. I didn't know if I was about to be ambushed by someone trying to hide themselves, or if there was actually someone in need of help. Moving in closer, my heart nearly stopped when I saw the dirty face of a little girl. Long, red hair hung in a tangle down her back, and I noticed her feet were bare. A quick glance didn't show anyone else in the area, but I was hesitant to put away my weapon. Wouldn't be the first time some asshole used a kid to lure in a victim.

"Is your mom or dad here?" I asked, trying to keep my tone as non-threatening as possible.

The little girl pointed to the dumpster and began walking that way. She stopped in front of it and lifted a hand to the opening on top. I braced myself in case someone leapt from inside to attack, but as I neared the metal container and peered inside, my breath stalled in my lungs. Holy shit!

"That your sister?" I asked the girl.

She shook her head.

"Your momma?" I asked again, barely believing the woman who was likely dead was old enough to be a mother. Then again, maybe she just aged really well. At first glance, I'd thought she was maybe sixteen or seventeen. Wouldn't be the first time a kid had given birth, if she really was as young as she appeared, but I hoped that wasn't the case. Kids should have a chance to be exactly that -- kids.

The little girl nodded.

"All right. I'm going to put my gun away and I'm going to get your mom out of there. Can you step back so you don't get hurt?"

She stared at me a moment before shuffling back a step, then another. It was eerie that she hadn't said a word, but at least she'd obeyed. I climbed the side of the container and reached inside, pressing my fingers against the pulse point in the woman's throat. I exhaled sharply when I realized she was still alive, and carefully extracted her. She shivered in my arms, her body barely covered except for the dried blood and bruises coating her skin. Her clothes were cut or ripped, exposing enough of her that I worried what might have happened to her. I hoped whatever asshole had done this to her would suffer.

"I'm going to get your mom some help. Can you follow me to my truck?" I asked the little girl.

She slowly approached and reached out to grip my jeans. She held on as I carried her mother to the front parking lot. The door to my truck was still ajar. If it weren't for the club's colors I'd added to my tailgate, someone likely would have boosted it. Most people around here didn't want to fuck with the club and gave us a wide berth.

I balanced the woman as I shoved the alcohol to the floor, not even caring at this point if the damn vodka and rum busted other than the fumes it would create. Whatever these two had been through was far worse than the demons I fought on this day every year.

"Get in. I'm going to buckle your mom up front," I told the little girl.

She had trouble getting into the truck, so I opened the front door and made sure her mom was secure before lifting the tiny girl into the vehicle. I didn't know a lot about kids, but she felt a little too light and fragile. I made sure she was buckled, then hurried to the driver's side. As the dome light came on, I glanced at my front seat passenger and nearly froze. There was something familiar about her. Too fucking familiar, even though I couldn't remember where I'd seen her. It would come to me, but right now I needed to get her somewhere safe.

I pulled my phone from my pocket and dialed Scratch as I started the engine.

"Need your help, Pres," I said as I pulled out onto the street, not giving a shit that I was driving while I was on the phone.

"The kind that requires bail money?" he asked, knowing the significance of today.

"No. The kind that requires your wife and a doctor. Found a woman beat to hell and left for dead in a dumpster, and her kid, though the kid seems to be in better shape. I'm on my way to the compound now." I paused a moment. "I think I know the mom, but I can't remember how."

Scratch cursed. "Take her to your place. The clubhouse is too rowdy for a kid right now. I'll have Chansy head that way."

I disconnected the call and met the somber gaze of the little pixie in the back seat.

"I'm taking you to my place and a doctor will meet us there. We'll get your mom fixed up."

She still didn't say a word, which I thought was weird as fuck. Didn't kids talk non-stop? I knew Jackal's daughter had some issues when he'd first found out he was a dad, but that kid was a ball of energy that never quit nowadays. She'd chatter anyone's ear off if they sat still for half a second. And Scratch's kids were rather vocal too. Couldn't really compare the kid to Havoc's demon spawn. I'd never seen anything like her before, and everyone in the club gave Lanie a wide berth for good reason. Even Cinder backed down from that little hellion. It would be funny as shit, if we didn't all feel the same way.

"What's your name?" I asked, hoping to draw her out, and possibly learn who her mother was, but she just stared and didn't say a word. I hated puzzles, and this one was starting to bother me. I knew the woman. She was too young for me to have ever fucked her, but there was something... a pull of sorts.

Looked like I wouldn't get any answers from the kid. I hoped her mom came through and woke up to tell us what the fuck had happened to her. If she didn't make it, I had no clue what the hell to do with a kid. Call social services? I didn't like to think of entrusting her into the government's hands. They fucked shit up too often.

Since I had precious cargo, I made sure I obeyed the traffic laws as I made my way to the compound and the house Cinder had assigned to me. I'd have been content staying in something smaller, but right now I was glad for the extra space. The Prospect at the gate let me through and I went straight to my house, grateful to see the doc's vehicle already in the driveway. He walked over as I stepped out of the truck.

"Heard you found a damsel in distress," Dr. Chansy said.

"Something like that. Heard the little girl and went to check it out. The mom was in a dumpster. She's been cut and beat to hell from what I can tell."

He grimaced, but I saw the flash of anger in his eyes. Dr. Chansy was a good man, and he definitely didn't like it when someone abused a woman. None of us did. We might be outlaws, but that was a line even I wouldn't cross. Then again, if the woman was hurting other people, like the one responsible for hurting Scratch's adopted son, then all bets were off. She deserved whatever she got. Evil wore many faces. For all I knew, the woman I'd just saved had done bad things, but until I knew for certain, I'd give her the benefit of the doubt. The fact she was so fucking familiar made me think she was a good sort. If she'd harmed me or mine in some way, I'd have never forgotten. No, I knew her from somewhere else.

I opened the back door and the little girl cautiously slid across the seat and held out her hands. I lifted her, setting her down next to me. She took one look at the doc, then grabbed my leg and tried to hide behind me.

Dr. Chansy grinned. "Looks like she trusts you."

"Yeah, but not you."

He shrugged, but I could tell it bothered him. He'd never hurt a woman or kid, but the little sprite clinging to me didn't know that. She just saw a big man, and I'd be willing to bet it had been a man who had hurt her mom. If not more than one. I'd seen some violent women in my time, but this just felt like a man's handiwork. I opened the front door of the truck and heard Chansy hiss in a breath as he got his first look at the mom. Carefully, I lifted her from the vehicle and carried her into my home, her daughter clinging to my leg.

Thankfully, my home was all one floor. I took her to the only bedroom in the house that was furnished, other than my own. Easing her down onto the bed, I found that I was reluctant to let go. That sense of her being important to me filled me, a gut reaction to hold on and never let go. I forced myself to take a step back, careful not to step on the little girl. She peered around me to watch Dr. Chansy as he checked her mom's pupils, listened to her heart, and began checking over her injuries.

"I'll have to finish cutting her clothes off, but the blood has started to dry and they're sticking to her. Renegade, I need scissors, a big bowl of hot water, and some rags you don't mind getting bloody. After I get these clothes off her and clean her wounds, I'll have a better idea of how to treat her."

I nodded and moved to get the items, but the woman's daughter tightened her hold on my leg. Looking down, I saw her eyes were wide and fearful, and her face had gone even paler. She needed reassurance, but I wasn't the greatest when it came to kids. I hunkered down so I was closer to eye level with her.

"Sprite, I need to get some things so the doc here can help your mom. You can come with me if you want, but I need to leave the room to get them."

She shook her head so hard I thought she might hurt herself.

"It's okay. Just tell me where everything is," Dr. Chansy said. "It's obvious she doesn't trust anyone but you to be alone with her and her mom. Seeing the shape these two are in, it's understandable. She sees you as her hero."

I wasn't a hero.

"There's rags and towels in the hall closet. Large bowl is to the right of the sink in the upper cabinet, and scissors are in the butcher block."

Dr. Chansy smirked. "Nikki set up your home, didn't she?"

"Yeah."

He nodded. "Figured. You don't seem like the type to care about butcher blocks, linen closets, or the various prints I've seen hanging on your walls."

Without another word, he left to get the things he needed. The little girl wrapped her arms around my neck, and I stood, holding her close to me. I leaned against the wall by the bed, so she'd be close to her mom while we waited for Dr. Chansy to return. He came back to the room about fifteen minutes later with all the things he'd requested, then set about removing the woman's clothes and cleaning her enough that he could assess her wounds. Some of the dark spots I'd thought were bruises, ended up being dirt. Though her cuts had bled badly, most weren't as deep as I'd feared.

"I'm going to stitch a few of these. Since I don't know her name, I can't exactly call anything in to help with pain or infection. I brought a few samples of some medications with me that should help with those two concerns. I'll need something for her to wear when I'm finished," Dr. Chansy said. "I'm not sure the little girl should see her mom being sewn back together."

"There are a few T-shirts in the dresser that should work. They're old ones I don't wear anymore, so it doesn't matter if they get a little bloody."

"I'll bandage what I can, but there's a cut on her forearm and another on her calf that will have to be sutured," Dr. Chansy said.

With one last look at the woman on the bed, I carried the girl from the room. She made a strange noise similar to a whimper but not quite, and held out a hand to her mom, clearly not wanting to leave the room. I pulled the door mostly shut, enough that we couldn't see inside, but we could hear everything going on. It felt like Chansy took forever, but he finally stepped from the room.

"I left the pills on the bedside table. She'll need to take the antibiotic once a day, and the pain reliever every six hours as needed." Dr. Chansy glanced at the girl in my arms. "Are you hurt too?"

Her arms just tightened, but she wouldn't answer. I'd have to ask Clarity to come check her over. Surely she wouldn't be afraid of the VP's old lady. Hadn't met a sweeter woman in all my life. Well, except maybe Meg, Cinder's old lady, but since their son wasn't very old I didn't want to disturb them.

"I don't think she'll let you examine her, doc."

The man seemed resigned as he headed out, not even speaking another word to me. The way he walked, his shoulders drooped, it was like the weight of the world was pressing down on him. I didn't know anything about him outside of the help he offered the club, and he never volunteered information. His reaction to Fawn and the woman had me wondering what his story was, and whether or not anyone in the club knew his background.

I was about to pull my phone from my pocket when the front door opened again. Clarity and Scratch came in, their two boys trailing behind them. Caleb was Scratch's adopted son, and was already six years old and in first grade. The youngest, Noah, was only three and a half. Seeing the two boys must have eased the girl's fears because her hold on me slackened and I set her back down. The moment her feet touched the floor, she seemed hesitant, but the boys approached slowly, both smiling.

"I'm Caleb and this is my little brother Noah," he said.

She pressed her lips tight together and didn't respond. Caleb looked up at me, but I shrugged. I didn't have a clue why she wouldn't talk, and I didn't know her name. I'd thought maybe the kids would draw her out, but that didn't seem to be happening. Was she just scared or was it something more?

Clarity came forward and knelt in front of her. "My name is Clarity and I'm their mom. I brought over a clean set of clothes I got from the mom of a little girl and thought you might like a bath? I can help, if that's all right."

The little girl looked up at me and I gave her a nod, letting her know that it was safe to go with Clarity. She slowly reached for Clarity's hand and let my VP's woman lead her down the hall to the bathroom.

"Clothes came from Jackal and Josie, so don't worry about us dressing her in a stranger's things. They were too small for Allegra, but you know Josie doesn't like to throw things out," Scratch said. "What's the story on these two?"

"Not sure. The girl won't speak, and the mom is pretty rough. She hasn't woken, but Chansy treated her wounds, stitched a few that were deeper, and left some meds for her. I don't know who they are or where they came from. For all I know, I was supposed to find them." My brow furrowed. "I still feel like I know the mom, but she's so young I can't imagine where I'd have seen her."

"Since when do you believe in that cosmic shit like Fate? Thought it was all bullshit?" he asked. "Maybe you met her through Nikki. Are they close in age?"

"I don't believe in that crap. I was thinking more along the lines of them being a Trojan horse. Though now that you mention it, it's quite possible she went to school with Nikki."

Scratch rubbed a hand down his face and sighed heavily. "Boy, when are you going to learn that sometimes the surprises in life can be a gift? If Clarity hadn't tripped the alarm at the shop that day, if I hadn't gone to check it out, I'd never have found the best thing in my life."

"I'm not you, VP. I'm not the settling down type."

He grinned. "We'll see. I have a feeling those two were put in your path for a reason, and it wasn't to detonate like a damn bomb."

I seriously hoped he was wrong. A bomb I could handle. A woman and kid living in my home? That scared the shit out of me. My parents had an awesome marriage, from what I could tell, and were the perfect example of how a family should act. It was the idea of having something special like that, then losing it that terrified me.

Clarity and the little girl stepped out of the bathroom. Caleb and Noah started to move forward, but Scratch reached out to tug them back. The girl's wet hair hung down her back, and now that she was clean, I could see a few bruises along her arms and one on her face. The jeans Clarity had brought for her hid her legs from view, but the look on Clarity's face told me the girl was in rough shape. I pushed open the mom's door and let the little girl go inside. Clarity sagged against Scratch and spoke in a near whisper.

"You can see her ribs, and there are so many bruises. I didn't see any cuts, but it's apparent someone beat that poor girl and starved her." Clarity rubbed her face against Scratch's cut. "We have to help them. Whoever did that, they can't be allowed to get their hands on either of them again."

I knew Clarity had lived on the streets and had suffered abuse. Even if she hadn't, she was tenderhearted and wanted everyone to have a happy-ever-after. Scratch had been that for her and Caleb, but I didn't think I was the right man to save that woman and her kid. Getting them here was one thing. Taking care of them? I'd never been responsible for someone else. The state hadn't awarded me custody of Nikki when our parents died. Even though I'd been there for her as much as possible, she'd been raised by a foster family. They'd been nice, and hadn't abused her. She'd been one of the lucky ones. Or maybe it was me lurking over her shoulder with the weight of Devil's Boneyard at my back that had made them toe the line.

"They're safe here," Scratch promised his wife. "And Renegade is going to make sure of it."

My jaw tightened. "Is that an order?"

The smile Scratch gave me would have scared a lesser man. "You're damn right it is."

It felt like someone was driving nails into my coffin, sealing me inside to be buried alive. The thought of that woman and her kid depending on me? It was the stuff of nightmares. If I failed them, I wasn't sure I could live with myself. This was the one time I definitely couldn't fuck shit up. The fact I was hard didn't help. The moment I'd lifted that woman into my arms, my cock had taken an interest. It was sick and made me feel like the worst sort of man. She was beaten and bloody, but something about her weight in my arms, the curves of her pressed against me, had made something inside me stir and come to life.

After they left, I made sure the kid was asleep on the couch and her mom was still resting. I went into my room and shut the door, twisting the lock to keep them out of my space. I quickly stripped off my clothes and went to take a shower. The hot water should have relieved the tension, but the fact my dick was hard as fucking steel didn't help matters. What kind of sick bastard got hard over an unconscious woman?

I slammed my eyes shut in hopes of thinking of anyone else. The blonde at the clubhouse who always wanted in my pants, the raven-haired beauty at the coffee shop, but nothing worked. I grabbed the lube off the top shelf of the shower and slicked my palm before gripping my cock. Stroking it hard and fast, I wanted to banish the demons, to chase away the image of the woman down the hall. In my mind she was healthy and whole, smiling up at me as she knelt at my feet. I groaned as I pictured her taking my cock into her mouth, sucking me off. I jerked my dick faster, the images in my mind shifting to her lying on her back, legs spread and begging me to fuck her. I'd drive my cock into her wet pussy and fuck her until neither of us could walk.

I came with a groan, my cum splattering the shower wall, but it wasn't enough. My dick was still hard and I stared down at it in annoyance. What the ever loving fuck? It hadn't shown interest in anyone in months, and now I wanted some nameless woman who'd been left for dead?

I was one sick fuck.

I finished showering and went to bed. After tossing and turning, I ended up tugging one out twice more, and still couldn't fucking sleep. I had the horrible suspicion that my life had just changed and not in a way that I wanted.

Maybe she'd wake up and tell me to fuck off, to keep away from her. Or maybe she'd be a royal bitch and my dick would stop getting hard just thinking about her.

Even I didn't believe that. I snorted. I was fucked. Well and truly fucked, and not in the fun way.

Chapter Two

Darby

Pain. That was the first thing I noticed. Lots of pain. It hurt to breathe, and my head pounded like someone was beating on it with a sledgehammer. I struggled to open my eyes and wondered if the bastards would succeed in killing me next time. Fawn! My eyes flew open and I immediately regretted it. Spikes of pain shot through my head and I groaned, fighting back nausea.

"Easy," said a soft voice. "You're safe."

Safe? There was no such thing. Not with the Mayhem Riders MC. At least, not with the Nomads. The ones belonging to actual chapters seemed decent enough, from what little I'd witnessed, but if I'd ever breathed a word of what Fawn and I suffered at the hands of their brothers, it would have meant a death sentence for us. I couldn't risk it.

I managed to open my eyes, and blinked as I tried to remember where I'd been taken. Nothing seemed familiar. Slowly, I turned my head and met the gray gaze of a beautiful raven-haired woman. She smiled softly, and all I saw was genuine kindness in her eyes. There was something familiar about her, but I didn't know why.

"My name is Nikki. Nikki Adams. My brother found your daughter in an alley, and then discovered you in a dumpster. He brought you to his home and had a doctor treat you. There's medication you need to take, but you should probably eat something first."

I wasn't sure what to say to all that. It was hard to process all the words, but I made somewhat sense of them. Nikki Adams. I remembered someone at school by that name, but she'd been older than me. Could it be the same person? It was her coloring and her eyes that made memories surface, but otherwise she looked different from the girl I remembered.

"Where..." My throat felt like sandpaper.

"My brother, Renegade, is part of the Devil's Boneyard MC. You're at his home inside the compound. Whoever did this to you and your daughter, they won't reach you here."

Instead of her words inspiring a sense of safety, they only scared me more. I hadn't heard good things of the crew her brother ran with, and I didn't know if they hurt women or not. I remembered seeing her with a man around town and at the school. I hadn't known for sure if it was her brother, even though there had been whispers about it. Scandalous with him being a biker. Honestly, I'd thought he was hot, even though he'd been a lot older than me. Nikki seemed happy enough, but for all I knew it was a ruse to lull me into a false sense of security. I'd learned the hard way that I couldn't trust anyone. It had been drilled into my head since the day the Nomads had taken me. I'd only been fifteen at the time, and they'd managed to get me pregnant almost immediately. I didn't even know the father of my child, not with certainty though I had my suspicions, and was grateful she looked like me and hadn't inherited their mean-spiritedness.

"Who did this to you?" Nikki asked.

"Mayhem Riders," I croaked and I immediately wished I hadn't said anything. What if they were allies to this club? What if they gave us back to Boomer?

Nikki frowned and her mouth opened and shut, then she shot up out of the chair she'd been sitting on and rushed from the room. Only a minute or two seemed to pass before a tall, broad-shouldered man came inside, a glass of water in his hand. He handed it to me. When his gaze locked with mine, I remembered him. I'd seen him several times when he'd been hanging out with Nikki at the local burger place, and I'd had a huge crush on him. He'd been too old for me, but even as a teen I'd noticed how sexy he was, and he was still mouthwatering.

"Sip it so you don't get sick," he ordered.

I took a few small drinks, then held it out for him to take, even though I really wanted to chug the entire thing. I glanced around wondering where Fawn was hiding. Nikki said that her brother had found both of us. They hadn't hurt my baby, had they?

"Fawn?" I asked.

His brow furrowed. "Your daughter? Her name is Fawn?"

I nodded.

"She's in the living room watching cartoons," he said. "I haven't been able to get her to say a word. My sister, Nikki, tried too, and so did my VP's wife, Clarity. She's been bathed, by Clarity, and has clean clothes on."

My heart ached for my baby girl. She'd been through so much. I didn't know how much I could trust the men with this MC. While I knew that not all of the Mayhem Riders were bad, I had only ever heard of the exploits of the Devil's Boneyard. None of it good, but also none of it as horrible as abusing women and kids. Just because the woman, Nikki, had seemed nice, didn't mean we were truly safe here. I might have gone to the same school as her, but people changed over time, and we'd never exactly been friends. I'd just known *of* her and seen her around.

Nikki came in with a plate. Two slices of lightly buttered toast were lying on it. I accepted the plate, my stomach rumbling. I was starving, couldn't even remember the last time I'd eaten something. Glancing at the toast, I wondered if they'd fed my daughter.

"Fawn. Did she eat?" I asked, my voice still raspy.

"She had some eggs, toast, and bacon," the man said. "And I fed her pasta last night. I hope she doesn't have any food allergies."

"Not that I know," I said, grateful they'd taken such good care of Fawn. I nibbled the toast until I managed to eat both pieces, then drank more water. Renegade handed me some pills, and I stared at them, not sure if I should take them or not. Was he trying to drug me? That's how I'd gotten into this mess in the first place.

"Dr. Chansy left those for you. One is to keep your wounds from getting infected, and the other is a pain pill. You can take the pain one every six hours as needed. He couldn't call in a prescription since we didn't know who you are. These are samples that were delivered to his office in town," Renegade said.

"Darby. My name is Darby Gillis."

"It's nice to meet you, Darby, though I wish it were under other circumstances. Although, you seem familiar to me. I don't remember ever meeting a Darby, though." Renegade paused. "Do you know how you came to be inside that dumpster?"

Nikki gasped and as I looked at her, I saw her pale. "Darby?"

I nodded.

"Oh, my God," she whispered. "You've been missing for five years!"

I licked my lips. Should I tell him the truth? I still didn't know if his club was an ally of the Mayhem Riders. Would I be returned to the Nomads? Even if I had to go back, if someone would just keep Fawn safe, then I could endure anything. I tried to see through the open bedroom doorway, wondering how far she was. He'd said she was watching cartoons. I could hear a TV from what seemed to be a few rooms away, or the volume was just turned down.

"Nikki, bring Fawn in to see her mom," Renegade said. "Then maybe you can take her over to the playground while Darby fills me in on their situation."

Nikki hurried off and returned a moment later with Fawn. My precious baby raced toward me and clambered onto the bed. I hugged her, not caring how much it hurt the bruises I was sure covered most of me. She smelled sweet and the clothes she was wearing were nicer than anything she'd owned, even though they didn't appear to be new. The fact they'd kept her safe, fed, and clothed meant a lot to me.

She patted my face, then pointed to Renegade.

"You told him where I was?" I asked.

She nodded, and I kissed her soft cheek. "Thank you, sweetheart. Go with Nikki for a little bit. Renegade said something about a playground. Won't that be fun?"

"It's inside the compound," Nikki said. "She'll be safe the entire time. No one is coming inside without approval from Cinder or Scratch."

I didn't know who Scratch or Cinder were, and since I didn't know if the Mayhem Riders were welcome, it didn't exactly make me feel confident that Fawn would be safe here. So far, they'd taken good care of her, but what if Boomer showed up and laid claim to us? Would they just hand us over to them?

"Take your phone, just in case," Renegade told his sister. She patted his shoulder, then held out her hand for Fawn. She clambered off the bed and went to

Nikki without any hesitation, which meant she trusted these people.

"Go easy on her," Nikki said. "She's one of the girls who went missing at my school all those years ago. You remember the ones? The police searched for a few weeks, but no one came forward with information. They gave up after a while. I have a feeling she's been through hell, Renegade."

Nikki left with Fawn. Once we heard the front door open and shut, Renegade focused his gaze on me.

"So, now we need to talk," he said. "It's obvious that someone did this to you, and there were countless bruises on Fawn as well. Who dumped you in that alley? Nikki said the Mayhem Riders had hurt you, but the ones I know would never condone this shit. If you've been missing for five years, where have you been?"

"I'm not lying," I said. "The Nomads kidnapped me five years ago. They got me pregnant, kept me caged or tied up until I gave birth, then they made sure I knew if I dared to defy them or tried to run, that Fawn would pay the price."

"Is that how she got bruised?" Renegade asked.

"Boomer doesn't like it when she gets in the way. He smacks her around." I felt like a horrible mom admitting what else he'd done to her. "He choked her one time until she passed out, squeezed so hard it must have damaged something. She hasn't been able to speak since then. Occasionally she can make some raspy noises, but she can't say words."

"I'll ask Dr. Chansy to take a look at her, but she was scared of him last night. He'd never hurt her, or you, but she didn't know that." He rubbed the back of his neck. "I didn't realize there were any Mayhem Riders in the immediate area. You said they were

Nomads, so it's possible they're just passing through, but I'll ask my Pres if he knows anything about it. If they hurt you, they won't be allowed inside these gates. We don't condone violence against women and kids. You said they kidnapped you?"

"I was fifteen when they took me. There was a flyer posted at the underage club on the edge of town about a party in a field. I went, wanting to escape my foster home for a while. Except it wasn't a regular party. Boomer and some of his friends used it as a way to lure in teen girls. They drugged and kidnapped us. I was the only one Boomer kept. He traded two others within days of taking us. I don't know what happened to everyone else at the party. When I woke up, we were already out of the state."

For the next half hour, everything spilled out. Not just about my time with Boomer, but also being in foster care and the atrocities I'd seen while being in the system. I told him about the abuse I'd suffered since Boomer took me, the rapes, starvation, the way the bikers had gotten me pregnant almost right away, then the fear I'd felt over Fawn being around them. I didn't understand why I felt safe enough telling him all that I'd been through, but I did. Maybe it was the old crush I'd had on him, or the fact he'd taken such good care of Fawn. When he looked at me, I didn't feel the fear I normally felt when a man was focused on me. With Renegade, I felt a sense of longing. Once I was finished, it felt like a weight had been lifted from my shoulders.

"They won't hurt you ever again," Renegade said. "We won't let them anywhere near you, or Fawn. I need to tell my President and VP everything you shared, and I'll need you to convince Fawn to let Dr. Chansy have a look at her throat. Maybe whatever was done can be reversed."

Part of me wanted to know why he'd go to so much trouble over someone he didn't know. Even though I'd gone to the same school as his sister, and he claimed I looked familiar, we didn't really know each other. Never had. At the same time, I worried if I asked, he might decide he didn't want us around after all, and this was the nicest place I'd ever been. Yes, he was a stranger for the most part, and maybe everything I'd seen so far was all faked. It wouldn't be the first time I was taken in by someone pretending to be something they weren't. The last time had changed my life forever, and not in a good way.

I fingered the shirt I was wearing, and wondered if Renegade had dressed me. I remembered Boomer ordering his brothers to hurt me, and my clothes had been cut and ripped. They hadn't been more than rags to begin with, but I doubted they'd survived the beating I'd received. He must have realized the direction of my thoughts.

"The doctor had to cut off your clothes, as much as he could. The blood was making the material stick to your wounds. He wet the rest and removed it before patching you back together. You have some stitches. One set on your arm and another on your calf. You need to keep them dry as much as possible, but there are ways around it if you want to shower."

"Do I need to stay in here?" I asked, wondering if he would shackle me to the bed, or just lock the door when he left.

"You can go anywhere in the house you want. Although, I'd recommend waiting to go outside until you have more clothing than my old shirt. While no one here would harm you, you still might get more attention than you'd like." His gaze lowered and lingered on my unbound breasts a moment. My nipples hardened, as if they could feel his gaze like a caress. I felt heat warm my cheeks. It had been a long time since I'd had that reaction. Life with Boomer had stripped me of any sense of modesty.

Right, so stay inside. I could do that. Only wearing his shirt was better than some options I'd had previously, but I certainly didn't want the attention of an entire MC. I knew that there would likely be a price I'd have to pay for anything I was given, or Fawn, but I'd do anything for my daughter. I'd endured so much already to try and keep her safe, and I'd go through so much more.

"Darby, I know that you don't have any idea if I'm who I really say I am. I don't even know if you remember Nikki from back before you were kidnapped. You have no reason to trust me. I'm not going to lie and tell you I'm some saint who has never done anything wrong. I have blood on my hands, but I'd never kill an innocent. I don't abuse or rape women and kids. No one in this club ever would." His eyes narrowed a moment. "In fact, I think you should meet Meg."

"Who's Meg?" I asked. Did he have a girlfriend? And why did that make me feel like someone had just stolen my favorite toy?

"The Pres's old lady. More than that, she's one of the women the club rescued in Colombia. She suffered much the way you have, and now she's married to Cinder. They just had a little boy not that long ago, but I'm sure Meg would come by when Tanner is napping."

His President and VP both had families, and there was a playground at the compound. It was hard to wrap my mind around a family-oriented MC. Didn't that go against everything bikers stood for? Or had my experience with the Mayhem Riders skewed the way I viewed everyone else? I'd already seen the difference in the Nomads and the actual chapter members among the Mayhem Riders. It was possible that other clubs were decent, even if they weren't law-abiding. Just because they didn't walk the straight and narrow didn't mean they couldn't be good men. Heaven knew I'd met enough "God-fearing" people during my time in foster care, men who sat in church on Sunday, then slipped into my room later that night to fondle me. If the good, upstanding members of society had that sort of darkness hidden from the world, then it stood to reason the men the town feared could be decent.

I'd learned long ago not everything was black and white. There were definite shades of gray in the world. I'd thought that maybe Nikki was just pretending, but what if she really was that nice and happy? It had been so long since I'd been around genuinely kind people. Even when the Nomads met with some of the chapters, I wasn't permitted to speak to many people. If Boomer thought I was getting close to someone, even an old lady, then he intervened. After receiving a few beatings after those meetings, I'd learned that he worried I would tell about the abuse I suffered at the hands of him and the other Nomads he traveled with from time to time. More often than not, it was just the three of us, but there were times he kept at least two other brothers with him. The larger the crew that ran with him, the more control he had over me and Fawn. I'd always thought a Nomad was just a lone biker, but Boomer didn't seem to care about what was normal, or rules of any sort. Boomer did what he wanted when he wanted, and fuck anyone who said otherwise. It was the reason he didn't belong to a chapter. He didn't want to be beholden to anyone. As long as he moved from place to place, then he felt like he was his own man, while still hiding behind the protection of the Mayhem Riders MC.

I hated that rat bastard, more than anything.

"You look close to Clarity's size before she had her youngest. I'll see if she kept anything that might fit you," Renegade said. "Or if you know your size, I can have someone pick up a few things for you."

My cheeks warmed when I thought about someone buying me bras and panties. With everything I'd been through, any embarrassment should have been burned out of me, but apparently it wasn't, at least not when the sexy man in front of me was so close. I tugged at the shirt I was wearing and knew I'd feel better fully clothed. If he was offering that option, then I'd gladly take it.

"I don't need anything fancy or expensive. The thrift store is fine."

He shook his head, clearly not liking my plan. "I'll get you a pen and paper. Write down everything from the skin out, including shoes, for both you and Fawn. Scratch and his family live outside the compound. If he's coming in today, I'll ask if he'll bring his wife and kids. Maybe they can pick up some things for y'all. I'm sure Clarity would do a better job shopping than any of us. If she can't come, I can send a Prospect after everything."

The fact he was concerned that Fawn and I would have clothing and shoes already made him better than Boomer. Then again, the fact he'd saved me, gotten medical attention for me, and had been worried that Fawn wouldn't speak was enough to prove he was a different caliber of man from the asshole who had taken me five years ago. I wasn't sure I could trust my instincts anymore. Just because

Renegade seemed like a decent guy, didn't mean he really was. I felt like I was at war with myself. Trust him. Don't trust him. It wasn't just physical damage that Boomer had caused, it was emotional and mental as well, and the scars ran deep. Yet there was a part of me that remembered watching Renegade and his sister, and wishing that I was old enough for him to notice me. I'd dreamed more than once about what it would feel like for him to kiss me.

I heard the front door slam, then the clatter of small feet. Fawn rushed into the room, her smile so wide that I couldn't remember a time she'd ever seemed this happy. Her cheeks were pink, and there was a brightness to her eyes that had been missing all her life.

"Did you have fun?" I asked.

She nodded eagerly.

"She really enjoyed the swing and the slide," Nikki said. "I had to help her with the swing, but she raced up the ladder and flew down the slide all by herself. I promised next time we go, if it's all right with you, I'll teach her how to keep the swing going by herself."

Tears misted my eyes as I thought about Nikki offering something so simple, yet she'd somehow known that it would offer joy to my daughter. No one had ever taken the time to do something with Fawn, other than me. My precious baby looked so carefree. I was torn between being elated that she enjoyed being here, felt safe enough to have a good time, and feeling like the worst mother ever because of how we'd lived prior to this. Deep down, I knew I wasn't really to blame. The few times I'd tried to escape, both of us had paid the price. There comes a time when you just accept your Fate and try to live through it the best you can, praying for a miracle to come. Had it only been me, I might have pushed Boomer enough that he'd have killed me, or I'd have succeeded in one of my escape attempts. I'd survived for Fawn, and done what I could to shelter her the best I was able. It wasn't enough, but I hoped that one day she'd understand.

Fawn cuddled close to me, and I held onto her. She smelled like sunshine. I couldn't remember the last time she'd been able to run free outside, or to use a slide at a playground. Boomer never let us loose long enough to go to a park. He certainly didn't care about Fawn, other than using her as a way to get to me. If Boomer wanted me to do something, all he needed to do was threaten Fawn and I'd fall in line. Regardless of what he wanted, I'd have done anything to keep her safe. I'd only dared to call his bluff once. It had taken him less than five minutes to find a buyer for Fawn, a man he said enjoyed taking in babies and raising them into his perfect little girls, girls that he trained to satisfy him sexually. I'd not gone against him again after that.

"Maybe you can go to the playground again soon," I told her.

"I'd be happy to come over and take her again tomorrow," Nikki said. She chewed her lower lip. "I'm really glad you're here, Darby. I don't know where you've been or what you've been through, but you're safe here."

"Come over?" I asked, honing in on the first part she'd said. "You don't live here too?"

Nikki smiled. "And cramp my big brother's style? Not a chance. Besides, he doesn't like me hanging out at the compound that often. Says I'm too much temptation for the single guys around here."

I could understand his concern. Nikki was stunning, and with her openness and infectious smile, I could easily see her as being a magnet for the men with the Devil's Boneyard -- or any men for that matter -- even if her brother was a patched member. I glanced his way, taking in his cut. I hadn't studied it before, but now that I looked closer, I saw he had a patch under his name. *Road Captain*. I'd been around the chapters long enough to know that not just anyone had a title.

The fact he was someone important, and I was staying in his home, gave me a little hope. If Renegade said I was safe here, that Fawn would be safe, then I knew his brothers wouldn't cross him. Although, if he worried over his own sister... I looked from him to Nikki, then back again. He'd said that his club would never hurt a woman. Perhaps it wasn't that he worried she'd be hurt in the physical sense, but more in the heartbroken way. Either way, I felt safer here than I had in a long time, and it seemed Fawn was of the same belief.

I only hoped that I wasn't putting my faith in the wrong people. Fawn had been hurt enough already. I didn't want to be responsible for placing her in yet another bad situation. Even if I hadn't come here voluntarily, if Renegade gave me the option to stay and I took it, then things went south, that would be all on me. I already owed her so much, my sweet baby. This was a chance at a better life for both of us, and I couldn't back down from it, not out of fear or mistrust. Sooner or later, I had to believe in someone. Might as well be Nikki and Renegade.

His cut *did* have wings on the back. Maybe he was my guardian angel in disguise.

Chapter Three

Renegade

Not only had Clarity been unable to shop for Darby and Fawn, but my traitor sister had insisted on staying at my house with them. If I hadn't known better, she'd done it on purpose. So now I found myself wandering the kids department at one of the big chain stores, picking up tiny jeans and shirts and wondering if the silent Fawn would like any of them. I didn't know a damn thing about the kid, other than she was covered in bruises and couldn't speak. Did she like pink? Purple? Or did she prefer boyish colors or neutral ones? And why the fuck did I even care? Kids were like little aliens as far as I was concerned, and I honestly never planned to have one of my own.

There was a purple long-sleeved tee with a kitten on a motorcycle. Checking for Fawn's size, I tossed it into the shopping cart before adding a few more animal shirts. Since the Florida weather was unpredictable, I added a few T-shirts and three sweaters. When I saw the mini-biker type leather jacket, I couldn't pass it up and added it to the growing pile. Buying a package of the tiny panties was awkward as fuck, but I found her size and threw them into the cart along with some socks, then headed over to the shoe department.

If I'd thought buying for Fawn was weird, then picking out bras and panties for Darby was by far one of the worst things I'd had to do. I'd honestly prefer to dodge bullets. It was hard to maintain the badass biker image while holding a pair of black lace panties. When it came to sleepwear, I found that the thought of her wearing the silky negligee hanging on the end rack was tempting. Instead, I chose things that looked like they would be comfortable while she healed. Before I went over to the other clothes, I stopped and stared at the nightgown again. This time, I found her size and tossed it, along with two other colors, into the cart, then hastened over to women's jeans. It wasn't like I'd ever see her in them, but damn if my imagination wasn't doing an adequate job of how she'd look in the sexy garments, minus her current cuts and bruises. Maybe it made me an asshole to be thinking of her like that. She'd not only been beaten to hell and back, but she was a mom who didn't need the likes of me panting after her. Her name hadn't sounded familiar, but the more I'd looked at her I'd finally started piecing things together. When she'd been younger, I'd seen her watching me and Nikki. There'd been interest in her young eyes, but I'd never let on that I saw her. She'd been a cute kid, but all grown up? Holy hell. Even under the bruises and cuts, the woman was more than just pretty. And too fucking young. If she'd been taken at fifteen and had been gone five years, then she was twenty. I could be her fucking father. Not that a big age gap seemed to bother Scratch and Clarity, or Cinder and Meg. Didn't mean I wanted to follow in their footsteps, though.

The shopping cart was nearly overflowing when I approached the front registers. I'd known the total would be high, but I hadn't counted on just how much this shit would cost. Good thing I'd brought the truck because no way in hell this stuff would have fit into my saddlebags. As the cashier handed me the receipt, I realized I hadn't bought a single toy or game for Fawn, and she didn't have a damn thing to do at my house except watch TV. I loaded the bags into the back seat of my truck, then reset the alarm before trudging back into the store.

I didn't know much about little girls, but the ones in the movies usually liked dolls and that sort of shit. I bought a baby doll, a dollhouse with the extra crap that went with it, two board games that looked appropriate for a younger child, and just in case she didn't care for girly things I grabbed a handful of cars. If she and her mother stayed with me for long, Fawn would need more clothes. As I exited the toy department, I saw the books and magazines. Darby was as much of an enigma as her daughter. I tossed in two of the fashion magazines I knew my sister liked, as well as two paperbacks I'd seen her read. Not that Nikki and Darby were necessarily anything alike, but I hoped it would give her something to do. Once she was feeling better, I'd let her come buy her own shit.

Assuming she was still living with me. After we dealt with the threat to her and Fawn, then there was nothing keeping her at the compound, or my house. It wasn't like I ever allowed the club sluts to come to my place. If I wanted a quick release, there were plenty of bathrooms at the clubhouse. A shower wall would work. My home was my sanctuary. And now it was overrun with unwanted guests. Except, if I really thought about, they weren't all that unwanted. It had been nice having someone in the house last night. I'd checked on Darby a few times, and Fawn, who had slept on the couch. It hadn't been ideal and I knew I should have something better for her.

I hesitated before going up to the front again. The store carried pretty much everything from clothing to automotive supplies, even things like plants and furniture. It wouldn't hurt to just see what types of beds they might have for a kid. And if she didn't stay long, then I could donate it to someone who could use it or let her take it with her. By the time I checked out a second time, I'd bought a twin platform bed, mattress, and dresser for Fawn, and since I had an empty room right next to Darby's I'd just put everything in there. She'd have her own space for however long she was at my house.

My truck was loaded down when I entered the compound. The look on the Prospect's face was humorous, but the knowing glint in my Pres's eyes as I stopped in front of my house was a different story. I shut off the engine, then took a breath to steady myself before facing whatever Cinder had to say on the matter. The second my boot hit the driveway, he started toward me.

"This doesn't look like a temporary situation," he said.

"Little girl needed a place to sleep. Her mom is healing so it didn't seem right for them to share a bed, and the couch didn't seem like a good option for her either."

He arched an eyebrow, but didn't say anything else, even though I could tell he was holding back. It wasn't like him not to just say whatever he was thinking, and it made me nervous as fuck. With Cinder's help, I unloaded the truck quickly, then the big bad Pres even got down on the damn floor and helped me screw the furniture together. It wasn't until the mattress was placed on the bed that it occurred to me I didn't have bedding. How the fuck did parents deal with this shit? Then again, they probably didn't buy everything all at once. I looked around the room, and realized there wasn't a damn place for any of the toys either. Her clothes fit in the dresser, and I'd put her shoes in the bottom of the closet. A toy box hadn't occurred to me while I was shopping.

"Well, fuck," I muttered.

Cinder smirked. "Need to make another run?"

"I really hate that fucking store. If she didn't need stuff tonight, I'd just order online and have it delivered."

"Did you buy a booster seat for your truck?" Cinder asked. "She's on the small side and should ride in one."

Fuck. My. Life. Kids needed too much shit. I ran a hand down my face and heaved a sigh. I pulled my phone from my pocket and opened a doc, then started making a list. With Cinder's input, I added things both Fawn and Darby would need that I hadn't considered on my first trip to the store. Then the Pres called his wife and she had me add even more. It would have been just as easy to ask Nikki, but she was doing her best to keep Fawn occupied. As I stared at the items, and the growing list, it was starting to feel like an elephant was sitting on my chest. I'd never wanted a wife and kids, not like some of the other men in the club, and having Darby and Fawn under my roof was starting to feel a little too much like I had a family.

Families died. I didn't want to survive that again. Mostly because I wasn't sure I *would* survive if it were my wife and kid who died. It had been hard enough losing my parents and brother. Knowing Nikki hadn't perished in the fire had helped to some extent. Even if we didn't suffer together on the anniversary of their death, we knew that we had each other when it counted. Like now. Nikki had really pulled through when I'd asked her to come over. I'd worried that Darby would freak the hell out when she woke in a strange place with a man she didn't know. Despite the fact she'd seemed familiar, I hadn't been certain that I knew her, or that she'd recognize me. It had been obvious someone had beat her to hell and back. Even though I'd assumed it had been a man, it could have easily been a woman. That didn't seem to be the case, since she'd spoken to me about the last five years of her life with Boomer. I'd found that typically men beat women like that, even though I'd heard of women being just as violent. The prisons were full of them.

With my list saved to my phone, and Cinder's promise to be at the clubhouse should Nikki, Darby, or Fawn need anything, I got back into my truck and went back to the store I liked to think of simply as hell. Each item that went into the cart, I removed from my list. Instead of a toy box, which the store didn't seem to carry, I found a storage trunk with latches. It wasn't ideal, but it would work for now. Meg had told me to add tear-free shampoo for Fawn, as well as some baby soap, even though she wasn't a baby anymore. Then she'd suggested some feminine scented hair and bath products for Darby. It was the last item she'd added that had me frozen in the middle of the aisle. I stared at the back wall and the wide variety of products, not knowing the difference from one to another.

Resigned, I called my sister, knowing I'd never hear the end of this.

"Did you get lost?" she asked.

"Kind of. When it's that time of the month, what do you use?"

Dead. Silence. Seriously, if I were in a cartoon, I'd have heard crickets right then.

"Nik? Meg said I should get something for Darby just in case, but I have no fucking clue what I'm looking for. All this shit looks the same to me, just in different packaging."

"I can assure you they aren't all the same," she said. "I'll text two images to you. Get both."

"Thanks," I muttered and hung up, but not before I heard her snickering. Yeah, I'd get teased over this one for a while.

My phone chimed a moment later and I matched the images to the products on the wall, tossing in a package of each. I ran from the department as fast as I could. Once I was in the bedding section, I felt moderately better. The kids section didn't seem to have those bed-in-a-bag things I typically grabbed for myself. I had no fucking clue who most of the characters were on the bedding, but I did recognize one from a cartoon Fawn watched earlier with Nikki. I grabbed the sheets and matching comforter, then decided to grab plain pink sheets and a plaid comforter that was purple and pink. Wouldn't hurt to have a backup. The kid hadn't wet the couch when she'd slept last night, but it didn't mean she'd never have an accident. Better to be prepared now and not have to return later.

Anything else they needed, I'd buy online and have shipped overnight if need be. I'd pay just about anything to avoid this place again in the next few weeks. I checked out and loaded everything, then headed to the compound. I fucking hated shopping. Or more accurately, I just hated shopping inside a store. I'd buy crap online all fucking day and have it shipped. Not that I'd ever admit it, but I tended to get one-click happy with shit after I got paid. When I needed groceries, I usually made a list and sent a Prospect. Some of them weren't twenty-one, so I made my own alcohol runs most of the time, but those were quick trips. Occasionally, one of the club sluts would run to the store for a few of us, but I noticed they acted special afterward, like they were better than the others. Even worse, they tended to get territorial, like we were going to claim them or something. Far as I was concerned, one hole was good as another, and I didn't favor one girl more than any other one.

Honestly, I hadn't gotten laid in a few months. One of the guys had a pregnancy scare with a club whore and I'd decided to take a break. I'd also gotten tested, just in case. If the girls were poking holes in the condoms, which we'd dealt with more than once now, then I wasn't taking any chances. Cinder had cleaned house and told those involved to never come back -- then immediately dumped the community bowl of condoms in the clubhouse -- and while we had a new crop of pussy to pick from, I just hadn't felt the urge to sample the latest batch. I'd bought a box of condoms and stashed them in my bathroom at home, but I hadn't opened them yet. I wasn't about to let some slut try to trap me into taking care of her. Not that it would work. I'd keep the kid and kick her lying ass to the curb. Half the women who hung around us did more drugs than we did. I'd not had more than a hit of pot here and there in years, and I sure as shit didn't want my kid's mom doing that crap.

Coming to a stop in my driveway, I started to unload everything, just piling it near the front door. It was easier to haul everything inside at once than to keep running out to the damn truck. I kept the carport clear for my bikes. I had a sweet Harley Fat Boy and a 1971 Triumph Tiger Daytona I'd found in a scrapyard. It had taken me for-fucking-ever, but I'd managed to fully restore it. The Harley was my everyday ride, but I liked taking the Triumph out for recreational runs when I just needed to feel the wind in my hair for a bit, hit the open road and drive for an hour before heading home. I didn't do that as often as I'd like.

What I really wanted was to get my hands on a 1950 Triumph 6T Thunderbird. They weren't overly pricey all things considered; it was more the problem of finding one in decent shape. Not to mention the guys already gave me shit over the Triumph I had. They preferred American bikes all the way, and while I'd never ditch my Harley, there was an elegance to the classic British cycles. Ever since I'd watched *The Wild One* with Marlon Brando, I'd wanted one. And I knew that one day, I'd find the perfect one, even if I needed to put some work into it.

Cinder opened the door right as I set the last of the bags near the door. I went back to close the truck door, then began hauling stuff inside. Fawn's stuff went to the room I'd set up for her. Nikki left the little girl watching yet another show and snatched the bedding from me.

"You should wash it before you put it on the bed. What if she's allergic to the dye in it?"

Shit. I hadn't even thought of that. I always just opened them and put them on the bed. Then again, her skin would be a lot more tender than mine. I followed Nik to the laundry room and saw that while I'd been gone, she'd emptied the dresser of Fawn's new clothes and washed those too. While she handled the bedding, I took the clothes back to the room and put them away again. Cinder was placing the toys into the storage trunk, but I noticed he'd broken the latches off and left the lid open.

"What the fuck, Pres?"

"Kids are curious. What if she crawled inside and accidentally locked herself in there?"

The more I learned today, the less I felt I should ever have offspring. I'd likely kill them the first day. Unintentionally, of course. If they lived to their teen years, then any deaths after that would probably be another story. I remembered Nikki's snotty attitude when she'd been younger. Even though she hadn't lived with me, I'd tried to spend as much time with her as I could, and there had been a lot of times I'd wanted to strangle her.

It took forever to get Fawn's room set up and all her stuff washed, but Nikki was making the bed when Fawn wandered in. Her eyes went wide and she stared at everything. I motioned her closer, then knelt so I'd be nearer to her level. The last thing I wanted to do was scare the kid, although she hadn't been fearful of me so far. If anything, she tended to cling to me whenever I was in the same room with her.

"Fawn, while you're here, this is your room. You have clothes in the dresser, shoes in the closet, and the toys in that chest," I said, pointing to the storage trunk, "are all for you."

Her lower lip trembled and I worried she'd start crying, but she threw herself into my arms and hugged me so tight that my heart stuttered for a moment. The kid really was sweet, and it sucked that she'd had such a rough life so far. If we could deal with the Mayhem Riders, then maybe she'd have a better future. Her and Darby both. They were both victims and deserved to live their lives without fear of Boomer and the others who had hurt them over the years.

She released me and went over to the toys, gently lifting the doll and holding her against her chest. While Fawn got acquainted with her room, I went to check on Darby, carrying in the bags of things I'd purchased for her. I set everything in front of the dresser as quietly as possible when I saw she was sleeping. Careful not to wake her, I removed the clothes and stacked them on top of the dresser so she'd see them, then lined up the shoes on the floor beside the closet.

The bathroom items I'd purchased for both of them went into the hall bathroom. I just set everything on the counter and figured they'd put it where they wanted it. By the time I had finished, something delicious teased my nose from the kitchen. I found Nikki standing over the stove stirring something.

"What did you make?" I asked.

"Well, you missed lunch earlier so I decided to make dinner a bit sooner than you typically eat. I thought homemade chicken noodle might be good for Darby and Fawn, but I also put a chicken and rice casserole in the oven in case that wasn't enough for everyone." She got a wistful look on her face. "It was Mom's recipe. One of the old neighbors had a copy and gave it to me."

That was news to me. I hadn't realized that Nikki had been over there since the fire. It made me wonder what else I didn't know about my sister's comings and goings. Maybe I needed to pay a bit closer attention.

"You staying for dinner?" I asked.

She shook her head, her cheeks flushing. My eyes narrowed, knowing that she was trying to hide something from me. Which could only mean one thing. She had a date. I hated her asshole boyfriend and wished I could feed him to the fucking sharks. He didn't hit her, but he did talk down to her all the time and controlled her, even if she didn't realize it.

"Give Chad a big 'fuck you' from me when you see him," I said, as I opened the fridge for a drink, pausing when I saw it was fully stocked with food as well as juice, milk, sodas, and my favorite beer. "Did you go shopping?"

"I made a list and asked Bane to pick everything up for me. He dropped it off while you were off buying stuff for your houseguests. I knew you wouldn't think about feeding them until it was time to actually cook something," she said. "And I'm not seeing Chad. Ever again."

Well, that was at least a bit of good news. As well as discovering I had beer. I wasn't sure which was the better news to be honest. I hated fucking Chad with a passion, but… beer. Yeah, the beer might win this round. I'd never brought in the alcohol after finding Darby and Fawn, and since the beer had been cold at the time, I'd had to toss it after it got hot.

"So who are you meeting when you leave here?" I asked.

She sighed, her shoulders drooping as she glanced at me. "I can't hide anything from you, can I? I didn't say a word other than I wouldn't have dinner with you."

"Nope."

"Fine. Yes, I'm going on a date, not with Chad, and that's all you'll get from me."

If Nikki thought that would be good enough, then she was slipping. No way I'd let her go off with some guy I've never met and not worry about her safety. I pulled my phone from my pocket and shot off a quick text to Dixon to keep an eye on Nik when she left today, and to make sure whatever asshole she was meeting knew that I'd rip off his balls if he fucked her over.

I knew that Nik was all grown up, but she was still my baby sister. I'd already been fully grown and out of the house when she'd been born. I'd been a surprise to my parents. They'd gotten married and struggled for a while. Then they'd had my brother, and

Nikki had been another surprise after my mom thought she couldn't have more kids. It seemed she'd had her tubes tied and they'd grown back, or some shit. She'd told me about it when she'd said she was pregnant again, but I'd only half-listened. There were some things a guy didn't want to think about. How his mom came to be pregnant was one of them.

She did her best to not look me in the eye as she finished making dinner, then she fixed me a plate, as well as making a bowl of soup for Fawn. When she tried to skirt around me to get the kid, I reached out and grabbed her arm. Not tight enough to hurt, but enough to draw her to a halt and let her know I wasn't playing.

"I don't like that you're going out with some jackass I haven't met. After Chad, I'm not sure I can trust your judgment when it comes to men, Nik. This new guy hurts you, he'll answer to me. And you *will* tell me what happened with Chad. I've practically begged you to drop that guy and you refused. So what the fuck did he do?"

She sniffed and tugged on her arm. "He fucked my best friend -- ex-best friend -- not two days after he asked me to move in with him. I stopped by to surprise him and caught him with his pants down, literally, thrusting away."

My jaw tightened. He'd cheated on her? And with Bethany? The two girls had been thick as thieves for as long as I could remember. I didn't understand women who couldn't follow a simple code. You don't shit where you eat, and you don't fuck your best friend's man or woman. Everyone knew that. Except Bethany it seemed. Now I was doubly glad I'd never accepted her blatant offers since she'd become legal.

"I'll be having a little talk with Chad."

She shook her head. "I already handled it."

"How?" I asked.

She shrugged. "There's a slight chance the police may be coming after me. I sort of went all Carrie Underwood on his car."

"The penis-mobile?" I asked, thinking of the little bright red foreign sports car he owned. Then I processed her words and remembered that song she listened to on repeat a while back. "Did you take a bat to that car?"

She grinned, and I had to grudgingly admit I was proud of her. It also meant I needed to make a few calls. If the cops were going to arrest her, then I wanted a heads-up. Wouldn't be the first time I'd offered a bribe to the local cops, but if it kept Nik out of trouble, I'd gladly do it again. Truthfully, I wished someone had filmed her beating the shit out of his car. I'd have loved to see it. I was glad she'd stood up for herself. The asshole was lucky I didn't rip his balls off, but he'd actually done me a favor by showing his true colors. At least Nikki was finally away from him, even if I didn't like the way it had come about.

I kissed the top of her head, hugging her tight, then let her escape. It made me wonder if Darby would ever stand up for herself again. From what she'd said, any disobedience had been dealt with in the harshest way possible. There were people who would criticize her for staying, for having a child in that environment, but I'd learned that sometimes it wasn't so much that a woman was weak when she stayed. Walking away wasn't easy. In Darby's case, it would have meant her death, as well as her daughter's, if not something even worse like her kid being sold to a pedophile. To me, the fact she'd survived and shielded her daughter as best as she could spoke of her strength. Too many people were eager to condemn someone like Darby without knowing all the facts, or having ever experienced something like that themselves. A person could never say one hundred percent for sure what they'd do until they were actually in that type of situation.

Fawn skipped into the room, the doll clutched in her arms, and she clambered onto a seat at the kitchen table. Nik came in right after her, setting the bowl of soup down. I glanced down the hall and saw that Darby's door was still closed.

"Darby not awake yet?" I asked. "I wasn't sure how long she'd been sleeping."

Nikki chewed her lip and glanced down the hall, then back at me. She did it twice more and I got the hint, forcing my feet to move toward Darby's room, the one place I knew I needed to avoid. The woman tugged on my heart and I didn't have time for that shit. I needed to deal with her issue and get her the hell out of my house.

Pushing her door open, I'd taken all of three steps before I froze in shock, then called myself an asshole when my dick got hard looking at Darby's naked body. She might be bruised and battered, maybe even a bit too skinny, but the woman had the perkiest breasts I'd ever seen. Her nipples tightened under my perusal and I knew I was going to fucking hell. If I'd ever had a doubt before, I didn't now.

"Shit," I muttered and took a step back, bumping into the door making it shut behind me. My gaze shot up to her face, and what I saw had me moving forward again, and not stopping until I had her in my arms.

Chapter Four

Darby

It hadn't occurred to me that I should lock the door before I got out of bed and removed the shirt I'd been wearing. Or maybe it was more accurate that I'd still been groggy and not thinking clearly. I'd woken and noticed the clothes on the dresser. Curious, I'd stood up to see what the biker had bought, and had just removed the shirt so I could put something on when he'd entered the room. It felt like the air was sucked out of the space. At first, my body had locked tight, my heart pounding. I'd felt like a rabbit the second it sees a coyote. Boomer had enjoyed catching me by surprise, and would do anything he could to humiliate me.

The moment Renegade froze, I realized he hadn't intended to catch me naked. Slowly, I relaxed. Enough men had seen me naked that I wasn't overly shy about my body anymore. Not usually. I'd been desensitized the hard way. Boomer delighted in ripping my clothes off in the midst of a gathering and letting his friends look and touch all they wanted. It took a moment for me to remember that this man wasn't Boomer. He hadn't hurt me, hadn't done anything inappropriate in the short time I'd known him. It didn't mean he couldn't or wouldn't, but so far, he'd proven trustworthy. If Fawn believed he was safe, then he probably was. She'd developed excellent skills at reading men, which made me feel like the worst mother ever.

As Renegade perused my body, it was the look in his eyes as he'd scanned me from head to… well, breast since he seemed to focus there, that got a reaction from me. I'd seen lust in men's eyes before, but Renegade looked at me with reverence, as if I were a flesh and blood goddess who had entered his home. No one had ever looked at me like that before. He wasn't reaching for me, wasn't leering or telling me to drop to my knees, or to spread my legs. He looked, yes, but I knew the moment he felt bad about it. He took a step back toward the door, reaching blindly for it but ended up bumping it shut instead.

My traitorous body reacted to him. I'd never been turned on, not the way a woman is for a man. There had been some crushes after I'd turned twelve, including the insane stalkerish one I'd had for the man standing in front of me, but nothing like this. I was aware of Renegade. Not as his prey, but as a woman who had never known the gentle touch of a man. I'd been used like an object with no feelings, just a hole for men to stick their dicks into. The way he watched me, it made me think that things might be different with him. I didn't delude myself into thinking he was a saint, he'd even claimed he wasn't one, but there was a kindness in his eyes that I hadn't witnessed in a long time. Not directed at me anyway. The fact I remembered the gentleness he'd shown his sister all those years ago, and the way he'd been with Fawn, made me want some of that kindness for myself.

I don't know if I made a noise or shifted, but he seemed locked in place and his gaze lifted to meet mine. My body warmed, and even though my mind was screaming that he was a man and men only ever hurt me, I felt myself grow slick between my legs. The hunger in his gaze, the uncertainty in them, as if he wanted me but felt like he shouldn't, made my skin warm. For the first time in my life, I wanted to know what it would feel like to be touched the way lovers touched in the movies. The next thing I knew, I was in his arms. With anyone else, I'd have felt fear. Renegade was a stranger for the most part, a biker at that. I should be terrified given my experience with men like him, or even men in general, but for whatever reason, the moment those arms closed around me, I felt... safe. Protected. And I couldn't help but melt against him, clutch at his cut, and wish that he wouldn't let go. His scent filled my nose -- spice and a bit of tang. It was the best thing I'd ever smelled.

All those old feelings welled up inside of me. The need to know what it would be like to kiss him, to be held like this by him, to just *be* his. It was what I'd wanted when I was too young to really understand. Being this close to him made me want him with the same feverish need I'd had five years ago, when I should have been giggling over high school boys and not crushing on a grown man with a beard and a motorcycle.

"Darby." My name was a soft caress with his deep voice. A shiver raked my spine and my nipples hardened even more. I'd never felt desire before, not this level of it. I'd thought boys were cute, had wanted Renegade even though I'd never met him, but being abducted by Boomer had cured me of ever wanting a man to touch me.

Until now. Until the man I'd once yearned for held me in his arms.

What the hell is wrong with you? He's a biker! A man!

Didn't matter what I told myself. His touch felt right. If he'd been holding me too tight, or rubbed himself against me, then maybe I'd have panicked. All Renegade did was clasp me to his body. I could feel the hard length of his cock where it pressed against me, but it seemed involuntary and not intentional. He rubbed his chin against my cheek, then trailed his nose along the column of my neck.

I gasped and felt my knees go a little weak.

"Tell me to leave," he said. "I shouldn't be here, shouldn't want you. Send me away, Darby. If you say the words, I'll go."

I licked my lips. "And if I don't?"

He groaned. "Darby, please. You can't want this. Not after all you've been through. I won't use you like they did. Tell me to go."

I opened my mouth, but the words that spilled out weren't what he'd demanded, nor were they what I'd intended to say. No, instead, my traitorous lips formed the words I'd wanted to tell him when I was just a kid with raging hormones.

"Kiss me." He sucked in a breath and pulled back so I could see his face. "Please, Renegade. Just a kiss. Nothing more."

He studied me a moment, as if trying to judge my sincerity. As his head lowered, it felt like my heart was taking off at a gallop. The moment his lips touched mine, it felt like fire flowed through my veins, my body awakening for the first time. His tongue flicked against my lower lip and I opened, letting him in. The taste of him made me press closer, needing more. His mouth devoured mine, left me hungering for more, craving his touch as much as I needed my next breath. The emotions swirling through me both scared and fascinated me. I wanted to run away and hold on all at the same time. His hand slid down my back and around my waist, his arm binding me to him. When he pushed against a bruise, I whimpered, making him stop and take a step back.

"Christ. I'm sorry, Darby. I never should have done that."

"I asked you to," I reminded him. "And… I'm not sorry."

He watched me, and I refused to look away. I wanted him to see that he'd affected me, and that while part of me was scared, I also wanted more. Regret what we'd just done? Not even a little. Want him to keep going? Maybe. I definitely wanted more of his kisses, even though I shouldn't. The smart thing would be to grab Fawn and run as far and fast as I could. There was a chance I would elude Boomer, but I couldn't risk my daughter. No matter how scary it was to feel something for the man in front of me, I needed to stay as long as he'd let me.

"No one's ever kissed me like that," I admitted. "You're the first man I've ever asked to touch me, and the first to make me want more. It's not what happens between a man and a woman that's scaring me right now. It's how you make me feel. I've never wanted anyone before, not with this intensity. Before, I just had teen crushes. This is different."

I didn't know why the words were spilling out of my mouth. I needed to shut up. Just get dressed and walk out of the room, but my feet led me to him and not the dresser. I placed my hand on his chest, feeling his heart thump against my fingers. He didn't look like the type of man to back down. He'd always been the bad boy. Sexy. Forbidden. Right now, I just wanted him to be mine for at least a few minutes. I wanted all those teen fantasies to come to life, to have some good memories to last me a lifetime.

"You pressed on my bruise. It wasn't distress over what we were doing that made me make that noise."

His gaze scanned my body and he grimaced. "I shouldn't have touched you if for no other reason than you have a lot of healing to do. Even if you did ask for the kiss, I didn't have to agree to it."

I cocked my head. "Why did you?"

It wasn't like a man who looked like him would be lacking for female attention. While he wasn't model-type gorgeous, there was a rugged, dangerous air about him that I had no doubt would draw the opposite sex to him, and possibly even the same sex. He had that type of sex appeal I'd seen on TV but had never truly witnessed in person, not as a grown woman at any rate. The man had been mouthwatering when I was a teenager, but raging hormones then compared to how I felt now? No comparison. And his voice? Dear God. When the man spoke, I wanted to ask him to never stop. He could probably sell ice to Eskimos. If he whispered dirty things in my ear, it might be enough to make me come.

I didn't think he would answer. Renegade looked away, staring at the wall. The silence dragged on and I was about to tell him to just forget it when he finally spoke.

"I haven't been interested in women the last few months. The women at the clubhouse have tried and failed to get into my pants. You're the last woman I should want, and yet I get hard just thinking about you, and I know that's all kinds of fucked up. You're too young. Been abused and sexually assaulted. You need help and a place to heal, not me sticking my dick in you."

"But you haven't demanded that I spread my legs for you. You haven't asked anything of me," I reminded him.

When he focused on me, the heat nearly seared me. "Maybe not, but I want to. Do you want to know what I want?"

I stared, unable to say yes or no, unable to look away.

"I want to grab a handful of your hair and tell you to get on your knees and open your mouth. I want to feed my cock to you, make you take all of me until you gag -- and you will because I'm not small -- then I want to fuck you until I come. Except with you, I don't think that would be enough. I'd still be hard." He growled and advanced a step. "Then I'd spread you out on the bed, put those shapely legs of yours over my shoulders and take you hard and deep, fuck you so good you'd not be able to walk. I want to see your tits bounce as I drive my dick into your wet pussy, make you beg me for more. You'd come so hard that you'd soak the bed, and I'd demand even more from you."

I knew my eyes had to be wide. My chest was heaving with my labored breaths, but it wasn't from fear. It should be, by all means, but it wasn't. No, his words were turning me on, or rather the images they evoked were making me hot and wet. I could see it just as he'd described. Rubbing my thighs together didn't ease the ache. Renegade closed the distance between us, one hand going to my hair and the other between my legs. I cried out as his fingers slid along the lips of my pussy, and found myself opening up wide for him.

The first swipe of his finger against my clit had me seeing stars. I panted and bit my lip to keep from making a fool of myself with words I shouldn't utter. He shifted, rubbing the hard bud with his thumb as he plunged two fingers inside me. It only took three strokes before I was coming, my body shuddering with the force of my release. I'd never had an orgasm, unless it was self-induced, even though I'd seen the faked ones on the porn Boomer watched. My fingers couldn't compare to what Renegade was doing to me.

"That's it, angel. Come for me."

As if his words alone were powerful enough, I felt another climax building and soon I was coming again. I ached from head to toe, had been through hell before he'd found me, but despite it all, I felt the most intense pleasure ever at his hands. I reached for his belt, unfastening it and unzipping his pants. Reaching inside the band of his underwear, I gripped his cock and gave it a little squeeze. Renegade hissed in a breath. I'd never voluntarily touched a man before, not like this, but I wanted to give him the same release he'd given me. His fingers still drove into my pussy and worked my clit. I was too selfish to kneel and take him into my mouth because I wanted him to keep touching me, wanted to come again and again. I needed that euphoria, but only if it was Renegade touching me.

"Darby." His voice was nearly all growl.

"I didn't want them, never asked them to do those things to me." I stroked his cock. "I don't know why, but I'm not afraid of you. I want you. So much."

He added a third finger and my eyes crossed. *Sweet Jesus!* He hit just the right spot and I came so hard it felt like I blacked out for a moment. When everything came into focus again, I was draped over the side of the bed, my breasts rubbing against the soft comforter as he nudged my feet apart.

I looked over my shoulder and saw the need etched on his features. He shoved his jeans and boxer briefs down his thighs, his cock long, hard, and thick. The head looked angry as he gave it a few strokes, then he was pressing against me.

"If you don't want this, tell me now," he said.

I didn't say a word and he thrust into me, not stopping until I'd taken every inch of him.

"Fuck!" He slammed into me again. "So fucking good. Never felt anything as amazing as your pussy."

I opened my mouth to warn him he hadn't put on a condom, but he stole the breath from my lungs with his frenzied thrusts.

Soon he was driving into me, and as I felt his cock swell, another orgasm hit me. I screamed out his name as he fucked me, taking what he wanted, what he needed. He roared out his release and I felt the hot splash of his cum inside of me. My breath froze. No. God, no. If I was carrying anything and gave it to him…

"Renegade."

He ground his hips against me, his cock as deep as it would go.

"Renegade, you didn't use a condom."

My words seemed to douse him in an icy dose of reality. He cursed and jerked free of my body. I felt his cum slide out of me and stood, turning to face him. He stared at the mess now trickling down the insides of my thighs with horror. My heart shattered in that moment. He'd been the only one to ever give me such a beautiful moment, but now it was ruined.

"We need to both get tested." I swallowed hard. "I don't know if I'm carrying anything from…"

He growled and jerked up his pants, storming out of my room and slamming the door shut behind him. I snatched a few pieces of clothing off the dresser and dashed across the hall to the bathroom. Someone had laid out plastic wrap on the counter. I used it to cover my stitches before starting the water. Showering off the evidence of what we'd done, I cried and called myself ten times a fool. Being with him had been wonderful, until I'd reminded him I was no better than a whore. I'd been used often, and not just by Boomer.

He'd give me to anyone if the price was right. And I'd reminded Renegade of how dirty I was, how unworthy of him. I was such an idiot. I needed to figure out where I'd take Fawn. After this, there was no way he'd let me stay here. When I'd let him take me, I'd never considered he wouldn't use a condom. Even though Boomer and his friends hadn't, Renegade had seemed like the cautious type. Until the moment I asked him to kiss me.

I got out of the shower and quickly dried off, removed the plastic wrap, then dressed. My stitches held up and hadn't gotten wet. As I stepped into the hallway, a wave of dizziness hit me, making me stumble. I reached for the wall to support myself, but it wasn't enough and I sank to my knees. Even though I'd eaten earlier, it had been too long since I'd had regular meals. Maybe I could at least get a few slices of bread before I had to leave, anything to hold me over. The thought of taking Fawn from this house nearly made me throw up. A gasp drew my attention and I looked up to see Nikki staring at me in horror.

"Renegade!" she screamed, then rushed toward me.

I heard a door farther down the hall slam open and heavy steps come toward me. Closing my eyes, I wished the ground would just open up and swallow me. The last thing I wanted was for him to see me like this. Not after what we'd shared and the way he'd bolted.

"What happened?" he asked, keeping a good foot of space between us.

"I found her like this," Nikki said. "I thought I heard something and came to check on her."

"I'm fine," I managed, but even to my ears my words sounded slurred.

Shit. It wasn't hunger. I knew what was about to happen and I couldn't stop it. Within seconds, my body tilted until I fell to the floor. When I came to again, I knew I'd only been out of it for a few seconds. The episodes never lasted more than a minute. When they'd first started, I'd had no warning and hadn't even realized what was happening until someone pointed out I was spacing out a lot. Turns out, I wasn't doing that at all. I was having a type of seizure. As I'd gotten older, they'd changed a bit. Now I'd get dizzy within seconds of having one. Then again, I got dizzy when I didn't eat as well, so sometimes it was hard to tell if I was about to black out or not. The slurred speech right before it happened was new, though. I'd only had that happen twice now.

"You're not fine," Nikki said. "What the hell was that?"

"It's nothing," I said, brushing off her concern as I struggled to my feet. The hallway spun a moment as I got my bearings, and then I was fine. Well, as fine as I ever was at any rate. I knew there was something wrong with me, but I didn't exactly have medical insurance, or money for a doctor.

"Anything I need to know?" Renegade said.

I glanced his way and wished I hadn't. His eyes flashed with anger and his jaw was tight. Yeah, he was still pissed at me, even if there had been two of us in that bedroom. It wasn't my fault he hadn't thought to use a condom. Or at least, it wasn't entirely my fault. I was willing to share the blame since we hadn't exactly had the sex discussion before things progressed as quickly as they had. If we had, then he'd have known ahead of time that I might be carrying something.

"I haven't kept anything from you. Nothing important."

"Nothing important," he repeated. "But something. What is it you haven't told me?"

"I sometimes get seizures. I just zone out for a few seconds, occasionally up to a minute. Lately, I get some warning signs before it happens, but that didn't used to happen. They're changing and I don't know what it means." I looked away. "You won't have to worry about it. I'll be out of your way soon."

"What's that mean?" Nikki asked. "It's not safe for you out there! What about Fawn?"

My heart ached at the thought of putting my daughter in jeopardy. But staying wasn't an option. It was obvious Renegade was pissed at me, and I doubted he wanted me to stay in his home another moment. Maybe he could return the things he'd bought for us, except the clothes we were wearing.

"You're not fucking leaving," Renegade said.

"You don't want me here," I said softly. "I never meant to cause any trouble. I should have left when I woke up."

"Why didn't you?" Nikki asked. "If you weren't going to stay, why not leave right then?"

"Fawn. She trusts the two of you and seemed happy. It was the first time she'd had a real home and I didn't want to take it from her." I tipped my chin up and stared at Renegade. "If I go, can Fawn stay with you? Just until I can make other arrangements?"

He stared at me, not a single emotion showing on his face. When he spoke to his sister, his voice was soft but still held a ring of authority.

"Leave, Nikki. I think I need to discuss a few things with Darby."

Nikki gave a quick nod and scurried away. I heard her speaking to Fawn and then the front door opened and shut with a *click*. Facing Renegade, knowing I was alone with him except for my silent five-year-old, had my heart hammering in my chest. I didn't know what was about to happen, but I hoped my daughter didn't pay the price. I'd never forgive myself if anything happened to her.

Chapter Five

Renegade

She wanted to leave? Not fucking likely. I'd never been inside a woman without a condom, and I was pissed as hell that I'd screwed up. That was on me, though. I wasn't mad at her. Didn't mean I was letting her walk out of here. If there was even the slightest chance she carried my kid, she wouldn't be going anywhere. It was the way she'd claimed I didn't want her here that had me wanting to bellow in rage, and it was my own damn fault. I shouldn't have run from her room, should have talked to her. It seemed she'd drawn the wrong conclusion over my reaction to the lack of protection.

My gaze scanned her body, noting the clothes I'd purchased fit her well. The leggings hugged her hips and the stretchy shirt clung to her breasts. Even with her hair wet and hanging down her back unbrushed, she was still beautiful, and far too fucking tempting. The thought of her carrying my kid had scared the shit out of me, but seeing her like this made me hard as fuck and all I wanted to do was bend her over again, consequences be damned.

"We're going to go eat with Fawn, then get her settled with a movie or her new toys. You and I need to have a discussion," I said.

She nodded, but her face had paled and I knew she was scared. As much as I wanted to reassure her, I had a feeling she wouldn't like what I had to say right now. Considering how bikers had treated her so far, it wasn't likely that she'd be thankful I was about to forbid her from leaving my house, at least until I knew if I'd knocked her up. Although, I had to admit the thought of her and Fawn out there on their own didn't give me any warm fuzzy feelings. Even if we were able to stop Boomer, it didn't mean she'd be safe. What if any of the others who had hurt her found her off on her own?

I followed her to the kitchen, then pulled out a chair for her beside Fawn. The little girl had already finished her bowl of soup and stared into the bottom of the dish. Reaching for it, I dumped it into the sink and took down a plate. I filled it with the casserole Nikki had made, then set it and a fork down in front of Fawn. The little girl's eyes went wide and she grabbed the utensil and started shoveling the food into her mouth as if it would be her last meal. It made me wonder just how many times she went without food. Clarity had mentioned that she was overly thin. No kid should ever go hungry. It's why I'd started a charity ride with the club last year. All the money earned went to the local schools with their promise to earmark it to pay for meals for anyone who couldn't afford breakfast or lunch.

Focusing on Darby, I realized that she was watching her daughter with tears in her eyes. Regardless of our issue, I knew that she would do whatever it took to keep her kid safe. That alone made things a bit tricky. If I did get her pregnant, then I knew she'd be a good mom to our kid. I couldn't just toss her out and keep the baby, which meant... Fuck. I'd have to claim her. I waited but the feeling of my heart being squeezed, of being unable to breathe never came. Typically, the thought of having a family scared the shit out of me. I wasn't ready to analyze why the thought of Darby and Fawn being here wasn't stirring that same feeling. Oh, I'd been scared shitless earlier, but the two were rapidly growing on me and it hadn't even been a full twenty-four hours yet.

"Do you want soup or the casserole?" I asked Darby. "Nik made them so they're safe to eat."

"Maybe the soup," Darby said.

I fixed a bowl and set it in front of her with a spoon. The way her hand shook as she fed herself told me plenty. Fawn wasn't the only one starving. It didn't take a genius to figure that what little food Darby had been permitted she'd given her to her daughter. The fact they'd lasted as long as they had was a miracle. I didn't think Darby would necessarily see her situation that way. She'd been through hell, but if she was anything like Meg or Clarity, then the experience would only make her stronger as she healed.

I scooped some of the casserole onto a plate and sat next to Darby. She tensed a moment, but kept eating. It was tempting to take the spoon from her and feed the soup to her, but I didn't think she'd appreciate the help. Even though we were still strangers, despite the fact I'd been inside her, I could tell that she was the independent type. The fact she'd even asked to leave Fawn here for a little while was astonishing. Not that Fawn was going anywhere, or her either.

"Fawn, your mom said someone hurt you and that's why you can't speak," I said. "The doctor who helped your mom might be able to help you too. Would you let me take you to his office so he can check your throat tomorrow?"

At first, I thought she'd ignore me, but she set the fork down and faced me. Her nose was slightly scrunched and it was obvious she didn't like the idea, but after a moment she nodded. I only hoped that Chansy could help the kid. I couldn't imagine being unable to talk, especially because some asshole had hurt me. Then again, I'd just kick the guy's ass. Fawn and Darby didn't have that opportunity. Not that I thought a woman couldn't take care of herself. Havoc's old lady could take just about anyone to their knees, and his daughter was well on the way to being just like her mom and dad. much to the horror of everyone who met her. The dickhead who had kidnapped Darby had used them against one another to keep them in line, and I couldn't wait to get my hands on him.

"I'll text the doctor after we eat and make sure he knows we're coming tomorrow. I'll stay with you the entire time if you'd like." I glanced at Darby. "I know you probably want to go too, but I think it's safer for you to stay here. If I take both of you, Boomer might try something. I'll make sure someone goes with us, and I'll ask a Prospect to stand outside the house in case you need anything."

Her lips thinned, but she didn't comment. Probably thinking about her plan to run off, but that shit wasn't going to happen. She obviously trusted me with her kid, since she'd asked to leave Fawn here. Now I just needed to make sure I put Darby on lockdown as soon as possible. The last thing I wanted or needed was her disappearing and Boomer locating her. I hadn't heard a peep from the Pres or anyone else since I'd relayed the info about Darby's situation. For all I knew, Boomer was long gone, but I somehow didn't think so. If he'd left Darby in a dumpster in this town, he was more than likely hanging around to see if news of a body surfaced. He had to know that Fawn couldn't talk, so she wasn't a threat to him. As badly as Darby had been beaten, if no one had found her, then she could have died. I didn't know why he hadn't finished the job, or if he'd just been careless. If I'd dumped a body, I'd want to make sure the person was really dead and find out if there were any leads when the corpse was discovered.

We finished eating and I let Fawn pick a movie to watch in the living room, then I took Darby by the hand and led her to my room. I shut the door, then leaned against it, arms folded, to guarantee she had to stay and listen to what I had to say. She looked around the room, her hands twisting the hem of her shirt. When her gaze locked with mine, I could see the vulnerability there, and the resignation.

"I should have been clearer when I told you what happened to me. I guess I assumed since I got pregnant with Fawn, you'd understand they didn't use condoms. You need to get tested and I understand why you're pissed, but --"

I held up a hand to stop her. "Yes, it's a concern that you could be carrying something, but an STD isn't what freaked me out earlier. I didn't run from that room because I thought you had herpes or anything else. It was the realization I'd taken you bare and you could damn well be pregnant right now."

Her mouth opened and shut.

"I told myself a long time ago that I would never have a family. I've used women for pleasure, but never let one get close. And the thought of kids? Not something I wanted. That being said, if you're pregnant, there's no way in hell I'm letting you leave here with my kid."

Darby seemed to shrink in on herself and I wished I'd been a little gentler in the way I'd phrased things. When she'd said she was leaving, it wasn't because she was trying to keep our potential kid from me. She'd thought I didn't want her here, and in some ways, she'd be right. I hadn't wanted houseguests, especially of the female variety, but now that they were here, that I'd had a sample of what it was like to be inside her, I didn't want to let her go.

Fuck me. I was so screwed, and I had no doubt that Scratch and Cinder would have fun at my expense for a while.

"I'm not angry with you, Darby, though you're right and we both should get tested. I'm upset with myself for losing my head and not remembering protection. I've never taken a woman bare, not even when I was a teen. Being careless has consequences, ones that neither of us are really prepared for. Yes, you have a kid already, but do you really want another one right now?"

She pressed her lips together. I didn't think she'd say anything, but then she blew out a breath and came closer.

"Fawn is my entire world, and even though she's the result of rape, I love her more than anything. If I'm pregnant again, I'll love this baby too."

"That isn't what I asked."

"No," she said softly. "I don't want another one right now. Things are too messed up. Boomer could still come after me, I have nowhere to live and a daughter I can't even feed most of the time. The last thing I need is more responsibility." Her eyes grew sad. "I feel like a horrible mom for saying that. Does it make me a bad person?"

I reached out and pulled her into my arms. The way she melted against me felt too damn good, but I didn't release her. She needed comfort and I had to admit I liked that I was the one to give it to her.

"You're not a bad person, Darby. And you're an awesome mother. You've suffered in order to keep your kid safe. We'll get Fawn whatever help she needs, but you're wrong about one thing."

"What?" She tipped her head to look up at me.

"You do have a place to stay. Here. I'm not throwing you out, and I damn sure didn't go buy a bunch of furniture and toys for you to just haul Fawn out of here. This is your home for however long you need it."

Tears welled in her eyes, but she slammed them shut to keep the moisture from trickling over her lids. She buried her face in my chest and held on tight. I wondered how long it had been since anyone gave a shit about her, or offered her a bit of help. We hadn't discussed her life prior to Boomer getting his hands on her. I knew nothing about her. Speaking of...

"You need to be seen about your seizures. If they're preventable, then we need to get them handled before something bad happens. I'll get Chansy to schedule you somewhere. I'm sure you'll need an MRI or something. Fawn can stay here that day with Nikki or Clarity and her kids. She'll be safe."

"Why are you doing all this?" she asked.

It had started out as an order from my VP. He'd wanted me to bring her to my home and take care of her. It was the last thing I'd wanted to do, even though I'd wanted to ensure they both got whatever help they needed. Then I'd gone and kissed her, and fucked her. Now Darby was under my skin and I didn't know what to think or how to feel. Part of me still wanted to fucking run as fast as I could, but the other half? The other side wondered what it would be like to have Darby in bed with me every night, to wake up with her in my arms, to teach Fawn how to ride a bike and watch her grow up.

Yep. Screwed. Most definitely fucked in all ways. Goddammit.

I knew what I needed to do. I wasn't ready yet to admit it's what I wanted. Who the fuck decided in twenty-four hours they were keeping a woman and her kid? Then again, there was Scratch to consider. He'd been tempted by Clarity from the moment he met her, or so he said. Fucking hell. I wasn't about to admit that he could have been right about that Fate shit.

As she stared at me, I realized I hadn't answered her question. What exactly did I tell her? That her pussy was the best I'd ever had? That her kisses made me want more of them? I didn't think she'd be too impressed that the sight of her in the leggings she had on made me want to bend her over the nearest surface and bury myself balls deep.

"When I saw you in that dumpster and saw how scared your kid was, I knew I couldn't walk away. You needed help and I was going to give it to you. Honestly, I'd thought I'd take you to the clubhouse and let someone else take over, but now that you're here in my home I don't want you to go."

She blinked, then her brow furrowed and her nose scrunched like her daughter's had earlier. "What does that mean exactly? That you don't want me to go?"

"I want you and Fawn to stay. In my house." I cleared my throat. "And I wouldn't be opposed to having you in my bed every night, but it's not a deal breaker if that's not what you want. I'm not going to kick you out because I can't fuck you."

I inwardly winced. I wasn't exactly known for my eloquence and I was proving that right now. It would be a miracle if she didn't run the other way, or even slap me. Although, she didn't seem like the slapping type. Maybe she had been at one time, but right now she was more like an abused puppy, waiting for the next person to strike her.

"In your bed."

I nodded.

"Are you going to share me like Boomer did?"

"What? No! Fuck, no! You'd be mine, Darby. Mine and mine alone. No one would ever touch you." I blew out a breath. I was fucking this shit up. "If you've been around clubs, then you know about old ladies, right?"

She nodded.

"I want you to be my old lady, Darby. My name, and that of the club, would give you protection. You and Fawn would have a home, a family, and you'd never want for anything ever again."

The minute I said the words I had to wonder if I'd just dug my hole deeper. I was making it sound like I'd be doing her a favor, and while it was true she would benefit from the arrangement, it wasn't like I didn't want her around. Jesus. Why was this so fucking complicated? Havoc just laid claim to Jordan and they lived happy-ever-after. Sort of. It didn't look like I'd have it that easy. Darby didn't trust anyone. Or at least she hadn't, and for good reason, but it wasn't making this any easier on me. I'd thought she was coming around, but it seemed it would take a while to break through the training Boomer had instilled over the last five years.

"And what do you get out of it?" she asked. "Because I'm not exactly a prize."

"I'd get to watch Fawn grow up and teach her things, as her dad. And I'd get you in my bed every night." And again with the eloquence. I made it sound like I was thinking with my dick, and while he certainly had an opinion, the brain above my shoulders was actually making the decisions.

"I find it hard to believe you can't snap your fingers and have whatever woman you want."

She wasn't wrong about that, except the only one I seemed to want was her. No one had tempted me until Darby. The whores at the clubhouse had tried their best. Even women around town who wanted to walk on the wild side would try to lure me into their beds, didn't matter if they were single or married. Not a single one had gotten so much as a twitch out of my cock. Then I'd held Darby and gotten hard as a fucking post.

"Maybe the only woman I want is you," I said. "I already admitted I lost control and took you without protection. I'm forty-four years old, Darby. I've been sexually active since I was fifteen, and not once have I ever gone bareback. You did that to me, made me lose myself and only think of getting inside you."

"You're... You're..." She shook her head. "There's no way you're forty-four. You look thirty. If that. I could tell you were older than Nikki, and definitely older than me, when I saw you back in high school. I didn't think you were that much older, though!"

"Want to see my license to prove it?" I pulled out my wallet and showed her.

"Cory Adams?" she asked, her lips tipping up a little at the corners. "You don't seem like a Cory. I think Renegade suits you better. The name Cory makes you seem tame. I don't think I've ever met a badass with that name before."

"Know many of those, do you?"

She shrugged a shoulder. "I've met a few, or at least men who thought they were. I think it was more that they were just assholes."

I fought not to smile. It seemed my little Darby was coming out of her shell. She was getting bolder and more playful. I liked it. It made me wonder what she'd be like in a few more weeks or months. Before that could happen, I needed to handle Boomer. Darby wouldn't feel safe until that dickhead was dead and buried, or locked up for the rest of his life.

"You're mine, Darby. Maybe I should ask you to stay, but I won't. If I give you the choice, you'll leave. Not because you want to, but because you don't think you belong here. You said you're unworthy of me? That's bullshit. You even think of leaving and I'll track you down, then paddle your ass until you can't sit for a week, then I'll fuck you long and hard to remind you that your place is right here with me. Understand?"

She slowly nodded. It wasn't fear in her eyes as she looked at me. It was hope.

Tangling my fingers in her hair, I tipped her head back, then brushed my lips against hers. I kissed her soft and slow. There probably hadn't been much of that in her life. I'd fucked her in the other room. Now I wanted to make it up to her. Unfortunately, Fawn was still awake and I wouldn't take a chance on her walking in here or looking for her mom while I was balls deep inside Darby. I'd lost my head once already, with both Fawn and Nikki in the house. I couldn't risk it again. I pulled away before I was tempted to do far more than kiss her.

"We should go sit with Fawn until she goes to bed," I said.

"You want to sit with us?" she asked.

"What did I tell you?" I asked.

"That I'm yours."

"And that means that Fawn is mine too. I want to be the dad she never had. I'll probably fuck it up somewhere along the way, but I want to try."

She smiled softly. "That's all any of us can do. Try. Do you think I knew how to be a mom when I was fifteen? I still don't have all the answers."

I grasped her hand and led her out of the bedroom. Fawn was still on the couch watching an animated movie. She didn't even look our way as we sat down. Darby claimed the spot next to Fawn and I sat in my recliner. There was something almost comforting about sharing my space with them. Seeing the pure enjoyment on Fawn's face, and the contentment on Darby's, made a warmth spread through me.

I wasn't perfect, and I had no fucking clue how to be someone's dad, but I was going to do my damnedest to give them both everything they could ever need or want. I hoped that one day they would be able to put the horrors of their past behind them. Until then, I'd have my work cut out for me. Starting with the Mayhem Riders.

Chapter Six

Darby

My heart felt like it was going to fly right out of my chest, along with the butterflies tumbling in my stomach. He wanted us to stay, to live here with him, to be his family. I'd never considered that anyone would ever see me as more than a piece of ass, and while he'd been clear he wanted me in his bed, Renegade treated me differently than anyone had before. For the first time in five years, I felt hopeful that Fawn might have a fairly normal life, and that I could stop living every day in fear.

He'd promised to keep us safe. More than that, he was giving us a home. The fact he was part of a motorcycle club scared me a little. I hadn't met the others and didn't know what to make of the Devil's Boneyard. Other than the whispers I'd heard as a kid living in this town, I didn't know anything about them. They didn't seem to be all that bad. He'd mentioned his VP had kids. Were there other families inside the compound? Would Fawn have children to play with?

My precious baby had started to fall asleep toward the end of her movie. The moment Renegade had noticed, he'd picked her up and carried her to her room. It was the first time I'd been in there and it amazed me how much he'd bought for her in so little time. It looked like she'd lived here for weeks if not longer. She snuggled under the covers and held her arms up to him. I bit my lip so I wouldn't cry as he gently hugged my sweet girl, then kissed her forehead.

Renegade came toward me and paused before leaving.

"I'm going to lock up. You need to decide where you're sleeping tonight."

My gut clenched. He was still giving me a choice even though he'd made it clear he was claiming us as his. No one had ever given me a choice in whether I wanted to be touched. Even in foster care, I'd had more than one foster dad think it was okay to grope me when his wife wasn't looking. Renegade was different from them and from Boomer. I didn't quite know what to make of him.

I told Fawn goodnight and gave her a kiss on her cheek. After I shut off the light, I stood in the hall and wondered if I was brave enough to go after what I wanted. I'd had a crush on Renegade when I hadn't known him. Now that I was seeing how kind he was, I wanted more of that, more of him. He might be rough around the edges, but he treated me better than anyone ever had. To some, he might be considered an asshole, but under his gruff exterior he had a good heart. If he didn't, then he'd have left me and Fawn in that alley to fend for ourselves.

My heart hammered as I took one step after another toward his bedroom. I heard him moving around the front of the house, checking the windows and doors, and I knew it wouldn't be long before he went to his room. I crossed the threshold and stared uncertainly. Should I strip down to nothing? Stay as I was? Boomer and his horrendous friends were the only men I'd known intimately until Renegade had taken me earlier in the other bedroom. I didn't have any idea what to expect.

"Are you sure this is what you want?" he asked, his rough voice making me spin to face him. He leaned against the doorframe, looking relaxed and unconcerned, but I could see the tension in his body.

"I'm sure."

"You're not doing this because you think I'll throw you out?" he asked.

I shook my head. "I want to be here, to share a room and a bed with you. I'm just not sure what you expect from me, what the rules are."

"Rules?" His brow furrowed.

I licked my lips and wondered if I should say something or keep silent. There had been a lot of rules when Boomer had owned me. With Renegade, I didn't quite understand my place. He said he wanted me to be his old lady, and while I sort of understood what that meant, I'd never had a chance to talk to the ones I'd met and had no idea how their lives differed from what I'd known with Boomer. I'd noticed their property cuts and that some were marked on their bodies.

In the end, I decided to clamp my mouth shut and not tell him what I'd meant. He'd heard enough about my captivity. If there were certain things I should or shouldn't do or say, then I hoped he would tell me so I wouldn't anger him or embarrass him in front of the rest of the club. Despite the fact I'd been living with a biker the last five years, I felt a bit out of my depth with Renegade. He wasn't like anyone I'd met before and I didn't know how to act, what to say, or what to do.

"Darby, the only rules I have are about your safety for the most part. In our home, you can call me Cory if we're alone, but you don't have to. In front of the club, I'm always Renegade. No one can call me Cory except you, or Fawn if she were able to speak. I don't mind you leaving the house, but until I have a property cut for you, I want you to only leave if you're with me."

I nodded my understanding and he continued.

"After you have the property cut, you need to wear it whenever you're outside of the house, even if you're outside the compound. No, especially if you're outside the compound. I'd prefer that you stay inside the gates unless you have an escort of at least two men, doesn't matter if they're patched members or Prospects. Same goes for Fawn when she wants to go outside the gates."

"Why do I need to wear the property cut outside of the compound?" I asked.

"For protection. It shows everyone you're mine, and that means I'll protect you with my last breath."

"What about Fawn?"

"Kids don't get one, but maybe we can come up with something if you think she'll feel left out. She's just as much mine as you are."

I took a shuddering breath and released it, letting the tension ease from me. There were still things we needed to address. I just wasn't certain how to bring them up.

"I saw your cut and know you're important. You have a title and not everyone does," I said.

"I'm the Road Captain for the Devil's Boneyard. Does that bother you? I know you said Boomer was a Nomad, so he wouldn't have been an officer for any of the chapters of the Mayhem Riders. Were you around the others very often?"

"Sometimes, but I learned early to keep my mouth shut and keep to myself. I just wondered if your club had to approve of me before you claimed me? What if they think I'm not good enough?" I hated baring my soul like that, letting him see that I was still vulnerable.

"My VP and Pres have already hinted that you were here to stay. They won't have a problem with it, but I do need to ask if they'll call Church so I can make everything official. I also need to discuss Boomer with them and figure out how we're going to handle him and the Mayhem Riders."

"Will I get to meet everyone eventually? Are there a lot of kids Fawn can play with?" I asked. I remembered him mentioning someone named Scratch had kids, but were there other families here too?

"I'll see if one of the old ladies will throw a family party at the clubhouse soon so you can meet everyone, and yes, there are kids for Fawn to play with. Jackal and Josie have a daughter named Allegra who is close to Fawn's age. Caleb is Scratch and Clarity's boy and he's around the same age too."

"Are those the only kids?" I asked.

"No, there are a handful of others, but they're all younger. Irish and Janessa have a girl who's a little younger than Fawn. The rest of the kids are three or under."

At least I understood why they had a playground. It seemed that quite a few of the club members had settled down and started families. It gave me hope that I had found myself in a good place, and that Fawn would thrive here. She deserved to have a dad and family who loved her, friends, and to know that she was safe and loved. Renegade had already given her far more than she'd ever had before. I'd been lucky to get a pack of crayons and a few coloring books from the dollar store here and there. Boomer had never cared if she had toys, or even if she ate for that matter. She'd just been a pawn to him.

He pushed away from the doorframe and came toward me, stopping close enough I could smell the leather of his cut and the scent of whatever cologne he used. Slowly, he reached out and ran his fingers through my hair. My eyes slid shut and I found myself leaning into that touch.

"If you're sure you're ready to move in here, to stay in my bed every night, then you should go get your things. I'll make room in the dresser and closet. Bring your bathroom stuff too."

I opened my eyes and turned to do as he'd said. He'd purchased so many things it took me several trips to move everything from the guest room and hall bathroom. As I put my things away, I left out one of the pajama sets he'd bought. He hadn't said anything about sleeping naked, but if it was a requirement I was sure he'd say something when I started to change clothes. Boomer had hated it when I wore clothes to bed, even though I didn't sleep in his every night, he liked me to be ready and available.

A shiver ran down my body at the thought of his touch. If I never saw him again, it would be too soon. I heard the shower running and changed for bed, then slipped under the covers. Far too nervous to sleep, I clutched at the blankets while I waited on Renegade to come to bed. He came out of the bathroom with a towel around his waist and went to the dresser, then pulled out a pair of underwear. Without a hint of modesty, he dropped the towel and put his boxer briefs on.

I admired the lines of his body, and the graceful way he moved, like a predatory cat in the jungle. He didn't come straight to bed. Instead, he grabbed his phone and started tapping on the screen, then made a call when he was finished. I tried not to eavesdrop, but it was hard since he hadn't left the room. I heard him request testing for both of us, and mentioned my seizures. I'd never heard of someone calling a doctor at home, but I had to wonder if that's what he'd done.

Then again, I'd never known a doctor to make house calls either.

By the time he slipped into bed next to me, I was wound so tight that every muscle in my body started to ache. Even though he'd asked for the tests, the damage had already been done. I didn't know if he would wait for the results before he touched me again, or if he'd ask me to strip at any moment. He turned to face me, lying on his side, and draped his arm over my waist, tugging me closer to him. His lips brushed my temple.

"Get some sleep, Darby. I have a feeling the next few days will be busy and you need your rest."

"You aren't going to…"

"Not tonight. And for the record, I'll never take something not freely given to me. If you'd told me to stop earlier, I would have no matter how badly I wanted you. Always remember that. You're safe with me."

I rolled over and clung to him, burying my face in his chest. Having him hold me, run his hand up and down my back, made tears spring to my eyes. He let me cry, murmuring words of comfort until I sniffled and wiped the last of the moisture from my cheeks. It had been so long since I'd permitted myself to have a good, hard cry. Admittedly, I felt a lot better, and while it was partly due to the man holding me, it was more than that.

"Was that the doctor on the phone?" I asked.

"His after-hours nurse. She said we can come in tomorrow to have the tests done and Chansy can speak to us then about a referral for your seizures. Fawn can go with us, but I'd prefer not to take you both out at the same time. Less temptation if Boomer is still lurking." He rubbed his beard against me. "The text was to the club Pres, Cinder. He said we'll have Church first thing in the morning. We can go to the doctor's office after that. You'll be alone here with Fawn for a bit, but I'll have a Prospect outside the front door to watch over the two of you."

Everything was changing, and so fast that I felt like my head was spinning. I didn't know why Renegade had found us, but I would be grateful to whoever had placed him in the right place at the right time. I didn't know that I believed in God anymore, not after all that had happened during my life. Truthfully, I didn't think I'd ever believed. But if there was a greater power watching over us, then I was thankful they'd chosen Renegade to keep me and Fawn safe. The thought of Fawn being in that alley, vulnerable as I lay unconscious in a dumpster, terrified me. What if someone as evil as Boomer had found her? I could have lost my baby forever if things had turned out differently.

"You're thinking too much, Darby. Sleep," Renegade murmured.

I knew he'd said I could call him Cory, but it really didn't suit him. I had to wonder if he had a middle name. Most people did. Would he get angry if I always called him Renegade? Even though he'd said it was my choice, he had to have a preference.

"Darby." There was a hint of warning in his tone.

"I'm sorry. My mind is racing."

"Then talk to me. Whatever is bothering you, just let it out."

I bit my lip and decided to start with the easiest question. "Do you have a middle name? Or something only your family calls you?"

He chuckled softly. "Still don't think I look like a Cory?"

"Not exactly."

"My middle name is Slater. I used that name in high school because I thought it sounded cooler," he said. "You're welcome to use that if you like it better than Cory and don't want to use my road name."

"Slater." I smiled. "I like it. I can see you as a Slater."

"What else is bothering you?" he asked.

"I don't think it's worries so much as just... I'm overwhelmed? I thought I would die when Boomer beat me this last time. Instead, I woke up here with you, my daughter safe and cared for, and I'm not sure how to act or feel." I pursed my lips. "Did you ever watch that show *Buffy the Vampire Slayer* with Sarah Michele Geller?"

"I'm not going to admit if I did or didn't."

From his tone, I could surmise that he had in fact watched it, and apparently enjoyed it. Good. We had something in common, even though the show had gone off the air before I was old enough to enjoy it, I'd caught a few reruns over the years and had gotten hooked.

"When she comes back from the dead in season six, the way she feels when she re-enters the world. That's sort of how I feel right now. I've been in hell most of my life and suddenly the world is bright, nearly blindingly so. She wasn't in hell, but the harsh difference between where she'd been and being alive again, that's how I feel."

"Makes sense, I guess. You didn't really say anything about your life before Boomer took you. Do you have family who might be looking for you?" he asked.

"No. I was raised in the system. My mother abandoned me at a fire station when I was only a few days old. No one knew who she was or anything about me. The person who took me in named me, and I had a good life the first few years. When I was four, the lady was in a car accident and died. After that was a different story. One home after another, all with daddies who couldn't keep their hands to themselves."

He squeezed me tighter. "I'm sorry, sweetheart. Nik was in the system for a while too. Our parents died and even though I was old enough to care for her, the courts wouldn't give me custody. I kept a close eye on her, though, and she was safe. You should have had someone watching over you, protecting you."

"I saw you," I blurted. "The times you were with Nikki at the school or at the diner. I had a crush on you when I was a teenager."

He went completely still and I wasn't even sure he was breathing. He eased away from me and I caught his gaze. What I saw stole the breath from my lungs.

"You're the girl who was always watching us. I'd thought that was you," he said. "When I pulled you from the dumpster, I knew you were familiar but I couldn't place where I'd seen you. It wasn't until you and Nikki mentioned going to the same school that it finally clicked."

My cheeks burned. "I didn't think you noticed. I wasn't trying to be rude back then. It's just that I couldn't seem to look away from you. Even though you were obviously too old for a thirteen-year-old girl, or fourteen and fifteen, it didn't stop me from dreaming about having you hold me, kiss me."

He smiled faintly. "And did it live up to your expectations?"

"Even better."

"As much as I hate to admit that Scratch was right, maybe he was. I've never believed in Fate or any of that crap, but the fact I found you must mean something. Not to mention that it's a bit ironic Boomer dumped you in the same town where he'd kidnapped you all those years ago."

I hadn't really thought of that, but now that he mentioned it... I didn't know why Boomer had come here. There weren't Mayhem Riders in the area. The men who had been with him that last night were ones I'd seen before. My brain hurt as I tried to force the memories of how I knew them, and when it clicked into place, I felt a spike of fear.

"Easy, Darby. You're going to hyperventilate. What's wrong?"

"The men. The ones with Boomer. They're the same ones who were with him the night he kidnapped me, the night of the party. What if they're here to do it again?"

He sat up and stared down at me. "You mean another party to lure in high school girls?"

I nodded.

"Fucking hell." He snatched his phone off the bedside table and made a call. "Shade, I need you to search for any disappearances in the area of young teen girls. Darby remembered something. The men with Boomer are the same ones who helped with her kidnapping before. Also see if you can find out about any parties being pushed to the high school crowd. That's how they lured in Darby and the others."

I didn't know what Shade was saying, but Renegade nodded his head and rubbed at his beard.

"Right. Thanks, brother. I'll see you in Church tomorrow."

- 83 -

He disconnected the call and settled back against his pillow, putting the phone away. I curled against his side and wondered if it was all right for me to ask about the call. Boomer never wanted me to know anything, and for all I knew Renegade shared that with him. I didn't know if it was a biker thing or not.

"If Shade can't find anything, there are others who will help him. Hackers with clubs we call family or friends. We won't let him take anyone else, Darby."

I didn't know if he could keep that promise or not. Boomer didn't exactly play by the rules, not even the rules other bikers followed. I hoped that I was wrong and he wasn't planning anything. I never wanted anyone to suffer the way I had.

Chapter Seven

Renegade

I hadn't slept for shit last night. Darby had eventually dozed off, curled against me. The thought of Boomer snatching more girls left a sour feeling in my stomach. Even worse, I worried that he'd come looking for Darby and Fawn. No matter what it took, I couldn't let him get his hands on them again.

Everyone had gathered for Church, except Cinder. Our Pres seemed to be running a bit late, and I had no doubt that his son was the cause. Tanner was a fussy baby and had a tendency to keep his mom and dad awake all night. Even though Cinder grumbled now and then about a lack of sleep, everyone could see he doted on his son, and his wife.

He stumbled in about ten minutes late and looked like he hadn't slept for weeks. Collapsing onto his chair, he leaned back and shut his eyes a moment.

"Better get this shit started before I go to sleep right the fuck here," he muttered. "Christ. If that boy doesn't start sleeping at night, I may lose my fucking mind."

Everyone wisely kept their amusement to themselves.

Cinder sat up and looked around the table. "A few of you are aware that Renegade found a woman and kid outside the liquor store. The woman was in a dumpster, passed out and beaten to hell. Dr. Chansy patched her up and the kid seems okay minus the fact she doesn't talk."

"Consider that a blessing," Shadow muttered.

I knew there was a story there, but I didn't have time to dig it out of him. Far as I knew, Shadow didn't have kids, so what the hell would he know about it? It seemed he was hiding something, and I wanted to know what it was. In due time. Right now, my concern was for Darby and Fawn.

"I'm claiming Darby and Fawn," I said. "I'll need a property cut for Darby, and I want something to give Fawn so she won't feel left out."

Scratch snickered and I fought the urge to flip him off. But I liked having my head attached to my shoulders and not kicked around like a soccer ball. Anyone who thought the silver in the VP's hair meant he was slow would realize their mistake quick enough, assuming they lived long enough.

"Tell us about Boomer," Cinder said. "Has she mentioned anything else?"

I relayed everything I'd learned, including her fear that he was back in this area in an attempt to snatch more girls. Made sense if that was why he'd dumped her. Maybe she'd gotten too old or become too much trouble. If he'd taken her when she was fifteen, it was possible that Boomer was a pedophile who enjoyed underage teens. Or maybe he was just an asshole who liked to rape women regardless of their age. A teen girl was less likely to cause as much trouble as a fully grown one, unless she'd been trained to protect herself.

"Find anything, Shade?" Cinder asked.

"There are no signs around town or by the high school about a party, however, I did discover that someone sent out word for a party through social media, targeting the freshman and sophomore girls," Shade said.

I didn't want to know how he'd discovered that. Something told me that he hadn't necessarily hacked someone's phone, which meant he had a contact at the high school. I sure the fuck hoped it was a teacher and not one of the students. I knew Shade well enough that I could say with absolute certainty he'd never cross a line with an underage girl, that didn't mean he wouldn't chat one up and get just friendly enough that she'd feed him information.

"The party is being held tonight at a warehouse just outside town. I have the time and address," Shade said. "No way we can sneak in there with our bikes, though. We'd have to blend and I'm not sure most of us could pull that off."

"There isn't a damn patched member of this club who could pass for a high school kid. Not even Renegade even though his ass gets carded everywhere we go," Scratch said.

"Which is why I'm going to suggest we use Bane and Dixon," Shade said. "Bane is ex-Navy and Dixon might be older, but he can pass for a high school kid."

"Why would they let boys in there if they sent out the invitation to girls?" Cinder asked.

"Because they're going to have some girls with them, or rather women who can pass for fifteen or sixteen if the lighting is right," Shade said.

"And which women are we sending into the viper pit?" Scratch asked. "Because none of our old ladies are going near that place. I doubt Renegade will let you send Nikki either."

"I was actually hoping that Nikki might want to help," Shade said.

"No fucking way are you getting my little sister involved in this," I said.

Shade shrugged. "Fine. Then I'll find someone else. Karley said she'd help."

Ashes shot up out of his seat. "What the fuck? Are you shitting me right now? You think I want my baby cousin going in there?"

Shade threw up his hands. "If we don't send some women in there, we'll never get through the doors. The second they see a bunch of bikers coming down the road, they'll scatter and we'll lose them."

"Fuck." Ashes sat back down. "You already talked to Karley and explained exactly what she's walking into?"

Shade nodded.

"Fine. If she wants to help, I won't stand in the way. But you better make sure Bane and Dixon know that I'll have their asses if she's taken or hurt in any way. She can hold her own, but not against a bunch of bikers who seem to follow no one's code but their own." Ashes ran a hand through his hair. "Where are you finding another girl?"

"I actually have two others lined up. One just graduated from the local high school. She's had extensive martial arts training," Shade said.

"Wait. Are you talking about LiLi Strong?" Charming asked.

"Yes. She's won several state and national championships." Shade leaned back in his chair. "In addition to her and Karley, I've spoken to Nikki and a woman by the name of Catori Windtalker."

"Why do I know that name?" I asked.

"She's the Hopi woman who was traveling through here with her family two years ago when their car careened off the road. Catori was the only survivor," Stripes said with his thick Russian accent. "Isn't she twenty-two? A little old to pass for a high school girl."

"She doesn't look her age. Her father was a bladesmith and as long as she's armed with a few knives, she'll be fine. Catori knows how to protect herself," Shade said. "I'd never pick a woman who would be completely defenseless, and let's not forget that Bane and Dixon will be there too. It will raise up red flags if they refuse to let the two of them in there. Boomer will want to keep a low profile so no one goes looking for him later."

"What exactly is the plan?" I asked. "Because putting those women in danger isn't going to do a damn thing that I can see."

"They're going to slip something into Boomer's drink, along with anyone else there with him. It will knock them out long enough for Bane and Dixon to toss them into the bed of a truck and bring them here," Shade said.

"And if they're caught?" Cinder asked.

"They won't be," Shade said. "But if they are, then Bane and Dixon can help protect them."

I rubbed my forehead, a headache starting to building behind my eyes. This was so fucked up. There had to be another way to get to Boomer. Shade slid a file down the table and I snatched it before it made it all the way to Cinder and Scratch. Flipping it open, I saw the address of a seedy motel on the bad side of town.

If they were staying there, and Shade knew their location, why go to all the trouble to infiltrate the party? I scanned the file, ignoring Cinder thumping his hand on the table in irritation. He could chew me out later. Right now, I felt like I was missing something. It was on the last page that I realized why Shade didn't want to just go in and grab the bastard.

"Are you fucking kidding me?" I glared at Shade. "He's related to motherfucking Destroyer?"

I heard Charming suck in a breath, as well as several others. Stripes let out a long whistle. If Boomer was kin to Destroyer, then we could all very well have our asses handed to us if anyone found out we caused him to go missing. No one fucked with the Pres of the Mayhem Riders' original chapter. I'd only met the guy once, but pretty much everyone knew *of* him. His exploits were legendary, and so was the trail of blood that he sometimes left in his wake.

"Now you know why we can't just grab the jackwad," Shade said. "We have to be stealthy and make sure none of this can come back on our club."

Cinder grabbed the file from me and scanned it, then snorted. I stared as he jerked his phone from his pocket and pulled up a number in his contacts, then turned on the speaker.

"You aren't dead yet?" a rumbling voice said on the other end.

"No, and apparently you aren't either, dickhead," Cinder said. "You're on speaker with my club present."

"What the hell do you want, Cinder?"

"Destroyer, I have a bit of a problem by the name of Boomer."

There was a growl and it sounded like a bottle smashed against something on the other end of the phone. Cinder chuckled and looked downright gleeful.

"That's what I thought," our Pres said.

"What's the little cocksucker done now?" Destroyer demanded. "I swear to Christ that kid is more fucking trouble than anyone else I know."

Kid? Just how old was Boomer? The file had said he was related to the Destroyer, but not *how*. Not that the man went by "the Destroyer" but it was how most people referred to him. I sure the fuck hoped Boomer wasn't his son. The way Darby had spoken about the guy, I was expecting a man in his thirties or older. Hell, maybe even someone older than me. It hadn't occurred to me that he'd be young and that's how he'd managed to snag Darby and the others. Then again, I'd been a little more focused on the fact that a woman and kid were in my house.

"He kidnapped a few girls about five years ago, then came back here to leave one in a dumpster with her kid standing nearby. My Road Captain is claiming Darby and Fawn. He'd like a little payback for the shit Boomer put those girls through," Cinder said.

"Wait." I heard rustling. "Are you telling me that shit stain kidnapped underage girls?"

"Darby was fifteen when she was taken and raped," I said. "She's suffered every day since then and has a kid with an unknown father because Boomer liked to pass her around."

"Motherfucker," Destroyer said. "I don't give a shit what you do to him, but leave him alive. I think it's time I have a little chat with my nephew."

"I couldn't find a picture of Boomer anywhere," Shade said, speaking up. "Unless the one he used on social media to lure in the latest batch of girls is really him. If that's the case, he looks about two seconds older than the girls he's trying to nab."

"Boomer is Sheldon Pierce, and he's a twenty-six-year-old pain in my goddamn ass," Destroyer said. "He's my older sister's kid and when she passed I promised to watch over him. Little did I realize he'd be an unredeemable fuckstick that didn't deserve to breathe much less reproduce. What does the kid look like?"

My gut tightened. "She's small. Really pale with red hair. Her mom is a redhead."

"Does she have a birthmark?" Destroyer asked. "Something that resembles a clover?"

I didn't have a fucking clue. It wasn't like I'd helped the kid bathe or get dressed. I'd figured it was better if women helped her. Weren't there rules about that kind of shit? I wasn't her birth father, even if I did plan to be the only dad she ever knew.

Scratch cleared his throat. "My wife helped the girl bathe the first night she was here. Clarity mentioned that Fawn had an unusual birthmark, a deep strawberry color, on her right hip. It looked a bit like a four-leaf clover."

"I'm going to kill him," Destroyer said.

"Does the clover mean something?" I asked. Obviously the man had asked about it for a reason.

"One of Boomer's friends patched in around the same time as my nephew. Shark was part of my club for a few years, and then he just up and left one day. Came back about four years ago," Destroyer said. "If he hadn't said that he was with Boomer, keeping an eye on him, then I'd have stomped his ass for pulling that crap."

"And that has what to do with this shit?" Cinder asked.

"Shark has a dark red birthmark on his forearm of a four-leaf clover. We gave him shit over it. Seems to run in his family," Destroyer said.

"He raped Darby," I said, feeling a burn start in my chest and work its way through my body. "He forced himself on her, got her pregnant. She was a kid and helpless."

"Shark will be dealt with. Permanently," Destroyer said. "Do what you want with the Mayhem Riders with Boomer. But I want my nephew alive when I get there. His Fate is mine to decide."

I didn't like it, but I couldn't very well tell the man no. Cinder wrapped up the call, but my head was filled with everything I'd learned. I didn't know if Darby would want to know about the father of her child or not. At the very least, it might give her some closure to know the man wouldn't be breathing much longer. Club business was just that, but I wouldn't leave her completely in the dark. If knowing that Shark would die, and that Boomer wouldn't be far behind him, would give her some sort of comfort, then I'd give that to her. Gladly.

"I'll speak with Bane and Dixon about going after Boomer at the party tonight," Cinder said. "But I want Phantom, Charming, Gator, and Magnus to go as well. We'll have an easier time of taking him by surprise under the cover of night than in broad daylight. The four of you are to hold back and not give yourselves away. I need you to blend with the crowd as much as you can. So roll your bikes to the warehouse and give Bane and Dixon some backup. Bring Boomer and any other men with him to our special interrogation room."

"Pres --" Before I could finish, he lifted a hand to stop me.

"I know you want to be part of this, Renegade, and I understand why. Let them bring Boomer here, then you can get your pound of flesh. Right now, you need to focus on Darby and Fawn," Cinder said.

I stood and left the room, but Shade stopped me on the way out to my bike. His hand was firm as he gripped my arm, not giving an inch even when I tried to jerk out of his grasp.

"There's something else you need to know. I didn't want everyone else privy to it," Shade said.

"What?"

He handed me another set of papers. Not just any papers. Copies of blood work.

"What is this?" I asked.

"Found this shit in one of Boomer's email accounts. The idiot doesn't keep his business protected very well. I've accessed everything he's touched online in the last five years, and then some. But there's good news. Boomer had Darby tested regularly." He tapped the top page. "The last results are from a week ago. Since she'd been raped I thought it might be a concern. It seems he wanted to make sure he didn't catch something from her after he let others have a turn. Don't know why the dumb fuck didn't just make them wrap their dicks."

"How would she not know about this? She's been worried that she caught something from those assholes."

Shade shrugged. "Maybe he did it when she was drugged. Only Boomer can answer the how and why. Just thought you might want to have those."

I thanked him and went out to my bike. Tucking the pages into my belt, I turned the engine over and drove back to the house. Jin was on the porch, a Prospect related to Phantom. The kid was dedicated and I knew he'd patch in before long. I sent him back to the clubhouse and went inside, eager to give Darby the good news.

Fawn was sprawled on the living room floor watching another animated movie, her doll beside her. I didn't hear any other sounds in the house and went in search of my woman. With Jin outside, I knew she hadn't left. The kitchen was empty, and so were the other rooms. When I reached the bedroom, I heard the shower running. I quickly stripped out of my clothes, tossing the papers onto the dresser, and decided to join her.

I opened the shower door and she squeaked, spinning to face me and nearly falling on her ass. I grabbed her to keep her upright, mindful of the stitches she'd wrapped, then stepped under the spray. Darby blinked up at me and reached over to shut the shower door.

"Is your meeting over?" she asked. "Are we leaving for the doctor?"

"The doctor won't be necessary for today. Still need a referral for your seizures, but..." I smiled and wrapped my arms around her. "Shade found copies of lab work in Boomer's email account. He had you tested a week ago for STDs. You're clean, sweetheart. Or at least you were then."

Her hands tightened on my arms. "I didn't know. How did I not know he'd had me tested?"

"Shade thought you might have been drugged when it happened."

"I guess that's possible. He gave me drugs if I started to get too hard for him to handle or started asking too many questions. I don't think it was the same thing back to back and must have been spaced out just right because I didn't get addicted to anything." She leaned into me, pressing her cheek to my chest. "You have no idea how glad I am that I didn't give you anything. He hasn't touched me in about three weeks, and neither has anyone else. I mean, not in a way that would have gotten me sick."

I didn't want to know in what way he *had* touched her, but I was thankful that she wouldn't have a lasting thing like herpes or HIV to deal with. It seemed Boomer had the same concern, at least for himself. I doubted that he gave a shit if Darby was sick, only that he hadn't wanted to catch something from her after passing her around. It wouldn't save him from the beating I would give him. I wanted to make that fucker bleed.

"Boomer won't be a problem much longer." I tucked the wet strands of her hair behind her ear. "He's being picked up tonight, and his uncle is coming to take care of the problem."

I didn't know if I should tell her about Shark or not. She'd claimed to not know who Fawn's father was, but if the man had the same mark on his arm as Fawn had on her hip, she had to have noticed.

"Shark will be dealt with as well. Permanently," I said.

Her face paled, but she didn't say anything.

"He's Fawn's father, isn't he?" I asked.

"I don't know. He liked to hurt me, and he's one of the ones who…" She clamped her lips tight, but I understood. Her gaze held mine. "Until now, Fawn didn't have a father. You said you wanted the job. Is that still true?"

"Yeah, sweetheart. I still want the job. Were you hoping that with Boomer gone you could leave?"

"No, but I thought… I just wondered…"

"You're mine, Darby. Both of you, and I'm not letting you go."

"I don't want you to," she said softly. "There's nowhere else I'd rather be."

Chapter Eight

Darby

Renegade backed me to the shower wall, every hard inch of him pressed against me. The fact he wanted me was more than evident. I'd just been concerned that all he wanted was sex, and he could get that anywhere. He'd told me that wasn't the case, more than once, but after only being an object for the last five years, it was hard to believe someone actually wanted me as more than their whore. The heat blazing in his eyes was enough to make my knees weak and my heart race. I trembled in anticipation. Until Renegade, I'd never experienced passion. A girlhood crush was one thing, but what I felt when his hands were on me? Or even when he just looked at me the way he was now… I'd never had something like this before.

The moment his lips touched mine, I knew I was doomed. No one would ever make me feel this way. It was him and only him who could do this to me. I'd wanted Renegade for too long. Maybe after just once I could have walked away, but with his hands gripping my hips and his mouth devouring mine, I knew that I never wanted to leave. Whatever was simmering between us was too powerful for me to ignore.

I felt the hardness of his cock press against me and I squirmed, wanting to feel him inside. I slid my hands up and down his arms before gripping his shoulders. Renegade lifted me and I wrapped my legs around his waist. The head of his cock brushed against my pussy and he rocked his hips, teasing me. The drag of the head of his cock against my clit sent sparks dancing along my nerve endings. I couldn't stop the moan that left me, nor hold back from digging my nails into him. There was a tightness coiling inside me, and I knew the only cure was for him to slide deep inside and fuck me until I screamed in pleasure.

"Please," I murmured as he broke the kiss. "I need you."

He stared down at me, his brown eyes darker than they'd been before, his desire making them nearly black. "I don't want to use a condom. I know I said I didn't want kids, but we already have Fawn. Being inside you, bare, was the most incredible thing I've ever experienced."

"You can't take something like that back later," I reminded him.

"I know, Darby. But you're mine. Fawn is too, as well as any other kids we have. I ran from your room earlier, but I won't run again."

"Then take me," I said. Having Fawn had been scary, but having a baby with Renegade would be different. I could tell from the way he was looking at me that he'd be with me every step of the way. He really did want this, want us. Whatever had spooked him before, he'd gotten control of it.

His gaze held mine as he slowly sank into me. The thick, hard length of him stretched me wide to accept him. There was a slight burn from the tight fit, but I was more than wet enough to take him and the moment he started thrusting, a slow slide of his cock, it was like I couldn't get enough. I wanted him harder, faster, deeper.

"Please, Slater." I didn't care that I was begging.

Saying his name felt right, and it seemed to trigger something in him. The moment I said the words, it was like his control snapped. He pounded into me, making pleasure spiral through me and leaving me dizzy. I gasped for breath as my release hit me, my pussy clenching down on his cock. Renegade didn't slow, just took me relentlessly, until I'd come twice more, the force of every stroke making my ass press harder against the shower wall. I would possibly have a bruise later, but I didn't care. It would be worth it.

I felt the warmth of his cum as his cock jerked and thickened. He groaned, burying his face in my neck. His breathing was ragged and I felt his heart racing. I wrapped my arms around him, digging my fingers into the hair at the base of his neck. For the first time in my life, I had a man pinning me to a wall and I just wanted to hold on and never let go.

He kissed me again, slower and softer than before. I'd never felt so cherished, so wanted. He hadn't said anything about how he felt, but I knew that it would really easy to fall in love with him. After having a crush when I was younger, being here with him was like living a fairy tale. Renegade was far from being Prince Charming, but he was *my* prince, albeit one who wore leather, and rode a motorcycle.

"Let's dry off and check on Fawn," he said. "I'm surprised she hasn't come looking for us yet."

"She hasn't had a lot of chances to watch what she wants. I'm sure she's in heaven having control of the remote. I know TV isn't good for her, or so they say, but I don't have the heart to take it away from her right now."

He kissed my forehead, then eased from my body. I felt a twinge between my legs, but it was the best kind of ache. Never before had I craved someone's touch the way I wanted his. If we could have stayed in bed all day and night, I'd have gladly done so. Renegade shut off the water and got out, quickly drying himself, then got a fresh towel to use on me. He wrung the moisture from my hair, then swiped the water droplets from my body. He gently unwrapped my stitches, checking to see if they'd stayed dry. I would be so glad when they dissolved.

"I was thinking that Fawn should have the chance to fix her room the way she wants it. I didn't have any idea what her favorite color was, or if there was a bed set she'd have preferred. There's no reason we can't put a small TV in there. You can turn on the parental settings to block certain content and even limit the times she's able to watch it." He tossed the towel over the top of the shower and took my hand, leading me into the bedroom. "I want her to be happy here."

"She is, Slater. So very happy." I was too for that matter, or at least, I was now that I wasn't so scared. "I've never seen her smile so much or look so carefree. She knows she's safe, and you've already given her far more than she's ever had." I turned into him, going up on tiptoe to kiss him. "You've been very good to both of us."

"Not quite. I acted like an ass with you. I'm sorry for that."

I drew away from him and took some clothes out of the dresser. He pulled on the underwear and jeans he'd left discarded on the floor, probably in his haste to join me in the shower. I smiled a little, happy that he'd been so eager. And if what he said about Boomer was true, and Shark, then soon I wouldn't have anything to worry over. I'd truly be safe. While there were others out there who would recognize me, I didn't expect trouble from them. Boomer and Shark had been the ringleaders.

"Something wrong?" he asked.

I jolted, realizing I'd been lost in thought and had stopped what I was doing to stare at him. My cheeks warmed and I shook my head, then finished getting dressed. I'd no sooner buttoned and zipped my jeans than Fawn opened the door. I froze, glancing at Renegade to see how he'd react. I'd explained to Fawn earlier that this was my room now, and she'd always just walked in whenever she wanted before. It hadn't been an issue since Boomer made me go to his room when he wanted me.

Renegade crooked his finger at her. "Come here, Fawn."

My body tensed as I watched, hoping that he wasn't about to hurt Fawn. He hadn't so far, and had given me no reason to think he would, but she'd just barged into his room uninvited. No matter how much I wanted to trust him implicitly, I had too many years of conditioning to overcome so soon. Men had never been kind to me, or to Fawn. Until Renegade. I hoped I wasn't about to witness that kindness coming to an end.

Renegade knelt down so he was on her level. "It's almost lunchtime. Are you getting hungry?"

Fawn nodded.

"Did your mom talk to you about what's happening? That you're going to live here?" he asked.

Fawn smiled widely and nodded her head so hard I worried she'd hurt herself.

"And she told you that I'm your dad? Your mom will be staying in here with me, and you get to sleep in your own room. We can paint it however you want."

I watched as Fawn's eyes turned glassy, and then a tear slipped down her cheek. Before I could react, Renegade reached for her. Fawn threw herself into his arms and he held her gently, rubbing her back and murmuring to her.

"It's all right, baby girl. You're safe, and you're home."

I sniffled and realized I was about to start crying too. I couldn't remember ever seeing a man hug Fawn until Renegade. And he was so careful with her. I felt the walls around my heart start to crumble, and the last of my fears of being here with him melted away. No matter how many times I doubted him, waited for the worst to happen, he kept proving to me that not all men were evil.

He stood, Fawn still clutched in his arms, and held out a hand to me. I went willingly, and snuggled into his side. Fawn turned her face toward me and gave me a smile. We were going to be fine. Happy even. If I didn't hate Boomer so much, I might have thanked him. Because he'd left me in the dumpster, Renegade had found Fawn and me, and he'd given us a home. I just wished I could have had this moment without all the pain and suffering of the previous years, not that I would trade Fawn for anything. If having her meant having to live through all that abuse, then so be it.

"I love you," I whispered, realizing in that moment that I really did love him.

His startled gaze met mine. The fact he didn't say it back made my heart ache, but I hadn't really expected anything else. We were strangers, and he hadn't even wanted a family. I knew he'd need time. Maybe someday he'd come to care for me, and eventually love me. As long as he kept giving Fawn the attention she craved, that would be enough. I'd lived without love my entire life, or most of it at any rate. I could barely remember the lady who had taken me in as an infant. Most of what I knew about her came from what my social worker had told me one day. I couldn't really miss what I had never had. At least, that's what I told myself, but I knew that one day it would break me if he never felt that way about me.

Fawn opened her mouth and then frowned when she couldn't speak. I felt so bad for her. Renegade had mentioned taking her to the doctor today, but he hadn't. I knew he'd gotten sidetracked with his meeting and the information he'd learned about Boomer, and before that he'd been concerned about my seizures and blood work. The trauma to Fawn's throat had happened a long time ago, but I was grateful she would get some help now.

"I think it's time we went to see Dr. Chansy, little one," Renegade said. "Your mommy needs to stay here today, but we can pick up lunch on the way home and come back to eat with her. Sound good?"

Fawn didn't look convinced.

"I'll even let you choose where we order lunch," he said. "Anything you want."

Fawn's eyes lit up and she nodded eagerly.

Renegade set her down and told her to go put shoes on. Once she'd left the room, he pulled me against his chest and stared down at me. Too many emotions flitted through his eyes for me to determine exactly what he was thinking or feeling. His lips firmed and he leaned down to press his mouth to mine. It was a hard, quick kiss, but it still made me tingle in all the right places.

"I won't say I love you, Darby."

I tried to hide my reaction, but I must have failed. It felt like my heart had just fallen to the floor and shattered into a hundred pieces.

"I won't say it because the last people I said that to died in a fire. My family. I lost my parents and my brother. Nikki was spared because she wasn't home that night. I don't do the 'I love you' thing anymore.

Not even for Nik. But I promise that I will always look out for you, protect you, and care for you. And I'll never hurt you."

I hadn't known that about his parents. Not the details anyway. Although, I did remember Nikki being absent from school for a week and hearing something about a death in the family. Back then, I hadn't realized what had happened. It wasn't until Renegade had said something about Nikki being in foster care that I'd put the pieces together. I'd mostly kept to myself back then, and since she'd been older than me, we hadn't really interacted at school. I'd never had a family to lose, but I could only imagine how much he'd suffered losing them like that.

Reaching up, I cupped his cheek, then ran my fingers through his beard. If he couldn't say the words to me, then I'd make sure to say them to him as often as possible. The tender way he looked at me right now told me enough. Even if he couldn't give me the words I wanted, it was obvious he felt *something* for me, and that would be enough for now. Maybe one day, he'd be able to tell me that he loved me. They said that time healed all wounds, but maybe it was love he needed in order to heal. And that I could give him times a million if he'd only let me.

He kissed me once more, his tongue tangling with mine until my toes curled and I was clinging to him, ready to beg for more. Renegade pulled away, give me a wink with a sexy grin, then he finished dressing and left the room. I trailed after him, watching as he swung Fawn up into his arms and stepped out the front door. A man stood on the other side, someone who looked close to my age.

"Darby, this is Dixon. He's a good friend, and a Prospect for the club. He's going to make sure you're safe and have whatever you need while I'm gone," Renegade said.

"Did you want to come in?" I asked Dixon. If Renegade trusted him that much, then so would I. Unless he gave me a reason not to.

Dixon's eyebrows arched and he looked at Renegade. My sexy biker gave him a nod and Dixon entered the house. Renegade paused a moment, then gave me one last kiss before carrying Fawn out to his truck. I stood in the open doorway and waved as they drove off, then shut and locked the door.

"She's in good hands," Dixon said. "He'd sooner cut off his arm than let anyone hurt her."

"I know," I said. And I did. Whatever doubts I'd still had were gone after witnessing him and Fawn together just now. "The only danger she's in with Renegade is possibly being spoiled too much."

Dixon snorted. "You aren't wrong. Big guy always said he never wanted a family. I knew one day someone would come along and change his mind. Don't give up on him. Losing his parents and brother is something he may never get over, but I think being with you and Fawn will help ease the pain a bit."

I hoped he was right.

Chapter Nine

Renegade

It was a bit unnerving to have a silent kid in the car, but hopefully Dr. Chansy could figure out a way to help her. I fiddled with the radio, glancing in my mirror with each station until I saw her face light up. Smiling, I realized the kid preferred classic nineties songs. Not exactly the type of music that a badass biker should be listening to, but it did remind me of simpler times.

I pulled into a parking spot in front of the clinic and turned off the truck. Fawn was staring at the building with fear stamped on her cute little face. I unbuckled and went to get her from the back seat, releasing her from the booster seat Scratch had insisted I should buy. If it kept her safe, then that was all that mattered. Lifting her into my arms, she clung to me like a baby monkey as I carried her inside.

The receptionist's eyes went wide when we walked in, and she pasted a falsely bright smile on her face.

"May I help you?" She glanced from me to Fawn and back again.

"My daughter needs to see Chansy. He's expecting us," I said.

"I-I see." She looked at the computer screen on her desk. "Did you have an appointment?"

Was she fucking with me right now? Everyone in this damn office knew that Chansy helped the club when he could. Of course, I hadn't seen this particular lady before, but surely someone had trained her. While I knew the old ladies tended to do the civil thing and schedule an appointment, the rest of us just dropped in whenever we fucking needed medical help. I'd only called last night since it had been after hours and I'd known Chansy was gone for the day. Chansy also came to the club when he was needed, but since I hadn't known if he would need to X-ray Fawn's throat, I'd decided that bringing her in would be best, and Chansy had agreed.

"Just tell the doc we're here," I said then turned to take a seat.

I garnered a few looks from the moms in the room, and more than one little girl stared at me in wonder and fear. I fucking hated that kids were scared of anyone in a cut, and I knew it was their parents' doing. Kids didn't fear someone based on their looks unless their parents had taught them to be afraid. Of course, the smaller ones could just be scared because of how angry I'd gotten. It pissed me off. I'd never hurt an innocent, but they just saw the leather cut and decided I was some asshole rapist who would murder them in their beds.

Fawn sat on my lap and looked around the room, a nervous energy thrumming through her sight frame. I wrapped an arm around her waist and hugged her to me. It made me sick that Boomer had done this to her. I'd watched her open up at the house, but out in public, she still acted like she expected people to lash out at her. Even the moms and kids in the room had her pressing as close to me as she could.

"I can't believe they have kids," one of the mothers muttered. "They should be neutered and not spread more violence."

Violence? So the kid had some bruises and it must be my fault? I arched my eyebrow and stared her down. I might not hit a woman, but her husband needed to paddle her ass. I'd be willing to bet she was one of those people who sat in church on Sunday, then badmouthed everyone on the ride home. I hated those types of people. The self-righteous ones who thought they were better than everyone else, when really their spot in hell was just as assured as mine.

The woman blushed and turned her face away, having been caught.

"Is there a Renegade here?" asked a nurse through an open doorway to the left.

I stood with Fawn in my arms. "That's me."

"Dr. Chansy will see you now." The woman smiled softly at Fawn. "Well, aren't you a little cutie."

Fawn turned her face against me and held on tighter. Poor kid. I patted her back and carried her down the hallway and into the room the nurse indicated.

"Just wait in here and he'll be with you shortly. He wanted to handle the visit himself, unless you think she'd respond better to a woman taking her temperature and weight?" the nurse asked.

"We'll wait for Chansy, but thank you."

She smiled again and backed out of the room, shutting the door behind her. Once we were alone, Fawn released me and I set her down on the padded table. The paper covering crinkled as her slight weight pressed down on it. She looked around and saw a stack of books across the room. Pointing, she looked at me, silently asking for them. I grabbed the stack and set them down next to her. Fawn picked through them, then held one out to me.

"The Poky Little Puppy?" I asked, vaguely remembering my mother having read this one to me when I was little.

Fawn smiled and nodded.

"All right, little one. I'll read to you while we wait."

I opened the book and began, trying to read it with the same animation I remembered my mother using. Fawn's eyes were bright and her attention was focused on the book in my hands as I flipped page after page. We'd just gotten to the end when Chansy walked into the room.

"And how is my most beautiful patient today?" Chansy asked, coming closer.

Fawn went stark white and her eyes went wide.

"Easy, baby girl. Dr. Chansy won't hurt you. He's going to look at your throat, remember? See if he can help you speak?" I gently reminded her.

Fawn held still as Chansy approached, but I could still see the fear in her eyes. Poor kid. She'd been through so much and didn't trust easily. I didn't understand why she was so fearful of Chansy but had come right to me. Shouldn't that have been the other way around?

I stayed close as Chansy examined her. He recommended a scope to determine the damage done to her larynx and if all looked okay, then she would likely need speech therapy.

"I honestly don't know why she can't speak," said Chansy. "Children tend to heal quickly from this type of wound, if treatment is given immediately. Since the trauma happened a while ago and she's not been able to speak since then, it's hard to say what's going on without taking a look at the inside."

I could feel the fear rolling off Fawn at his words.

"I know that Fawn wants to be able to speak, but maybe we can wait a little on those tests?" I asked, glancing down at her. "Give her time to adjust to the idea? Maybe I can find some kid-friendly explanations online that she can watch."

The doc nodded. "That's a good idea. Just call me when you're ready for the next step and we'll move forward. As for Darby, I placed a call with a neurologist I've known for years. He understands the situation she's in and said to bring her by when you're able. He'll work her in, but expect a long wait that day. His appointments are booked for the next seven months."

I thanked Chansy and left with Fawn, stopping at the front desk to pay the bill. On the way home, she pointed to Wings 'N Things so I pulled over. She pointed to what she wanted on the menu, and since I wasn't sure what Darby liked, I ordered four other flavors as well. We walked out with seventy-five wings, but I knew Dixon wouldn't mind helping me eat whatever the girls didn't want.

At the house, I heard the TV going in the living room and paused on my way to the kitchen. Darby was curled up in the corner of the couch, sound asleep, while Dixon stared at the sports stats rolling across the bottom of the screen.

"Everything okay here?" I asked.

He turned toward me and smiled. "Yep. She lasted about ten minutes before she fell asleep watching some Rom-Com. Once I was sure she wouldn't wake up right away, I changed the channel. What's in the bag?"

"Wings. Thought you might want to stay and help us eat them."

Dixon got up and stretched. "You know it. Better wake Sleeping Beauty here, though. Her stomach has rumbled a few times since she dozed off."

I handed the bag to Dixon as he passed, and Fawn trailed after him. Kneeling in front of Darby, I ran my hand up and down her thigh before leaning in and brushing a kiss on her cheek.

"Time to wake up, angel."

Her eyes fluttered and slowly opened. "Slater?"

"It's me, sweetheart. Fawn's appointment is finished and we brought wings back with us for lunch."

She sat up and rubbed at her eyes, looking too damn adorable.

"What did the doctor say?" she asked.

"Fawn needs further testing before he can say what's going on, or if she can learn to speak again. She looked terrified at the idea of having someone see the inside of her throat, so I asked for a little time. Thought we could find some videos online, kid-friendly ones, that could explain what will happen so that she won't be scared."

Darby wrapped her arms around me. "You're such a good daddy. And to think you didn't want kids."

I hugged her to me. "It still scares the shit out of me, but Fawn's a good girl and I only want what's best for her. I might not be perfect, but I'll give her the best life I can."

"I know," Darby said, then she kissed me. "Let's go eat."

Lunch was filled with laughter and conversation as Dixon got to know Fawn and Darby better. I had to admit, it was nice having them around the table with me. Only having Nik here would have made it better. Speaking of my sister… I checked my phone. I hadn't received any texts or calls from her since she'd gone on her date. Frowning, I shot off a text asking her if everything was all right. I didn't get a response right away, nor did I get one a half hour later.

When my phone finally rang, it wasn't Nikki like I'd hoped. It was Cinder.

"We have a problem," he said.

"What kind of problem?" I asked.

"The kind where Bane and Nikki are in some trouble."

Everything in me went tight and cold. What the fuck? Why were Nikki and Bane in trouble? Had he seen something on her date? I'd asked another Prospect to watch over her, but maybe they'd handed it off to Bane for some reason?

"What the fuck is Bane doing with Nik?" I asked.

Cinder was quiet a moment. "I think that's a discussion for another time. Right now, we need to extract Nikki and Bane from the warehouse where Boomer has that party scheduled for tonight. It seems he decided to get things going a bit early."

I felt ice fill my veins. If he hurt her the way he'd hurt Darby… I didn't care if Destroyer wanted his nephew left alive. The man had just crossed a line, and I wasn't about to leave him breathing if he harmed Nikki. He'd already hurt my woman, and now my sister? No. He was done.

"I need you to go to the warehouse, but you'll need to get there quietly. Take your truck since we don't know what condition Nikki and Bane might be in right now. I'll have the others meet you there. Dixon still at your place?"

"Yeah, he's here."

"Good. Have him stay with Darby and Fawn."

I glanced at the three sets of eyes focused on me and hung up the phone. With a nod of my head, I asked Dixon to step outside with me. Darby was worried, I could see it in her eyes and the pallor of her skin, but I'd talk to her in a minute. Right now, I needed to ensure that she and Fawn stayed safe.

I told Dixon everything Cinder had shared and what I needed from him. Then I went to find my woman. She was in our bedroom, pacing from one end of the room to the other.

"I have to go for a bit," I told her.

"Why? What's going on, Slater?"

"It's club business. I can't give you the details, but Nikki is in some trouble and needs my help. I don't know how long I'll be gone, but Dixon is going to stay here with you and Fawn. He'll keep you safe until I come home. Don't leave the house. You or Fawn."

Darby flung herself into my arms and held on tight. I kissed her, and wished I had time for something more. When I left the house, Fawn's door was shut and I decided to leave her be. She must have heard enough to know I had to go somewhere for a bit, and the closed door told me enough. If she'd wanted me to say goodbye to her, then she'd have left the door open or waited in the living room.

As Cinder had suggested, I took the truck, knowing it was quieter than the bike. The warehouse was only a few minutes outside the city limits and I pulled over along the roadway just before I reached the long gravel drive. I saw Stripes, Charming, Phantom, Havoc, and Ripper were already here and waiting for me. I gently closed the door so I wouldn't give away our presence.

"Anyone have a plan?" I asked.

"I did some recon when I got here," Havoc said. "They beat the shit out of Bane. Not sure if he'll live or not. Nikki looks kind of rough, but she was awake. They've gagged her and tied her to a chair in the center of the warehouse. She's got some bruising and a bit of blood on her, but they mostly seem to be taunting her."

I flexed my hands, ready to commit violence on the assholes who dared take my baby sister.

"Looks like her lessons with Jordan didn't help," Havoc said.

Wait. What? "Lessons with Jordan?"

He nodded. "Remember when she was snatched? When she came back, Nikki went on and on about how brave Jordan was and how amazing that she'd been able to handle herself so well. So my woman started teaching your sister how to defend herself."

I knew exactly what Havoc was talking about. We'd thought we'd need to rescue Jordan, and some of the club had gone after her, only to arrive too late. She'd incapacitated her captors, those she hadn't outright killed. Anyone who decided to tangle with that woman had to be a fucking moron. She'd cut off your balls and feed them to you if you so much as looked at her wrong. I hadn't realized she was training Nikki to take care of herself, though. I'd taught her a little, but apparently not enough.

"How did they get Bane and Nikki?" I asked. "Bane isn't the Prospect I asked to tail her."

Phantom snickered. "Oh, he was tailing her all right. Or rather, riding her tail."

What. The Fuck.

"Are you telling me that little shit is fucking my sister?" I demanded.

Phantom shrugged. "From what I understand, it's a new thing. Sort of. Bane has had a thing for Nikki since he met her, but she was seeing that asswipe Chad. Now that she's single, she agreed to a date with him."

That little shit. I'd asked her about her date, and she'd said it was someone new. She never once said a fucking thing about dating someone from the club. Once I got her out of this mess and she healed, I was going to beat her ass until she couldn't sit for a week. She might not have outright lied to me, but she'd lied by omission.

"How many are in there?" I asked, jerking my chin toward the warehouse.

"Boomer and three others," Charming said. "They don't look like much of a threat, but I can see how he lured in those teen girls. He's got a pretty boy face."

That was saying something, especially since it came from Charming. The man could talk any woman out of her panties, no matter if she'd protested at first or not. One smile, one whisper in her ear, and she melted. At least the only thing he ever did was fuck them and leave them. Charming wasn't the type of guy to rape a woman. If any of his conquests had refused to undress, or told him to stop even mid-fuck, then he'd have backed off.

"How many entrances?" I asked.

"Four," said Stripes.

"So, four entry points, four men inside, and there's six of us. I'm liking our odds. Everyone armed and ready?" I asked.

Havoc grinned. "Always. I'll take front with Renegade. Phantom and Stripes get the back entrance. Charming and Ripper each take a side."

"Let's do this," said Ripper, slapping his hands together with an evil glint in his eyes. He hadn't earned his name by being a choirboy, and I had no doubt that blood would be shed today.

We stuck to the dense grass and trees on either side of the drive and approached the building. Once everyone was in position, we burst through the doors, startling the men inside. Did the assholes really think they could take our Prospect and my sister without us coming for them? The look on Boomer's face was priceless as he gaped at us.

"Get away from my sister, asshole," I said.

"S-sister?" Boomer asked, glancing at Nik. "No, she's just some club pussy we caught with the Prospect."

"Nope, that's my baby sister. I already had a debt to settle with you, but you've just added to the level of pain I'm going to dole out."

"What debt?" he asked, backing toward Nikki.

"Darby and Fawn."

Boomer went deathly pale and looked like he might piss himself at any moment. This was the asshole who had struck fear in my woman? The one who had hurt my daughter? He seemed rather pathetic to me, or maybe he was only big and tough when it came to beating women and kids. Faced with six men he looked like a little pansy. I'd bet he screamed like a girl once I got started on him.

The others went after the three men Boomer had with him, and I lunged at the man who had treated Darby like a piece of trash. My fist slammed into his face, blood spurting from his nose as he stumbled back. I caught him before he landed on Nikki and jerked him away from her. I landed blow after blow. The sight of his teeth and blood on the floor only made me want to hurt him more. I wanted to watch him take his last breath. With a well-placed kick to his ribs, I watched him fall to the ground.

I turned to check on Nikki, then heard a scream.

"Daddy!" said a shrill little voice.

I spun in shock and stared at Fawn, standing just inside the warehouse front door, her gaze focused off to the side. I looked over in time to see Boomer pointing a gun at me. In slow motion, I watched as he pulled the trigger and felt the bullet slam into me a moment later. He gave me a sickening smile as he turned the gun toward Fawn and I let out a roar as I charged him, but the blasts from five guns ended his life before I could reach him.

A little body hurtled toward me and latched on as I sank to my knees, everything spinning.

"Daddy," she murmured, her little voice hoarse from lack of use. It seemed my little Fawn *could* talk but had chosen not to.

"I'm okay, little one. Daddy's fine." My words sounded slurred even to my ears, and then I started to slide the rest of the way to the floor. It felt like my head bounced on the concrete floor like a basketball and stars burst across my vision.

Havoc leaned over me. "Phantom has Nik and Stripes is handling Bane. We need to get you patched up quick. You're losing a lot of blood."

"Darby," I said. "Tell her I love her."

It was the last thing I said before everything went dark. As I sank into unconsciousness, I heard Fawn crying as she clung to me.

I'd been so worried about having a family leave me, that I hadn't thought about me being the one to leave them. I hoped the club would protect them after I was gone.

Chapter Ten

Darby

"What do you mean he's been shot?" I asked, panic rising inside me as Dixon told me about the shootout at the warehouse, and how Boomer had put a bullet in Renegade.

"There's more, Darby. Fawn was there," he said.

I raced down the hall and threw open her door, only to find her room empty. It felt like I couldn't breathe as I sank to the floor. My baby. How had she gotten past me? Why? It was too dangerous for her to do something like this, and she should have known better. Renegade had specifically said to stay here. She'd never defied an order before. What if she'd been killed?

"She somehow showed up at the warehouse," Dixon said, kneeling next to me. "Havoc thinks she hid in the back of Renegade's truck before he went outside. No one knew she was there until she screamed a warning to Renegade."

I blinked at him. "Fawn can't talk."

He smiled faintly. "Oh, trust me. She can talk. She's just chosen not to for whatever reason."

"Is he… is Renegade dead?" I asked, my tongue feeling heavy just trying to force the words out.

"No. He lost a lot of blood and they had no choice but to take him to the hospital. The club has a friend at the police department so Cinder placed a call. The officer was meeting them at the hospital to take a statement and try to gloss over the details as much as possible. All gunshot wounds have to be reported, so Cinder decided to get ahead of them," Dixon said.

"Can you take me to him?" I asked. "Is Fawn with him? Is she safe?"

"She's fine, but she keeps asking for her daddy. Demanding to see him, actually." He smiled again. "She seems rather fond of Renegade."

I nodded. My daughter wasn't the only one.

"I'll have someone bring one of the club trucks or SUVs over. Renegade would have my ass if I let you ride on the back of my bike."

"Just hurry," I said. I needed to get to him, to let him know I was there and that I loved him. I couldn't lose him after just having found him. And I really wanted to hear my daughter speak.

Dixon made the call and I ran to the bedroom so I could put on my shoes and run a brush through my hair. Once it was tangle-free, I rushed back to the front of the house, peeking out the window to wait for the truck or SUV to arrive. When I saw a big black Tahoe pull into the driveway, I ran for it. Dixon was shaking his head as he got behind the wheel, the other Prospect choosing to walk back to the clubhouse.

"How long until we get there?" I asked.

"Patience, Darby. If I speed or drive recklessly, Renegade will have my ass. The last thing I need is to wreck or get pulled over while I have you in the car with me. He'd lose his shit if anything happened to you," Dixon said.

I knew he was right, but it didn't make me feel any better. It seemed to take forever to get there. Dixon pulled into a parking space as close to the emergency room doors as he could get. I bolted from the vehicle the moment he'd put it into park and heard him yelling after me, but I didn't stop. All I could think about was possibly losing Renegade.

I skidded to a halt inside and saw several of the Devil's Boneyard members. I hadn't met them yet, but I approached them anyway. Two of them had officer's patches on their cuts. Treasurer and Sergeant at Arms. I went straight to them, hoping they would know who I was, or would at least have heard of me.

"How is he?" I asked. "Please tell me he's still alive."

"Who are you?" the Asian man asked.

"Momma," a raspy soft voice said, then Fawn was wrapping her arms around my legs.

I dropped down to hug Fawn, tears threatening to spill over as I heard my sweet girl say my name. I'd never thought to hear her voice, and even though it was rusty from lack of use, it was the sweetest sound I'd ever heard.

"You're Darby," said the Sergeant at Arms. His cut had *Havoc* on it. I read a few of the others. *Phantom. Charming*.

I looked up at him. "Yes. I'm Darby."

The Asian man wearing the cut that said *Phantom* smiled. "Welcome to the family. Renegade is in surgery right now. We haven't heard anything yet, even though we've asked. I think Havoc scared the sh--" He paused and looked down at Fawn. "Uh, scared the snot out of the lady at the desk."

My lips twitched at how quickly he'd corrected himself because Fawn was here. No one had ever bothered to temper their words around her, and I didn't expect these men to change for her either, but it was sweet.

"Thank you, Phantom, but I promise she's heard all those words before."

He nodded.

I looked at the man called Havoc. "Where's the person I need to see about a status update?"

He pointed behind him to a desk in the corner with a frazzled-looking woman in scrubs. I headed her way, Fawn's hand clasped in mine. Stopping and waiting, I cleared my throat when the woman wouldn't acknowledge my presence.

"Daddy," Fawn said.

I gave her hand a squeeze and felt my heart constrict at her plea. She wanted Renegade, and this woman needed to give me *something* to ease the worry filling me and our daughter. It wasn't right to not tell us whether or not he was alive and stable, or if they'd nearly lost him. Or maybe he was dead already and no one had come to speak to us yet.

"Patient name?" she asked.

"Cory Slater Adams," I said. "Or Renegade. I'm not sure what name he's under. He was brought in with a gunshot wound. Please, our daughter is really worried about her dad. Is there anything you can tell me?"

The woman's gaze went from me to Fawn and back again, her eyes narrowing. It was obvious I'd been really young when I'd had her, and I could see the curl of disgust on the woman's lips. *Uptight bitch.* I held my tongue, though. Telling her exactly what I thought of her wouldn't do me any favors right now.

"You'll have to wait for a doctor to come speak to you. I already told *those men* that. You can't intimidate me into telling you anything."

My back straightened and for the first time in years, I allowed my anger to surface. I'd had enough! After all I'd been through, and now finding out I could lose the only man who had ever been kind to me, I was done being a doormat.

"Listen to me, you uptight frigid bitch, that is my man in there, my child's father, and I want someone to tell me what the fuck is going on. Now!"

There was a slow clap behind me and I turned my head in time to get a wink from Havoc, then I faced the shrew once more.

"I don't know if he's dying, or already dead. All I know is some psycho who kidnapped his sister shot him and he was brought here. My daughter is terrified of losing her dad, and I'm…" My throat grew tight and tears pricked my eyes. "I could lose the man I love. I need answers."

The woman's face grew pinched but before she could speak a nurse came forward. I didn't know where she'd been sitting, but I could tell she'd heard the conversation. She placed a hand on the shrew's shoulder and I saw her fingers go white with the pressure she applied. The shrew let out a squeak and shrank down in her seat.

"What's the patient's name again?" the nurse asked.

"Adams. Cory Slater Adams. He was wearing a Devil's Boneyard cut that says Renegade when he was brought in," I said. "I just need to know if he's still alive and if he's out of surgery yet."

The nurse nodded, then shoved the shrew out of the way. After a few clicks on the keyboard she looked up at me, her eyes sad. I felt my heart stutter and I sank to my knees, Fawn clasped in my arms. Please, no. Not Renegade. I couldn't lose him. I just couldn't.

I felt the presence of the Boneyard members behind me. Phantom knelt down and put a hand on my shoulder. I couldn't hear what the nurse was saying over the buzzing in my ears. The room started to spin and I couldn't breathe. The next thing I knew, I was lying on the floor with seven men in cuts peering down at me, and Fawn clutching my hand.

"What happened?" I asked.

"You fainted," said the nurse.

I winced. Being weak in front of Renegade's club wasn't the way I'd wanted to introduce myself. They weren't going to think much of me after this. I slowly stood with the assistance of Phantom. Fawn released me and latched onto Havoc's leg. The big man looked scary as fuck, but he gently lifted my daughter and cuddled her against his chest.

"Is the family of Cory Adams here?" asked a man in scrubs with a surgical mask tucked under his chin.

I moved forward cautiously, not certain my legs would hold me.

"You his wife?" the doctor asked.

Before I could say anything, Havoc answered for me. "Yeah, she is. And this is his daughter."

The doctor gave me an encouraging smile. "I wasn't sure we'd be able to keep him stable, but he's in recovery. He lost a lot of blood. The bullet missed his heart and went straight through. He flatlined twice on the table, but we were able to bring him back. Once he's moved to a room, you can go see him. Just not everyone at once."

"Thank you," I mumbled, sagging against Phantom.

He was alive! Tears blurred my vision and I couldn't hold them back anymore. I sobbed in relief, so thankful he hadn't been taken from me.

It was another hour before someone came to get me, taking me to Renegade's room. I wanted Fawn to come too, but they said she was too young. Until he woke, they'd placed him in the Intensive Care Unit. There was a chair beside his bed and I sank onto it, reaching for his hand.

The steady beep of the machines was a comfort, since it meant he was alive and breathing. He had a tube in his nose and far too many wires coming from various places. I just rubbed my fingers against his and tried to think of what to say. The nurse who had brought me up here said I should let him hear my voice.

"Our daughter can talk," I said. "She keeps asking for her daddy, but they won't let her in here."

His chest rose and fell, but his eyes stayed closed.

"I met some of your brothers. Phantom and Havoc seem nice. There are more out in the waiting room, but I haven't had a chance to introduce myself yet. I've been worried about you." I licked my lips. "When Dixon said you'd been shot, I was so scared. I can't lose you, Slater. I love you. So much. Please don't leave me."

His fingers twitched and I leaned closer to him.

"Can you hear me? Open your eyes, Slater. Please. I need you to look at me."

He moaned and his entire hand twitched. I watched as he seemed to struggle to open his eyes, but slowly his lids lifted and he focused on me.

"Darby," he said in a near whisper.

"I'm here." I felt a tear slip down my cheek and hastily wiped it away. "I'm right here, Slater."

"Love you," he said, then his eyes shut again and I nearly died as the blue light started flashing outside his room and the *beep beep* of the monitor for his heartbeat went to a constant sound.

"No. No!" I screamed. "You come back right now!"

Doctors and nurses rushed into the room, shoving me out into the hall. The doors were slid shut and the curtains drawn. I sank to the floor and sobbed, terrified that he was gone for good this time. The flashing light went off a few minutes later and all but one doctor came out of the room. A nurse paused and gave a nod to go inside.

I cautiously stepped over the threshold and looked at the bed. He looked paler than before, but I noticed his heart was beating again. The doctor crossed his arms and studied Renegade.

"He's a stubborn one. That's a good thing." The doctor gave me a faint smile. "He'll be in the ICU until we're sure he's stable and on the mend. I hear there's a little girl who wants to see him. We don't permit anyone under the age of fourteen in here, but I'm going to make an exception. Next time he's awake, press the call button. A nurse will bring your little girl in to see him."

"I don't have to leave?" I asked, thinking about the visitation hours I'd noticed at the front of the unit.

"Normally, yes. Before he went under for the surgery, he kept asking for Darby. I'm guessing that's you."

"Yes."

"You being here may be what he needs. His recovery is going to be touch-and-go for a bit. I'm concerned if he doesn't know you're here and we lose him again, he may not fight to come back."

My heart ached at those words. I didn't want to think about seeing that blue light again, or watching him die.

"I thought the bullet didn't hit anything important. Why is he having so much trouble?" I asked.

"He'd lost enough blood that he was on death's doorstep when he came in. While the bullet itself didn't cause as much damage as it could have, the blood loss is what we're fighting. We gave him blood, but his body is weakened." The doctor moved to the door and stopped. "If you pray, now would be a good time."

I sank back onto the chair next to the bed and took Renegade's hand again. If me being here would help, then I wouldn't leave until there was no chance of losing him. Someone left a bag next to my chair one of the times I fell asleep, and I woke to find the gift bag. It had a fashion magazine and the latest thriller novel inside, as well as a puzzle book and pen. I didn't know who had brought it, but I was thankful.

Days passed and Renegade didn't wake up again. The police came twice, wanting to speak with him. I made sure they were sent away. I wasn't in the right frame of mind to deal with them, and Renegade wasn't awake to talk. I was starting to worry, and I could tell the medical staff were concerned as well. Something was wrong. I could feel it in my gut. People came and went, visiting when they were allowed. The day Nikki came, I gasped in horror at how bad she looked. She had a black eye, a bruise on her cheek, more along her arms, and I could see a cut peeking out of the top of her shirt.

I remembered Renegade saying she was in trouble, but I hadn't realized she'd been hurt. I'd been so focused on him that I never thought to ask about Nikki. I felt horrible about it.

"How is he?" she asked, coming farther into the room.

"I don't know. They say his vitals seem good, but he won't wake up again. I've tried talking to him, reading to him. He won't open his eyes."

She nodded. "He saved me. And… Bane, he…" She trailed off, a look of utter despair on her face.

"How's Bane?" I'd remembered hearing the name before. A Prospect for the club, and if the look on Nikki's face was any indication, someone important to her.

Nikki shook her head, her eyes glassing over with tears. "He tried to protect me."

"How did they get you, Nikki?"

Her cheeks burned. "I'd been on a date with Bane the night before, and I'd invited him to stay over. We spent the entire night in bed together, until I heard a noise outside. Bane went to investigate and didn't come back."

I didn't understand. Why had they gone after Nikki? Or was it Bane they'd been after and she'd just been a bonus?

Nikki took a shuddering breath. "It was Boomer and his friends. I don't know if my brother said anything to you or not. Bane and a few others were supposed to infiltrate some party, but somehow Boomer heard about the plan. I don't know who could have said anything. No one knew except the members of Devil's Boneyard."

"Not quite," said a voice from the doorway. His cut said *Shade* on it. "There were some women who knew as well. I did some digging after I got the call about you and Bane. One of the women I reached out to turned on us."

"Who?" Nikki asked.

His lips thinned in to a hard line. "Karley."

Nikki seemed shocked as her mouth dropped open. "Ashes' little cousin? Why would she betray the club?"

"I don't know, but Ashes is going to find out." Shade reached out and pulled Nikki into his arms, giving her a hug. "I'm sorry about Bane. He was a good man."

So the club had lost a man, and someone close had betrayed them, and I could very well lose Renegade because of it all. I was angry, but more than that, I felt defeated. Something good had to come of all this. It just had to. There was too much pain and suffering surrounding me. I'd thought by getting away from Boomer that things would be different, but it seemed that I brought the destruction with me.

"Boomer's dead," Shade said. "As well as the men who were helping him. Destroyer is coming to get Boomer's body."

I felt my heart stop a moment. "The President of the Mayhem Riders? Why is he coming?"

"Boomer was his nephew."

I felt the world tilt and I fell out of the chair. Shade was quick to help me up, concern in his gaze as he looked down at me.

"Darby, what's wrong?"

"Will he want vengeance? For your club killing his nephew?" I glanced at Renegade. "Will he try to hurt Renegade?"

"No. He was going to deal with Boomer himself, but he understood when we explained what happened. The club is safe, Darby. So is your family, including Renegade."

I nodded and sat down again.

"I'll get her something to eat," Nikki said.

"I'll come with you." Shade squeezed my shoulder. "We'll be back."

I didn't acknowledge them as they left the room. A few minutes later, I wished they'd stayed. The room spiraled into chaos as sirens went off and I nearly lost Renegade yet again. The doctors wheeled him out of the room for more testing once he had a heartbeat again. I only wanted the nightmare to be over. I didn't realize just how long it would drag on.

Chapter Eleven

Darby
Three Months Later

I stared at Dr. Chansy, thinking I must have misheard him. "Do what?"

"You're pregnant, Darby. About three months I'd say." He paused. "The medication the neurologist prescribed for your seizures isn't safe to take right now. You'll need to make another appointment with him, but for now, I need you to stop taking that medication."

I placed a hand over my belly. I'd been losing weight and felt sick all the time, unable to hold anything down. I'd thought it was stress at first, then wondered if I'd picked up a bug at the hospital, so I came to see the doctor, not wanting to take a chance on giving something to Renegade.

"You need to take better care of yourself. I know you're worried about Renegade, but you have two kids now who need you." He looked over my file. "If the seizures come back, there are alternatives while you're pregnant, but I'm hoping the neurologist will agree to keep you unmedicated during the pregnancy. It would be better for the baby."

Renegade had been placed in a coma once it was discovered that he'd had swelling on his brain. The doctors had asked those present during the altercation exactly what had happened, making them walk through it step by step. After Renegade was shot, he'd fallen and hit his head on the floor of the warehouse. It had caused brain trauma that had gone unnoticed since they'd been more focused on the hole in his body.

The swelling had receded and the doctors had tried to wake him, but it hadn't worked. He still slept, in a coma, no matter what anyone tried. He was breathing on his own and the doctors didn't have a clue why he wouldn't wake up. It was freaking me out and stressing me more than just a little. Poor Fawn didn't understand. She tried so hard to wake him up, and it scared her when he wouldn't.

I still went to the hospital every day, but the club refused to let me stay there all the time. The police had been something of a pain that first week, until Nikki talked to them. Whatever she said, it must have been enough to make them look elsewhere and clear Renegade of any wrongdoing. Fawn and I had done our best to turn Renegade's house into a home, hoping he'd get to see it soon. Cinder had given me money to buy whatever we needed or wanted, and he arranged for groceries to be delivered each week. The men of the Devil's Boneyard had been beyond kind to us, and I'd gotten to know each of them a little over the last few months.

"Darby, I don't know why Renegade won't wake up, but when he does, he'll be upset if you haven't taken care of yourself. You've lost a considerable amount of weight. It's not good for you or the baby you carry."

"I know. I'll do better about eating. It's just hard to keep stuff down." And I'd definitely call the neurologist who had managed to squeeze me in when he'd had a cancellation two months ago.

He nodded. "Morning sickness. Try some gingersnaps or drink a little ginger ale. It might settle your stomach. Not in large quantities, though. That would only make you feel worse. I'll call in a prescription for prenatal vitamins."

I thanked him and went out to the waiting room. Dixon had come with me and guided me out to the truck. Renegade's truck. Someone had brought it to the house after he'd been shot. It didn't feel right riding around in it without him, but I knew Dixon had been right when he'd said that Renegade would be pissed if I rode on the back of anyone else's bike. And now that I knew I was pregnant, I had a feeling I'd be riding in the truck until the baby was born and a few months old.

"Can you take me to the hospital?" I asked. "I have some news I need to share with Renegade."

"Sure." Dixon cast me a worried glance, but drove straight to the hospital. I was grateful he didn't push for answers. What I needed to say was between me and the man I loved. It wasn't right to tell anyone before him, even if he couldn't hear me. The doctor insisted he could, but wouldn't he have woken if he knew I was there pleading with him to open his eyes?

When we arrived, I went up to Renegade's room and shut the door.

He looked the same as he always did. I'd learned to trim his beard and kept it neat so he wouldn't look like a wild man when he woke up. His hair was growing out, but I couldn't do much about that. I reached out for his hand, running my fingers over the back of his, feeling the crisp hair tickle my fingertips.

His hand twitched and the breath in my lungs froze. He'd not done that since the time he'd woken before the coma. My gaze shot to his face, but he seemed to still be asleep. I stroked his hand again and gasped as I saw the bedding start to tent. I glanced around, making sure we were alone, and lifted the covers and his gown. His cock was fully erect, something that hadn't happened since he'd been shot. I knew men didn't always think with the head on their shoulders, but it had to be a good sign, didn't it? If he was responding to my touch in that way, then he had to wake up soon.

"Stop staring at it and give it a lick," said a voice raspy from lack of use.

I dropped the bedding and looked at his face again. His eyes were open and he had a slight smirk on his face.

"Slater!" I wanted to fling myself into his arms, but I didn't want to hurt him. His wound had healed completely, but being in a hospital bed for three months had weakened him.

"No kiss for your man?" he asked.

I paused. "Did you seriously just ask me to lick your cock? You've been in a coma for three damn months and those are the first words I hear from you?"

He chuckled and reached out to take my hand. "Missed you."

"I've been here every day." I drank him in, so thankful he was talking to me. "I need to let them know you're awake."

"In a minute. First I need your lips on mine."

I leaned down and kissed him softly. "I love you, Slater. You scared the shit out of me."

"Love you too, angel. I'm sorry it took me so long to come back to you. Three months? Is that what you said?"

I nodded.

"Nik and Bane?" he asked.

"Nikki is fine. She's healed, physically. Emotionally..." I bit my lip. "She and Bane were starting a relationship. He didn't make it. I think Shade feels guilty for his part in things, and Ashes blames himself since Karley is the one who turned traitor. He checks on Nikki all the time, makes sure she eats."

He frowned. "Karley turned on us?"

"It seems she had a drug problem no one knew about. Ashes was able to drag it out of her. She'd heard the party would have drugs, so she approached Boomer. In exchange for supplying her with enough drugs to last her a few weeks, she told him the plan to infiltrate the party and take him down. Even gave him the names of the men who would be there."

Dixon had told me about it one of the times he'd come to check on me. I'd wondered what happened to the woman, but I wasn't sure I really wanted to know. I had no doubt the club had punished her harshly, regardless of her being related to a patched member. What she'd done had gotten a man killed, and had seriously injured Nikki. I couldn't even imagine doing something like that, turning my back on people who had loved and supported me.

I reached over and pressed the call button.

"May I help you?" asked the nurse on the other end.

"He's awake."

In less than a minute, several nurses had filed into the room and the doctor shortly followed. They checked his vitals, looked at the machines, and asked him a million questions. Through it all, he held my hand, refusing to let go. The doctor wanted to keep him a few more days for observation, but just knowing he was awake would be enough to give me peace of mind.

"I need to call Cinder," I said.

"Not yet. I just want some time with you."

I leaned down and kissed him again. "There's something I need to tell you."

Renegade caressed my cheek. The tender way he looked at me made me feel warm all over. I'd worried I'd never see his brown eyes ever again. He pulled me down for another kiss, then another. Soon he was tugging my lower lip with his teeth and I opened, letting him kiss me the way he wanted. As much as I'd missed him, I was thankful I'd managed to help keep his teeth clean the last few months. Not that even three-month-long morning breath would have kept me from kissing him.

"I'm pregnant," I said. "Three months according to Dr. Chansy."

He smiled and tightened his hold on my hand. "So Fawn is getting a little brother or sister. Does she know?"

"No. I came to tell you first. I just left Dr. Chansy's office. I'd been feeling bad for a while now and I worried I'd get you sick during one of my visits to the hospital. It didn't seem right to tell anyone before you knew."

"Where's Fawn?" he asked.

"At home. Dixon drove me to the doctor and then here so Charming offered to stay with her. Dixon's down the hall in the waiting room. He's good about giving us space when I come visit every day."

Renegade scooted over in the bed and patted the mattress. I slipped off my shoes and crawled onto the bed next to him, careful not to jostle him too much. His arms curled around me and for the first time since he'd been shot, a feeling of peace filled me. We lay there long enough Dixon came to investigate. His eyes went wide when he saw Renegade was awake.

"You were just going to keep this to yourself?" he asked me.

"I wanted some alone time with my woman," Renegade said.

Dixon pulled out his phone and I heard him telling someone that the club needed to come to the hospital. He hung up, not giving them any details, and I had a feeling Cinder would chew his ass out later for worrying everyone. For all they knew, Renegade had died. It was a dick move, but Dixon was a big boy and could handle the fallout.

The rest of the day passed in a blur. Fawn got a chance to hug her daddy and talk to him. Her voice had grown stronger over the last few months, and while she still didn't talk as much as other kids, I was just thankful to hear her voice. The club was thrilled to have Renegade back, and gave him hell about taking so long to wake up. Eventually, he fell asleep, his arm still curled around me. He'd refused to let me leave the bed unless it was to use the restroom, then go right back to him.

Nikki promised to stay at the house with Fawn until Renegade was released from the hospital, and Dixon would return with an overnight bag for me. So I stayed in bed with Renegade, enjoying the fact he was holding me, something I'd thought I'd never feel again. The rest of the day and night passed with us dozing here and there, and me telling him everything he'd missed when he was in a coma.

It took two days for the doctor to release Renegade from the hospital, but he didn't get to go home. He'd grown so weak from lying in the bed for three months that he had to go to physical therapy. Even though the nurses had made sure his muscles didn't atrophy, he was too weak to walk on his own. The facility seemed nice, and he had a private room, but it had a very cold feel to it. There were no cheerful colors. Everything was utilitarian, the walls a stark white, and the furniture a plain brown. I hated it on sight and I knew he did too.

"I have to be with Fawn as much as possible," I told him, "but I'll come sit with you every day."

He shook his head. "Stay home with our daughter. I'm going to bust my ass to walk again, and I don't want you seeing me like this."

"But, Slater…"

He kissed me to shut me up. "Three weeks. In three weeks I'm coming home and I'm going to fuck you so hard, give you so many orgasms you'll be blissed out for days."

"Shh!" I glanced around, hoping no one had heard him.

He winked at me, then ordered me to leave. I hated walking out, but if that's what he wanted, I'd do it. He did permit Dixon to come visit, and I sent pictures Fawn drew and other things that might make his stay more comfortable. When Renegade wasn't looking, Dixon would take a few pictures and send them to me. I'd gotten a cell phone in the last month, courtesy of Cinder and Scratch. They'd insisted with all my trips to the hospital. I'd held out as long as I could, not wanting anyone to spend money on me. In the end, I'd seen the wisdom in it, even if I couldn't have the phone on in the ICU area of the hospital.

Over the next few days, he sent pictures of Renegade drenched in sweat as he trained himself to walk again, a look of anger and determination on his handsome face. As the weeks passed, I received more pictures, my sexy biker looking more and more like the man he'd been before the incident. According to Dixon, he'd been lifting weights when he wasn't working with his physical therapist. My man was on a mission to come home to us, and it seemed nothing would stand in his way.

While Renegade worked on getting better, Fawn and I made a few plans of our own. Since her daddy had been in the hospital, in a coma, for our first Christmas together, we decided to have Christmas when he came home. Dixon had bought us a tree and a few boxes of ornaments. I'd never taken it down, not having the time or energy, and now I was thankful it was still up. We shopped and bought Renegade a few things, wrapped them and placed them under the tree.

I hadn't been in much of a mood to celebrate on Christmas Eve or Christmas morning, but Nikki and the club had ensured Fawn had a good time. Each and every patched member and Prospect had bought her a gift, and Meg had somehow talked Cinder into dressing like Santa at the club's Christmas party, which Fawn had loved. She'd never had a chance to sit on Santa's lap before, and even though she knew it was Cinder, it had still been a thrill for her.

I hated that Renegade had missed all of it, but I knew people had taken pictures. In fact, there was a stack of prints in a kitchen drawer. Nikki had gotten a bunch together and placed them there, knowing I would eventually want to see them. As part of the preparation for Renegade coming home, I bought a few frames and set out pictures of Fawn, and one of the two of us together. Now that he would be here with us, we could take a family picture, assuming I could convince him to do it. Dixon had to sneak the pictures he took because Renegade threatened to geld him each time he pulled up the camera app on his phone.

"Not much longer," I murmured as I looked around the house. Soon, our little family would be whole again.

Epilogue

Renegade

Two weeks and five days of physical therapy. That's how long it had taken for me to walk on my own without assistance from even so much as a cane, and to gain back some of my muscle. The first time I'd looked in the mirror after waking up, I'd known that I didn't want Darby to remember me like that. I'd worked hard, pushed through the pain, and now I'd get to see my family. Kiss my woman, hug my daughter. Fuck. It would be great to be home again.

Dixon was in the truck at the curb, having offered to pick me up. I dumped my duffle into the back seat and climbed in. I'd no sooner buckled than he pulled away and started down the highway toward the compound. He'd mentioned something about a club party, but I'd had him ask the guys to hold off. I wanted a few days with Darby and Fawn, just the three of us, before I was swarmed with everyone else. I'd even asked Nikki to give me a bit of space for at least the first forty-eight hours I was home. She'd understood, but I'd heard the disappointment in her voice.

When we pulled into the driveway, I bailed out of the truck, not even stopping to tell Dixon bye, and I rushed into the house. I froze in the living room doorway when I saw a Christmas tree lit up and standing in the corner. It had hit me hard when I'd realized I'd missed their first Christmas here. I didn't know if Darby and Fawn had presents that morning or not. It was something I'd have to fix, and quickly. They deserved the best, and I intended to give it to them.

"Daddy!" Fawn saw me and flew across the room toward me, tackling my legs and holding on tight.

Tears burned my throat, not that I'd ever admit it. I scooped up Fawn, holding her close and breathing in her sweet scent.

"Hey, baby girl. I missed you."

"Missed you too," she said.

"Where's your momma?"

"Room."

I took that to mean the bedroom and set Fawn down. I pointed to the TV and told her to finish her movie while I went to check on Darby. Walking down the hall, there was a tightening in my gut. What would I find when I entered the bedroom? Did she even still sleep in there? I'd been gone so long, and so much had changed. We'd barely been together when I'd been shot. What if she hadn't felt comfortable remaining in our room while I was in the hospital? I'd noticed the difference in the house, and I loved that she'd made it into a home. The fact she'd made the place her own, and the way she'd stuck by my side, made a warmth spread through me. I only wished I'd been here to help.

Darby was humming in the bathroom, so I quietly closed the door and toed off my boots. Padding across the floor as silently as I could, I leaned around the bathroom door to watch her. She was in the process of straightening her hair, leaving it in a long, silky curtain down her back. Her eyes were smoky from some sort of makeup, and she looked so damn good. She leaned in closer to the mirror and I couldn't resist another moment.

"Stay just like that," I said, making her gasp as her gaze met mine in the mirror.

I worked my belt loose as I moved in closer. Shoving my jeans and underwear down to my thighs, my hard cock led the way. The dress she had on was sexy as fuck. I carefully gathered the skirt in my hands, lifting it to reveal her shapely thighs and her luscious ass. Her *bare* ass. Fuck. Me.

"Naughty girl. Were you anticipating my return home?" I asked, rubbing my cock along the crack of her ass.

"Yes. God, Slater. I've missed you."

"Spread those legs for me, angel."

She parted her thighs and I slipped my hand between them. She'd either waxed or shaved and the lips of her pussy were smooth. I parted the lips and stroked her clit. Darby moaned and pressed her ass back against me. I plunged a finger inside her, groaning at how fucking tight she felt. Stroking it in and out, I wasn't sure which of us I was teasing more.

"This is going to be quick, sweetheart. I'll make it up to you later."

"Just fuck me, Slater. Please. I need you so much."

I lined up my cock and eased inside. *Fuck*! She was so damn tight, squeezing me as I slid a little deeper. It took several strokes before I was balls deep, and it took every bit of control I had not to come right then and there. I pinched and rolled her clit between my fingers as I drove into her. When I'd said it would be quick, I hadn't lied. My dick was about two seconds from erupting, but I wanted her to come with me.

"Harder," she begged.

I didn't know if she meant my cock or my hand. I pinched her clit tight as I pounded into her. Darby screamed out her release and I followed, spilling inside of her. Had it felt that incredible before? It seemed like a lifetime ago that we'd been intimate. Slowly, I withdrew from her body, and grabbed the hand towel on the counter, placing it between her legs. While she cleaned up, I moved over to the other sink to rinse off my dick and straighten my clothes.

"You're not supposed to be doing anything that strenuous, are you?" she asked.

"I'm one hundred percent, angel. Fucking my woman isn't going to put me in the grave." I turned to face her. "I'm sorry I missed Christmas. And Thanksgiving for that matter. Hell, it was Valentine's Day while I was in rehab."

"Speaking of that…" She folded her arms over her chest. Her attempt at looking stern just turned me on again. "The doctor said your rehab was supposed to last four to six weeks. You weren't supposed to push yourself that hard. When you told me you'd see me in three weeks, I figured they would slow you down and make you stay the full time."

I went to her, pulling her into my arms. "Angel, nothing was going to keep me away from you and Fawn. I didn't want to miss another moment with the two of you. There was no way in hell I was staying in that place a month or more."

I leaned down and kissed her, taking my time to savor her taste and the feel of her against me. This was heaven. I didn't know why I'd run so far and so fast from having a family. Darby and Fawn were the best things to ever happen to me, that and the kid growing inside her.

Even though I knew we needed to get back to Fawn, I couldn't help but explore her curves a bit more. I'd have loved nothing more than to strip her bare and fuck her again, and again. I had three months of making up to do. It took another few minutes before I could take a step back.

"Let's go see Fawn. The two of you can show me the tree you put up."

She smiled up at me. "There are a few things under there for you."

"You got me presents?" I asked. "Darby, I didn't get a chance to shop for you and Fawn."

She pressed her lips to mine. "You already gave us the best gift ever. You. No one has ever been as kind to us as you've been. We love you, Slater, and the fact you love us back is more than enough of a gift. It's more than we've ever had before."

Dammit. My throat was getting that tight feeling again, and I was not going to fucking cry! I took her hand and led her back to the living room. Fawn's movie was just ending and she hurried over to us. My daughter latched onto my hand and practically dragged me to the Christmas tree.

"Sit," she said, pointing to my chair.

I sat down on the recliner and smiled as she handed me a stack of presents. Fawn settled at my feet, watching me expectantly, and Darby eased down on the couch nearby. With both of my girls watching, I opened every gift they'd gotten for me. My favorite was the Harley sculpture Fawn had made from clay, at least that's what she'd said it was supposed to be. It was a misshapen lump, but it was the most beautiful thing I'd ever seen, because she'd made it for me.

"Thank you, baby girl," I told her, pulling her onto my lap for a hug. "I love it. Best Christmas present ever."

There was a knock at the front door and I stood to answer it. Scratch was on my doorstep, a smile on his face as he handed a large paper shopping bag to me.

"What's this?" I asked.

"For your woman and kid. It's what you asked for before you went and got shot. Didn't seem right to give it to them. You needed to do it."

I looked inside and saw Darby's property cut, and a T-shirt in Fawn's size that said *My Daddy is a Devil* with the Devil's Boneyard colors on the back. They were both perfect, just like my girls.

"And if I hadn't been here to give it to them?" I asked, my gaze meeting his. From what I'd been told, I'd died several times both during and after surgery.

"Then we'd have given it to them, but only if there was no way you could do it yourself."

"Thanks."

The VP gave me a nod.

"Tell Fawn that my kids are looking forward to seeing her again. Clarity has picked her up for a few play dates while you've been recovering. I think Fawn and Caleb have become especially close."

I glowered at him, not liking the thought of my little girl being close to a boy, even if the was the VP's kid. Scratch smirked at me and stepped off the porch. I shut the door as his Harley rumbled to life and went to find Darby and Fawn. Neither was in the living room, but I followed my nose to the kitchen. I hadn't noticed something was cooking earlier, too focused on seeing the two of them. Darby pulled a pan of cornbread from the oven and I saw a ham, as well as several vegetables already out on the table.

"Before we eat, there's something I need to give the both of you. You were supposed to have these before I went into the hospital."

I took out the T-shirt first and handed it to Fawn, who squealed and ran from the room, only to return a few minutes later wearing her new shirt. I smiled, thinking she looked too fucking cute.

Darby approached me, interest lighting her eyes. I pulled her cut from the bag and held it up for her. She slipped her arms through the holes and ran her hands down the leather as she admired it. She'd been mine since the day I pulled her from that dumpster, but now everyone would know it.

"You know, in about six more months, you'll need another one of those shirts," she said, placing my hand on her belly. "We have a bit longer until we know if you need to get a pink or blue one. I was thinking we could name a boy after your dad or brother, and name a girl after your mom. You ready for late night diaper changes and walking the floor when the baby won't stop crying?"

"Looking forward to every minute of it," I told her. My throat was tight with emotion again. The way she'd thought of including my family in our lives touched something deep inside.

Her lips twitched as if she fought back a smile. "I'll remember that. No complaining about nasty diapers or not getting enough sleep."

I kissed her softly, slowly. "As long as I have you in my life, then nothing else matters. You're my one and only, Darby. I love you and Fawn, and I'll love the kid growing inside you. You've given me the one thing I thought I never wanted, but what I needed. A family."

She clung to me, holding on tight, and Fawn wrapped her arms around our legs.

I closed my eyes and breathed in Darby's scent. This was home. Not the house I'd lived in since the new compound opened, but Darby and Fawn… they were my home, my heart, my everything.

And what do you know. I hadn't fucked it up after all.

Wire (Dixie Reapers MC 13)
Harley Wylde

Lavender -- My parents weren't the type to win any awards, but I did learn a few things. Like how to read lines of code and get through the backdoor of pretty much any site or program. I also learned about the man my mother had dated when she'd met my dad, someone who has intrigued me for years. I never thought I'd get the chance to meet him, until my parents end up dead and I can't think of anyone else who might be able to help. I know too much, know my parents' deaths weren't an accident, and now I've been targeted. If the infamous Voodoo Tracer can't help me, then I'm screwed.

Reality is so much better than fantasy, and with one look, I know the reason I haven't dated is because I was waiting. For him.

Wire -- I never really expected my past to come knocking at the front gates, nor did I expect it to be in such a sexy package. Lavender isn't what I'd call a siren, but with her glasses perched on her nose, her messy hair, curvy figure, and adorable tees, she's exactly what I want and don't need. A nerdy, geeky, superintelligent woman who craves me as much as I crave her. So I did what any man would do... I claimed her. Now she's mine, and if an enemy from my past thinks he can hurt her, I'd like to see him try. He might have killed her parents, but I will destroy anyone who tries to take her from me.

Chapter One

Lavender

The infamous hacker, or more accurately cracker, Voodoo Tracer, hadn't been all that hard to find. My mother had always said if anything happened to her I should track down the guy she'd dated before marrying my dad. I'd heard the story a million times, about how they'd all been friends but she'd fallen for Dad and hurt the guy she'd been dating. He'd left and never returned. Mom had lost track of him, but it hadn't take much digging for me to find his current location, which told me he wasn't really hiding. A guy like him didn't leave a door open unless he wanted someone to use it.

While my mom and dad were hackers and worked for a lot of companies, trying to find the weak spots in their security so the companies could improve them, men like Voodoo Tracer took advantage of those weak spots to get whatever information they wanted. Mom had never approved of Voodoo's need to crack government and banking sites. From what she'd said, back then, he never took anything vital. He'd mostly done it because he could. I couldn't say for certain what he'd been up to lately.

I didn't really walk either path, but tended to dabble a bit in both. Like the infamous Voodoo, I mostly liked to see how far I could get somewhere I shouldn't be. If I were as nice as my mom and dad, I'd then turn that information over to the companies so they could keep other people out. Then again, they weren't exactly paying me for my help, so why give it? I wasn't an angel by any means, but I wasn't precisely a devil either. I operated in those murky shades of gray.

I'd known how easy it would be for some to trace my phone, or the built-in GPS on my car, so I'd left both behind. The bus hadn't been the most comfortable option to ride to Alabama, and I'd paid cash so there wouldn't be a credit card trail, but now that I was here, I had to wonder if I'd made a huge mistake. The walk to the Dixie Reapers compound wasn't that far, but the place seemed a bit imposing as I approached the gates. I'd walked what felt like miles of fenceline, although that was surely not the case. Razor wire topped it, and I had to wonder just what they were trying to keep out. Or was it more what they wanted to keep in?

The guy standing guard didn't seem much older than me, and I noticed the way he scanned me from head to toe. I probably wasn't the type of woman who typically came to this sort of place. My Converse were well-worn, my jeans ripped along my thighs and knees, and I had on my favorite *Dark Crystal* T-shirt, which had faded over time. I hadn't thought much about my appearance and had tossed my hair up in a messy bun. With my thick-lensed glasses perched on my nose, I probably looked like I should be in school right now. If it weren't for my curves, I'd never pass for my real age.

"You must be lost," the man said, then pointed back behind me. "Town is back that way."

"I'm not lost." I hitched my bag higher on my shoulder. "I'm here to see Voodoo Tracer."

The man stared and rubbed at the stubble on his chin. "No one here by that name. So I think you really are lost."

My brow furrowed. I'd assumed his club would know him by that name. From what little research I'd managed before taking this trip, I'd learned that some clubs preferred to use a road name and kept their real names private. If Voodoo followed that belief, this guy may not know his birth name. It was foolish to think whatever the club called him would be the same name he went by when he was cracking codes.

"Hang on. I have a picture, but it's really old." I slid the strap off my shoulder and dug in my backpack. I withdrew the picture of Voodoo with my mom, Seraph, and my dad, Doc Paradox. I'd stared at this picture a lot over the years. I'd found it shoved into a box in the top of Mom's closet a while back. The ginger-haired young man had drawn my attention. He couldn't have been older than sixteen or seventeen at the time it was taken, but even back then he'd been more than just cute. I knew he'd be my parents' age now, but I'd often wished I could meet a guy like him.

Showing the picture to the guy, his eyes went wide.

"Holy shit, is that Wire?" he asked.

"Um. Maybe. I don't know his club name. I only know his hacker name."

The man nodded. "That would be Wire, then. I'll have to call him down here. I'm not letting you in uninvited. You don't exactly look like the type to party at the clubhouse."

If that was code for sleep with random men, then no, I wasn't. Not even a little. I took a step back as he made his call and took the time to check out the place behind the fence. There was a building with *Dixie Reapers* across the top in neon letters, and a lot of houses down either side of the road. As I strained to get a better look, I thought I saw a playground, but that was ridiculous. What type of biker compound had a playground? The fatigue must be getting to me. It seemed I was now hallucinating.

"He asked who else is in the picture," the guy said.

"Tell him Seraph and Doc Paradox." I swallowed hard. "They were my parents."

He relayed the information, and I hoped that Wire would come and hear me out. If things had really ended as badly as my mom had said, then he might refuse to see me. She'd not gone into a lot of detail, just said she'd picked my dad over Voodoo. Knowing my mother, there was a good chance she'd omitted part of the story. Coming here was a gamble I'd been willing to take. Whatever Mom and Dad had been into, it had gotten them killed. Thanks to me nosing around, I now worried that I might meet the same fate. I didn't know anything about the man Wire was now, but the kid who had grown up with my parents had been the type to help those in need, even if he hadn't done it the legal way. I was counting on that still being true.

The rumble of a motorcycle started out faint and then got louder. I saw a rider with copper-colored hair approaching from down the road and as he came to a stop on the other side of the gate, my heart flipped, flopped, then took off at a gallop. *Holy hell*! Mom had thrown over this guy for my dad? What the hell had she been thinking? He didn't even remotely look like a hacker. Nor was he the gangly teen from the photo I'd brought. Yeah, he'd been handsome back then, but now? Shit. I was almost certain my panties were getting wet just looking at him. His heather gray tee stretched tight across his broad chest, and the leather cut just added to the sex appeal. The denim hugging his thighs was as worn as mine, with a few well-placed holes, and did nothing to hide how muscular he was, especially for a geeky computer nerd.

Definitely nothing like my dad. I'd loved my father, but time hadn't been kind to him. He'd had lines around his eyes, and what my mother fondly called his spare tired around the middle, from long days and nights at the computer. This guy didn't have that problem. Hell, he didn't even look my parents' age.

Wire swung a leg over his bike and came closer, removing the sunglasses that had shielded his eyes from me. Green, and so damn pretty. It was a sin for a man to have eyelashes that long and thick. Dammit. My nipples were getting stiff. I swallowed hard, wondering why my body was betraying me. I'd never had a physical response to a guy, even when I thought they were hot. Until now. The beard covering his jaw made my fingers itch to reach out and touch it. Would it be coarse or soft? I'd always had a weak spot for gingers, and he had to be the sexiest one I'd ever seen.

"I haven't heard the names Seraph and Doc Paradox in a long-ass time. What the fuck do you want?" he demanded.

A knot formed in my throat at the biting tone of his voice. Okay, so this wouldn't be a friendly conversation. It seemed he was still bitter about my mother's betrayal. Not that I could blame him. I'd often thought that it was shitty the way my parents had gone about things back then. Maybe if they'd been honest from the beginning, then Wire would have never left.

"My name is Lavender Narcissa Roberts. I'm --"

"Krista and Mark's kid," he said, his lips thinning in displeasure. "So I was told. You need to go home. I don't know why you're here, and I don't fucking care."

"Please, my mom always said if things went bad to come find you," I said.

"Tell her she was mistaken. You never should have come here."

"I can't," I said softly. "She's dead. They both are."

There was a flash of pain in his eyes, then he turned away from me. I wondered if he still loved my mom after all these years. It had to have hurt, catching her and my dad kissing, but I didn't know how he'd missed it. Anyone who saw them together could tell they were meant for one another.

"I think whatever they were digging into is what got them killed," I said. "They weren't as careful as they'd thought. It wasn't hard to trace their IP address, even though they'd bounced it around a bit. Anyone with decent skills could have found them."

"What happened?" he asked, not turning to face me.

"Someone blew up their hideaway. It's where they did all their work and was supposed to be untraceable, but I think they got sloppy. Maybe they were too cocky. I'm not really sure. If it hadn't been for my dad's backup laptop being at the house, I might have never figured out what happened. The police determined it a gas leak and refuse to investigate. I got into Dad's email account and pieced together their current job. It can't be a coincidence the day they find a weird strand of code they get blown up. Gas leak? That's bullshit."

He snorted. "What would you know about it?"

"I found you, didn't I?" I arched an eyebrow, even though he refused to look at me. "What? Because I'm a woman I'm completely useless? Is that it? I thought you were different from the others. You dated my mom! She knew her shit, so why would you think other women couldn't hack into systems or read lines of code?"

"What's that supposed to mean?" he asked, turning around, his eyes snapping with anger.

"I've been hacking since I was eight years old, and I'm a damn sight better at it than either of my parents ever were. But because I have breasts I must be a clueless bimbo who's just pretending, right?" I sneered at him. How could Mom have been so wrong about this guy? He was just another douche like all the others. "Dark Labyrinth can't possibly be a girl, right?"

He moved closer, not stopping until he was nearly touching the gate. "Are you trying to tell me that *you're* Dark Labyrinth?"

I wanted to look down at my shirt, as if that made it obvious. When I'd come up with my name, I'd been a kid, and had combined two of my favorite movies. Although my name could just as easily mean the shadowy paths of the Darknet. My dad had constantly played all the popular 1980s movies, and I'd fallen in love with the Goblin King and Fizzgig, among others. When I'd gotten to be around thirteen, I'd had a big crush on Maverick from *Top Gun* and Dean from *Overboard*.

"Wouldn't matter if I did. You wouldn't believe me. No one ever does." I crossed my arms under my breasts. I was sick of assholes like this one.

"Lavender… is that what you said your name is?" Wire asked.

"Yes. Lavender Narcissa Roberts."

He shook his head and looked up at the sky. "Your mother and her damn obsession with fictional characters. I take it she got into the *Harry Potter* craze?"

"You could say that." Seeing as every room in our house, except mine, had some sort of collectible from the movies, it was a safe bet my mother had been a wee bit obsessed with the wizarding world. I'd always preferred the classics from the eighties myself. Like father like daughter. Couldn't get any better than *Dark Crystal, Labyrinth*, and *The Last Unicorn*.

Wait a minute. The fact he recognized my names meant he was into *Harry Potter* too, or at least had seen the movies. I had a hard time picturing the tough-looking biker in front of me watching something like that, much less reading the novels. Then again, if he really was Voodoo, then he had a geeky side. It just wasn't visible to the naked eye. I wore my geek badge with honor, but I could see how that would be detrimental to a guy like him. It would dent that bad boy image he had going on.

"Can we talk?" I asked. "If not here, then somewhere safe? My mom and dad were working a job when something happened. They ran across a line of code that shouldn't have been there, and when they tried to follow it, I think it tipped their hand to someone."

"You really think whatever they were working on is what got them killed?" he asked.

"Yeah, I really do, and now that I've been poking around…" I bit my lip. "I started to feel like someone was watching me, but I brushed it off as paranoia. Until other things started to happen. I think whoever left that line of code isn't happy it was discovered, and now they're after me."

"Diego, let her in," he said. He took a moment to scan the surrounding area. "Where's your car?"

"Left it behind, along with my phone."

"Then I guess you're riding behind me on the bike."

Was it wrong a little thrill went through me? The guy was my parents' age, but I couldn't help ogling his ass as he walked back over to the Harley. Yeah, my panties were definitely wet. I'd gone past damp and straight to needing to change them. The man had to be the hottest guy I'd ever seen. Being wrapped around him while he drove us back to his place wouldn't be a hardship in the slightest. In fact, I was going to enjoy every second of it. If there were a way to make it last longer, I'd have done whatever was necessary to make that happen.

As I climbed on behind him and wrapped my arms around his waist, he revved the engine and the vibrations that shot through me nearly made me moan. If this was what it felt like to ride on a motorcycle, I wanted to do it as frequently as possible. Way better than B.O.B. Between the scent of the sexy man, the bike, and the way my nipples rubbed against his back, I was seconds away from coming. The bike shot forward and I squealed as I held on tight, pressing myself as close to Wire as I could get. I felt the rumble of his laughter, then his hand pressed over the two of mine. The bike wasn't the only thing racing after that. I thought my heart my explode from my chest.

My clit pulsed, my nipples ached, and for the first time in my life I seriously wanted to have sex with a guy. Not just any guy. Wire. Holy hell, the man was setting me on fire and he wasn't even trying.

He sped up and the trees flew past us in a blur, until he skidded to a halt outside a cute house. It was the type of quaint home people thought of when picturing a small American town, and looked completely out of place in a biker compound. But then, all the homes seemed to be similar. It looked more like a well-maintained neighborhood than anything else.

When I'd discovered he was a biker, this was the last thing I'd expected to find. Drugs, alcohol, and naked women would have been more of what I'd thought I'd see.

I got off the bike, my legs shaking a bit, and watched as he easily dismounted the machine. I'd probably looked like a newborn colt trying to get off the damn thing, while Wire was all lethal, predatory grace like a big jungle cat. So not fair. I followed him up to the front door and stepped inside. The inside looked... normal. And boring. I'd had no real picture in mind of what his place would look like, but I'd figured there would be pizza boxes and beer cans everywhere. It's how our house had looked when Mom and Dad were working on a big project. I was too much of a neat freak. If I knew I'd be sitting at the computer for hours or days on end, then I put a big trash can nearby.

Wire sank onto a recliner that looked like something my dad would have picked, and I eased down onto the couch. Now that I was in his space, I was a bit nervous. I'd spent the last few days worried about arriving here in once piece, and hadn't given myself the time to consider how it would feel to face this man. Someone my mother had loved at one time, even though she swore they'd never been intimate beyond kisses.

I wasn't sure if that was true or not, and I definitely wasn't going to ask.

"Why would your mom send you to me? I should be the last person she'd want you near," he said.

"She hated how things ended between the two of you. While she adored my dad, she once told me that she'd never meant to break your heart. She'd been trying to find a way to tell you and end things amicably." I shrugged. "I wasn't there so I can't say for certain."

He snorted. "Oh, you were there. It's just that you weren't born yet."

My eyes went wide. "What?"

"They never told you?" He cracked his neck. "Fucking figures. Saint Krista wouldn't dare tarnish herself in your eyes. Probably spun the entire thing as some sort of fairy tale with her as the princess."

He wasn't entirely wrong, but I seriously wanted to know what he'd meant by I was there. My mom had always said that she and my dad didn't go beyond a bit of making out until she and Voodoo were over with. Had she lied to me? Maybe he was right and she hadn't wanted me to see her in that light, but the thought of her cheating on this guy made my gut churn. It was no wonder he'd told me to leave. I'd have done the same in his place.

He leaned forward, bracing his elbows on his knees. "Let me tell you about your precious mother. She led me on for years, and the day we broke up was the day I finally saw the true Krista. She'd kept me at arm's length for the most part, insisting that she was a virgin and wanted our first time together to be perfect. Fuck, she barely even let me kiss her. I respected her wishes, thinking she just needed time or maybe was waiting on me to pop the question or something."

"But it wasn't true?" I asked.

"No. She'd been screwing your dad for months before we broke up, and from what I learned after that, she'd been with several other guys during our years together. She liked that I understood her, could speak her language, but she wasn't the least bit attracted to me."

I blinked, not knowing what to say to that. I thought he was the hottest guy I'd ever seen, and if my mother couldn't see the same thing, then she was a blind moron. I'd always known she was far from perfect, but what she'd done to Wire was beyond wrong. It made me wonder what else I didn't know about her. Of course, I was glad she'd ended up married to my dad or I wouldn't exist. It didn't mean I had to agree with how she'd lived her life though. The way she'd blatantly hurt Wire made me wonder if I'd ever truly known her. It was downright cruel that she'd strung him along.

I'd like to think there were extenuating circumstances, but I wasn't sure how she'd have justified cheating on her boyfriend. I'd never do something like that. Well, if I ever actually *had* a boyfriend. When guys hit on me, it tended to make my skin crawl. Then again, I hadn't known any guys who looked like Wire. If I had, then maybe I'd have dated someone by now. The ginger sitting near me sent my heart racing and made me ache. I'd never experienced true desire until now.

"When I said you were there, it's because your mom was already pregnant with you," he said. "If you didn't look a little like a combination of your parents, I'd wonder if she even knew who your dad was. Looks like she married the right guy."

I winced, but I couldn't hold it against him. My mother had royally screwed him over, and it sounded like my dad wasn't much better. Maybe my dad's betrayal was even worse than Mom's. He'd knowingly taken another guy's girl. Wasn't there some sort of code about that crap?

"Does that mean you won't help me?" I asked.

He sighed and ran a hand through his hair. "No, it doesn't mean I won't help you."

Chapter Two

Wire

Fuck my life. Of all the people to show up looking for me, it had to be someone tied to the two people I hated the most. With her big blue eyes, I couldn't very well turn her away. It wasn't her fault that her parents were shitheads. The fact my cock had been semi-hard since I'd gotten a good look at her wasn't helping matters. I didn't exactly live like a monk, but Lavender was the last person I should want in my bed.

She was young enough to be my kid!

Not that it had stopped most of my brothers. Every last one of them had fallen for a woman younger than them. It didn't mean I wanted to follow in their footsteps. I'd never really planned to settle down. Not since Krista had fucked me over all those years ago. Women were fun, and I was more than happy to blow off some steam with one, but that's where it ended. They weren't allowed in my house, and I sure as fuck wasn't going to fall for one. Didn't matter if seeing all the happy couples around me did make my chest hurt sometimes. That life wasn't for me.

But this one… she was different.

And while I was right and she did resemble both her parents, she was also uniquely herself. Krista hadn't had Lavender's curves or blue eyes. Lavender's paler skin came from her dad. Then again, neither of her parents had blue eyes. If she didn't have the shape of Mark's nose or the shape of her mother's eyes, then I might wonder if she'd been adopted. I'd never met Krista's parents, but she'd said that her mom was half-Malaysian and her father was Tahitian. They'd given her some killer genes that made one beautiful woman. Too bad her heart had been the size of a marble.

Lavender's skin was paler than Krista's yet more golden than Mark's. More the color of coffee when you added a shit ton of milk. She was beautiful. When I looked at her, I didn't see either of them. I just saw her. Which was a big fucking problem for me. Even behind the lenses of her glasses, her eyes were stunning and I had to force myself to look away. I swallowed hard. I couldn't remember anyone ever affecting me this way before, and I needed to get her the fuck out of my house. Now.

"Where are you staying?" I asked.

Her lips pressed together, but she flinched slightly. Dammit. God fucking dammit. She'd come all this way with no plan what-the-fuck-ever. Torch would kick my ass if I sent her off on her own. The motels in town weren't in the best areas, and without transportation, she couldn't get very far. This was motherfucking bullshit.

"Where's your stuff?" I asked.

She reached behind her to pat the backpack slung over her shoulder and I inwardly groaned. There was no way her problems would be solved in a day or two, and I wasn't sure she even had enough stuffed in there for that much time. I knew people on the run did desperate shit and didn't always think things through, but I seriously wanted to put her over my knee and paddle her ass.

My cock jerked at the thought and I turned away from her, hoping she wouldn't notice I was getting harder by the minute. It was like I was fourteen years old again and checking out my first girl. What the fuck was wrong with me? *She's the enemy*. But was she? Yeah, her parents were complete shits in my opinion --

or had been -- but that didn't necessarily mean she was too. Hell, I knew plenty of people who weren't a damn thing like their birth families.

"There's a guest room," I said, not turning around.

"You don't want me here," she said, and I heard her move closer.

I turned around and nearly collided with Lavender. A soft smile curved her lips and she placed her hand on my chest. Jesus. Could she feel my heart pounding?

"Maybe I can change your mind," she said.

Holy. Fucking. Shit.

I was so screwed. Possibly in the literal sense.

I was a grown-ass man, nearly forty years old. There was no way I was going to let some twenty-two-year-old woman lead me around by my dick. I took a step back, then another, but Lavender just advanced on me. When her gaze locked on mine, what I saw made me stop. I'd had plenty of women flirt with me, want the bragging rights to having been with a member of the Dixie Reapers, but I'd never once had a woman look at me like I was the best thing since Gottfried Leibniz invented the binary number system. I knew my brothers wouldn't think much of her, with her geeky shirt and the retro black-framed glasses. She was the type of woman who dressed for comfort and to please herself, not to chase after a man. And that was part of the problem.

She had the sweet, girl-next-door type of persona, with a touch of nerd and geek. It was my kryptonite. The fact she was a hacker was just icing on the fucking cake. I couldn't think of anything sexier than a woman who knew her way around a computer. The fact she'd been able to follow the trail her parents had left was impressive. It was also why I needed to get the fuck away from her. She could be in trouble, needed my help, and I wasn't about to take advantage of her.

I placed my hand over hers, marveling at how soft she felt.

"You don't have to offer up your body in exchange for a place to stay," I said. "I'm not that much of an asshole."

"Is that what you think?" she asked, her eyes flashing with annoyance. "I'm not some whore who spreads her legs for anyone."

She jerked free of my grasp and turned. She made it all of three steps before I reached out to draw her to a halt. It seemed that I was determined to say and do the wrong thing with Lavender. As much as I wished I could forget she'd shown up here, I couldn't. If Torch found out I'd ignored a woman in need, he'd have my ass. We might not walk on the right side of the law a bit of the time, but women were a soft spot with the club.

"I wasn't trying to imply that you're a whore. You don't exactly look the type, unless we're talking cybersex."

Her back stiffened and I winced. Yeah, that hadn't been too smooth.

"So the only way men would have sex with me is over the Internet?" she asked, her voice tight, but her acerbic tone got her point across. I'd hurt her, and it hadn't been my intention. "First I'd give it up to anyone, and now no one would want me? Is that what you're saying?"

I turned her to face me. "Lavender, I didn't mean it like that. I keep saying all the wrong things with you. I just meant that you seem like a sweet girl."

Her eyebrows arched. "Girl?"

"Girl. Woman. Female. Whatever. The point is that you're too soft to be a whore. You don't have that sharp edge that women have when they use men, whether it's for sex or money." She opened her mouth and I placed a finger over her lips. "Again, not trying to offend you, sweetheart. I'm sure you're downright wicked with a keyboard, but like you admitted, you aren't the type to spread your legs for anyone."

"What's your point?" she asked, her words muffled since I hadn't removed my finger yet. I glanced at that plump mouth and wondered what she'd taste like.

Dammit, focus!

"You can spend the night in the guest room. Get some sleep. Tomorrow, you can tell me in detail everything you discovered and why you think you're being watched or threatened. The more I know, the easier I can help you. That's what you want, right? To find the threat, eliminate it, and you can go home?"

She hesitated.

"What aren't you telling me?" I asked.

"I don't know if I can go home. Not without my parents nearby. At least, not right away. We weren't exactly close, but I'm still coming to terms with the fact they're gone."

I sighed and pulled her into my arms. She tightened but eventually relaxed against me. Resting my chin on her head, I breathed in her scent and wondered how the fuck I'd gotten into this predicament. The moment I heard someone was looking for me, and how they knew me, I should have told the Prospect to send them away. I didn't need whatever trouble Lavender had brought to my door, and neither did the club. While we still had some illegal dealings, we'd also started two legitimate businesses. With more and more kids popping up at the compound, and more of my brothers falling for women, Torch was trying to keep danger off our backs if at all possible.

Then again, it seemed to find us even when we weren't looking. Like now, with Lavender. I'd have never thought my past would come knocking on the door. Not like this. The government had no qualms with reminding me of my transgressions when it came to taking the back door into various places, like the US Treasury. They used it to their advantage, and called on my services from time to time. When the club got into some hot water a while back, I'd volunteered to do whatever Uncle Sam wanted, as long as they didn't put any of my brothers in jail. Not the perfect plan, but at least everyone was safe.

"I'm going to help you," I told her. "But not until morning. You need to sleep, Lavender. You have circles under your eyes and I'm sure you haven't slept much since you lost your parents. Even if they were the shittiest people on earth, they were your family."

I felt her hands grip my cut as she held on. The first sob came out so softly I almost missed it, then she stopped holding back. Her body shook from the force of her tears, and my shirt was soaked within minutes. I didn't care. It was obvious she'd been keeping it all in. Even if I didn't want her here, I wasn't going to be a complete dick and toss her out. The fact I enjoyed holding her was a problem, though. I didn't need her sort of complication in my life.

When she sniffled and wiped the remaining moisture from her cheeks, I couldn't help but notice her eyes looked bluer. Shit. She was one of those women who could look pretty while crying. No splotchy mess for her. Of course not.

"I wasn't offering myself to you earlier because I wanted a place to stay," she said. "I did it because you're the hottest man I've ever seen."

Her cheeks flushed, making her downright adorable. Then her words registered. She thought I was hot? Sure, other women had said the same thing, right before trying to grab my dick. They weren't Lavender. The sweet, smart, tempting woman in front of me knew all the right things to say.

I lowered my head, giving her time to pull away, then brushed my lips against hers. The soft gasp she made was enough to snap my control, what little I'd had. I deepened the kiss, taking what I wanted. The way she clung to me said she didn't mind. She pressed closer, her soft curves making the last of my reasoning fly out the door. I wanted her. She wanted me. What harm would there be in taking her to my bed?

I pulled away and stared down her. Lavender's eyes were still closed, her lips parted, and that charming flush had worked its way down her throat and across what I could see of her chest, which wasn't nearly enough in her tee.

"If you come with me to my bedroom, you're going to get fucked. Now's the time to back out," I said, knowing damn well I'd stop anytime she said to, but I really fucking hoped she gave me the green light all the way to the finish line. I would gladly take was what offered, but I wasn't the kind of guy who took a woman when she'd clearly changed her mind.

"Show me your room," she said, reaching for my hand.

I drew her down the hallway and to the master bedroom. Kicking the door shut, I pulled her back into my arms, kissing her until we were both gasping for breath. My chest heaved as I panted and tried to think of reasons I shouldn't do this. Then she trailed her fingers down my chest, farther down my abdomen, and dipped them inside my pants. I had her shirt off not even ten seconds later, admiring the swells of her breasts and the slight roundness of her stomach. She was tiny, barely reaching my shoulder, but I loved the fact she was curvy. Her breasts nearly spilled from her bra, practically begging me to free them.

My gaze locked on hers, looking for any sign she wanted me to stop. When she started working my belt loose, I had my answer. I unfastened her bra, dropping it to the floor, before getting my hands on the most perfect breasts I'd ever seen. She felt like silk against my rougher skin, and I knew that I would remember this night for a long fucking time.

She took a step back and stripped out of the rest of her clothes, then she turned and walked over to the bed, her ass swaying with every step. The way she crawled to the center had me pulling off my clothes as fast as I could and joining her. Lavender stretched out on her back, and held her hands out to me. I paused a moment, trying to not do anything overly stupid. The brain in my head was still somewhat functioning, but I didn't know for how much longer.

"You clean?" I asked.

She nodded. "You?"

"Yeah. Been a while since I was with someone, and I get tested regularly."

I reached for the bedside drawer and withdrew a condom, but Lavender put a hand over mine.

"I'm on the pill. You don't have to use that if you don't want to. Mom made me start taking them when I was fifteen."

Probably because her mom had been a slut at that age, but I wouldn't think of that right now. As tempting as Lavender's offer was, I'd heard way too many stories of women getting pregnant while on birth control. No way I was taking that chance. I'd avoided the "oops I'm pregnant" trap this long and I wasn't about to fuck it up now.

"I always wrap my dick," I said. "No offense."

I tossed the condom onto the bed, then settled on the mattress next to Lavender. The way she spread across my bed made me ache in a way I'd never felt before. I wanted her, but it felt like more than that, which was completely insane. I didn't know her, didn't believe in that love at first sight bullshit. Lust maybe, but that's all it was. There was no room in my life right now for anything else. Once upon a time, I'd wanted to settle down, have a wife and kids. Now I got a release when I needed it, and if I sometimes wondered what it would be like to have a woman in my house every day, well, that was a secret I wasn't sharing with anyone.

Taking my time, I explored her curves, loving the feel of her. Her body arched as my palm slid between her breasts. So fucking pretty. Her nipples were already hard little points, just begging for my attention. Lavender's lips parted as my fingers glided across the slopes of her breasts, not quite touching where she wanted me to the most. A soft whimper escaped her as she tipped her head back and thrust her breasts upward.

I leaned down and took the peak of one into my mouth, drawing on the bud. Lavender tasted sweet. So fucking sweet. I tongued her nipple, flicking it, before sucking on it again. She moaned and her fingers wrapped around the back of my neck, holding on as if she were afraid I'd get up and leave. Not fucking likely. Now that I had her in my bed, I wasn't going anywhere. Not until I'd fucked her hard enough to get her out of my system. The second I'd seen her at the gate I knew she'd be a temptation I should avoid. Yet here we were.

I lavished attention on her nipples, loving the soft sounds she made, then worked my way down her body. She giggled and squirmed as I brushed my beard against her ribs.

"Tickles," she murmured.

Using my tongue to trace her hipbone, I gave it a nip as I ran my hand up her thigh. I'd barely touched her, compared to what I wanted to do, and already she trembled. I glanced up, wondering if she was rethinking this, but the look of pure bliss on her face dispelled that fear. No, she wanted me every bit as much as I wanted her.

The curls at the juncture of her thighs had been trimmed short. I liked that she still had some hair, even though most of the club sluts shaved it all off. With a gentle nudge, I got her to part her legs and I settled between them. Her hands were fisting the bedding and I couldn't wait to see how she responded to my mouth on her pussy. I parted the lips and used my tongue to circle her clit. She jumped and squeaked, but I noticed she didn't tell me to stop.

"If I do anything you don't like, then tell me," I said. "I want you to enjoy this, Lavender. It's okay to talk to me and make noise."

"Don't stop," she begged. "Just… don't stop."

I grinned before I went back to tasting the sweetness between her thighs. I licked, sucked, nipped, working her pussy until I had her crying out for more and thrashing under me. She was nonsensical as she babbled, her body twisting. She'd jerk away from me only to press closer a moment later. When she came, I lapped up her juices, then flicked her clit with my tongue again.

"Too sensitive!" she cried as she tried to pull away from me.

I chuckled and wiped my hand down my beard before levering myself over her. She looked up at me with wonder in her eyes. Had no one ever gone down on her before? Jesus, what kind of fucking idiots had she been dating? Punk-ass kids most likely, since she was so damn young. Most guys didn't know what the fuck they were doing until their mid-twenties, or later. Some didn't learn at all.

"You still okay with this? Want to keep going?" I asked.

"Yes. Please, Leven."

I froze, having not heard my birth name in so fucking long. I knew her parents had to have told her. They'd known me not just as Voodoo Tracer, but as Leven Crawford. But no one had called me that since the day I left her parents behind and forged a new life for myself.

"What's wrong?" she asked, her brow creasing.

"Nothing. Just took me by surprise hearing that name."

She tensed under me. "I can call you Wire."

For some reason, I liked the sound of my name on her lips, and the thought of her calling me the same thing the club sluts did was... wrong. I didn't know why it felt wrong, but it did.

"You can call me Leven. As long as no one else is around."

Kissing her softly, I reached for the condom and ripped the package open before rolling it down my cock. I lifted her legs so that her feet were flat on the bed and her thighs were spread wide, then I gripped her ass to raise her up a little. I sank into her one inch at a time, groaning at how fucking tight she was. Lavender dug her nails into my arms and canted her hips, taking more of me. Fucking hell! I'd never felt anything so exquisite in my life. Her inner walls clasped me so tight it was nearly to the point of pain. I wasn't going to last at this rate.

"Yes! Yes! I need more," she begged.

I didn't stop until I was balls-deep inside her, then I was thrusting, driving into her wet heat. Our bodies slapped together, but it was the way her gaze held mine that made me breathless. I got to not only see her body flush a deeper shade, but seeing her fall over the edge when she orgasmed was the hottest thing I'd ever witnessed. I'd fucked plenty of women, but with Lavender, it felt like I was sharing more than a moment of pleasure with her. There was a connection, a need to ensure this was the best experience she'd ever had.

I reached between us and worked her clit, wanting her to come at least once more. She met each plunge of my cock, seeming almost frantic as she chased another release.

"Come for me, sweetheart. Let me feel that pussy squeeze my cock."

My words alone seemed to set a spark to her. She clawed at me, screaming my name, as her pussy clenched tight on me. I growled as I drove into her, fucking her hard and deep until I came. Part of me hated that my cum went into the condom, but I knew it was for the best. My dick twitched inside her and I reluctantly pulled out, holding the latex to make sure we didn't have any accidents.

I kissed her briefly, then rolled off the bed to get rid of the rubber. I tied it off and dumped it in the bathroom trash, rinsed my cock in the sink, then grabbed a warm wet rag for Lavender. She still lay sprawled across the bed, her legs splayed open. I used the cloth to clean her up, smiling a little at the cute blush that rose to her cheeks. Tossing the rag into the bathroom, I slid back into bed and pulled her into my arms.

I'd never given a fuck before what a woman did after we screwed. Making Lavender leave seemed wrong, though, so I held her as she curled against me. I didn't know what tomorrow would bring, but we'd at least have this one moment. It would be a night I would remember for years to come, if I ever was able to forget. Something told me that Lavender was unforgettable.

"Thank you," she murmured.

"For what?"

"Making my first time so wonderful."

Everything in me went still. First time? What the fuck? I'd not have missed virgin blood on my dick. How the hell was I her first? She must have sensed my confusion because she blinked up at me.

"I've used vibrators before. Decided to pop my own cherry when I was eighteen and hadn't had a boyfriend. But you're the first man I've ever been with."

Well, shit.

"If I'd known that, I would have done things differently. Taken my time."

"If you'd made that any better, I think I'd have melted right through the bed and turned into a puddle on your floor. Stop stressing, Leven. It was perfect, and I'm glad I waited for you."

I swallowed the knot in my throat.

I ran my hand up and down her back, letting her cuddle against me, and knew I wasn't going to ask her to go to the spare bedroom. Not after what she'd just said. There were times I could be an ass, but I wouldn't let tonight be one of those days.

Tomorrow I'd deal with the reality of what we'd shared right now.

For now, I would enjoy having her in my arms. But this couldn't happen again. I had a feeling if I let Lavender into my bed even one more time, I'd not want her to leave. Hell, I wasn't sure I wanted her to leave now. Knowing I was her first? It made me want to fuck her again, without the condom, and fill her with my cum. I wanted everyone to know that I'd been the one she chose, to brand her, mark her with my scent.

It was fucked up, that's what it was.

Screwed. So fucking screwed.

Chapter Three

Lavender

Waking up with Wire's arms around me had both made me feel all warm and cozy, and sent a sliver of fear through me. I'd liked it. Too much. He wasn't the type of man to stick around, to just want one woman. Or at least not a woman like me. I'd seen enough TV and read enough books to know that guys like him could have anyone they wanted. It wouldn't surprise me if women fell at his feet. So, I'd eased out from his embrace, gathered my clothes, and taken a shower in the hall bathroom.

I knew that I would never forget the night we'd shared, and I was so glad that he'd been my first, but I was realistic enough to know that it wouldn't happen again. There was a twinge between my legs. Even though I had several vibrators at home, none were the size of Wire and I was still feeling him this morning. It was a good ache.

"Stupid," I muttered. "You're stupid."

I didn't need to dwell on what we'd shared. All it did was make me want more from him. Not just sex either. I liked waking up in his arms, and had enjoyed cuddling with him last night. Getting attached to him was a mistake, but I already felt myself wanting more time with him. I was a fucking idiot. The second I'd seen how hot he was, I should have turned around and walked away, should have known the temptation would be too great. The fact my body had awakened after just one look at him should have been warning enough to turn tail and run.

This is what happened when I denied myself real sex for so long. Maybe if I'd let a guy take my virginity years ago, then I wouldn't feel the need to cling to

Wire. He wasn't the type to enjoy that kind of behavior. From what I knew of bikers anyway. Not that I had firsthand experience, but all the books and movies couldn't be completely wrong, could they? He might be a computer geek, but that wasn't all that he was, and I couldn't forget that.

By the time I'd washed, rinsed, and dried off, my stomach was rumbling. I couldn't remember the last time I'd eaten. Well, more than crackers I'd grabbed at a gas station on the way here when the bus had stopped to give everyone a break. I didn't hear a single sound in the house so I went exploring and found the kitchen. His fridge and pantry were well-stocked, especially for a bachelor. I pulled out eggs, ham, cheese, milk, onion, red and green bell pepper, then got to work prepping omelets.

I was bad about eating a lot of junk, especially when I was at the computer for hours on end. Getting the chance to eat something like this was a treat, even if I did have to be the one to make it. I'd always been terrible about keeping my kitchen supplied with nutritious food, or any food for that matter. Good thing there was a twenty-four hour shopping mart near my apartment, otherwise I'd likely starve.

I looked down at my pudgy belly and decided that missing some meals wasn't necessarily a bad thing, but I did need to lay off the junk food. It wasn't doing me any favors. If I packed on too much weight now, I could only imagine how hard it would be to lose it ten or twenty years from now. I'd heard enough women in their forties complaining about the difficulty of dropping weight to worry that might be my fate one day. My metabolism wasn't the greatest at twenty-two. I envied the women who still looked like runway models in their seventies and older. And I knew it took a lot of work for them to be in that shape.

The smell of food must have woken Wire. He shuffled into the kitchen, his hair and beard mussed, and looking like he wasn't completely awake yet. He paused and squinted at me before moving over to the coffeepot. I'd worried that he was upset I'd taken over his kitchen, then realized he'd only been trying to see me as he tried unsuccessfully to hit the right buttons on the machine.

"I can do that," I said as I flipped one of the omelets.

"Got it," he said, his voice still thick from sleep. "Forgot to set it up last night."

"Not a morning person?" I asked.

A grunt was my only answer. Good to know. Don't speak to Wire before coffee. He had that in common with my dad. I typically woke up alert and ready to tackle the day, regardless of the time or how much sleep I'd gotten. After he poured himself a cup, he pressed a button on an under-the-cabinet radio I hadn't noticed. Bad Wolves version of "Zombie" came on and I couldn't help but sing along. My nape prickled and I glanced over my shoulder to see Wire with the cup halfway to his mouth, frozen in place as he stared at me.

"What?" I asked. "I can't like good music?"

"I figured you'd be into pop or something," he said. "Isn't that what most women your age enjoy? You don't look like the rocker type."

He mumbled something else that sounded like, *or the singing type.*

Like I'd know a damn thing about what women liked? I didn't really have any female friends. Or guy friends for that matter. Most of the people I spoke with on a regular basis were miles away from where I lived, and I'd never even met them in person. Not that I would admit that to anyone. Whenever I told someone that, I got a look full of pity and a pep talk about how I'd make friends soon enough. As if I hadn't tried to make friends most of my life? Yeah, if it hadn't happened by now, I didn't hold out hope for the future. I'd just stick to talking to people through my messaging app. It was easier to be myself when I wasn't face-to-face with someone.

"I wouldn't know," I said, then focused on the food again before I burned it. I plated the omelet before starting another one. After topping the first one with shredded cheese, I handed the plate to Wire.

"You made me breakfast?" The tone of his voice had me glancing in his direction again. He looked… surprised? No, it was more than that.

"You act like no one has ever cooked for you before."

"Been a while. It wasn't like I expected you to do something like this."

I snorted. "Sit down and eat."

Despite what he'd said last night about not being with anyone recently, I was certain he'd had girlfriends before. Other than my mother. It was highly doubtful I was the only woman he'd slept with who had cooked for him the next day. Unless he threw them out afterward. Anything was possible. I liked to think that I was special in some way, but I wasn't that dumb. I'd been convenient last night and nothing more. I had to tell myself that or I might start getting ideas, the type that would have me daydreaming about more mornings like this one. The only way we were sharing another morning meal would be if I slept in a separate bed.

When my food was done, I joined him at the table. He gave me a contemplative look as he ate the last bite off his plate, then focused on his coffee. It seemed he'd said all that he'd planned to for now. Which was fine. It gave me time to tell him about my problem in more detail.

"I think what my parents found was a line of code that shouldn't have been there," I said. "The company hired them to test their firewall and security measures. Along the way, they found something, a bug of sorts that was siphoning money from the company. I didn't discover where it originated, but I think I dug just deep enough to tip someone off. They were probably being vigilant after my parents stumbled across it, and I fucked up by not covering my ass more."

"When you say siphoning…"

"The way it was designed it only took a few cents here and there. Enough to drive an accountant insane trying to piece it together, but it didn't happen frequently enough from the same accounts to really raise a flag. The missing money was probably written off as clerical error," I said. "However, the company in question had a lot of different locations and bank accounts. Dozens. From what I could tell, that little bug had the potential of stealing millions of dollars by end of the year. It was snatching a few cents from advertising at one location, then it would jump fifteen minutes later to another location and steal a few cents from a different department. It was all over the place but in a purposeful way, if that makes any sense. With the constant jumping, they were able to access various accounts at each location without tipping anyone off."

"What's the company?" Wire asked.

"LTX Communications," I said.

He choked a little on his coffee. "Shit."

Yeah, he had that right. They were one of the largest tech companies in the country and were about to branch out into the UK as a test run. If that little bit of code had gone undetected, over several years, someone could have become rich enough to never work again. And who's to say they'd have ever removed that bug? Once you started making that kind of money with little to no effort, it was addicting. I doubt they'd have given it up. Not to mention that if it had already been there for a while, they may have been cocky enough to think no one would ever find it.

But my parents had, and so had I.

"I don't think I covered my tracks good enough, which means whoever put it there is really fucking good. At first, I thought it was all a coincidence."

"What was?" he asked, his gaze sharpening.

"A window AC unit fell and nearly hit me. I got out of the way in time. There was maintenance being done on the building, so I just figured someone hadn't screwed it in tight enough. No biggie, right? Accidents happen. Then a car almost hit me as I crossed the street about two days later. Again, accidents happen. People get hit by cars often enough that it didn't seem suspicious."

"So what tipped you off?"

"My apartment was unlocked when I got home. The place wasn't tossed, but I did see something out of place. A box that I used for special little mementos. I'm a horrible housekeeper so the shelf was dusty. There was a dust-free mark near the box where it had been moved about half an inch."

"And that couldn't have been an accident too?"

"No. I don't have company and I hadn't touched that shelf or the box in months."

He arched his eyebrows and I realized what I'd just admitted. That not only did I not have friends to invite over, but that I hadn't had anything special for that box in a long-ass time. God, I was so pathetic. He probably wondered why he'd slept with a loser like me. Awesome. I was on a roll at making him think the worst of me.

"Anyway..." I licked my lips. "That's when I started paying more attention. After two more 'accidents' I decided that I was in danger. I grabbed what cash I had, hopped on the bus, and came to find you."

"Why would your mom send you to me?" he asked. "We hadn't spoken since before you were born, and we weren't exactly on good terms."

"I guess she thought you were a decent enough guy that you wouldn't turn me away." Because if she'd had even a hint that I would sleep with her ex-boyfriend, then she would have never told me about him. I loved my mom, but she couldn't have handled Wire finding me attractive, and not because I was her daughter but because she'd think of me as competition. Yeah, it was fucked up, but so was she. Mom had a competitive streak a mile wide. If I mentioned an accomplishment, then she'd done it bigger and better.

He tapped his fingers against his coffee mug, but the look in his eyes said he didn't think that was it. I honestly had no idea why she'd said I should find Wire. There were other people she was close to, people she'd still talked to up until her death. Unless she'd just known that Wire was the best at what he did and figured he could protect me. She wasn't wrong about that, I didn't think. Even though I hadn't witnessed his skills firsthand, I'd heard enough about him over the years, and read even more.

"Look, we'll never know for sure why she did it. The important thing is that I'm here and you said you'd help," I said, starting to wonder if he regretted bringing me to his home last night.

Wire nodded and glanced down at the table. "Yeah, I did. I need you to write down everything you remember about finding that line of code. I'm going to look into it, see what I can find, but I don't want you actively participating. If this person is already trying to find you, no sense in drawing more of their attention your way."

"Do you think you can get by them undetected?"

The look he shot me made me clamp my mouth shut. Yep. He did and would get by whoever it was with them none the wiser, and I was an idiot to have questioned him. The guy was the best in the world and I'd just insulted him. Wonderful. There were times I wished that someone would tape my mouth shut so I wouldn't say stupid shit. Like now.

"Right," I said. "Of course you can. Forgot who I was talking to for a moment."

"While I'm working, you should relax. Watch a movie, grab a book off the shelf in the living room, something…"

Which translated into *give me space*. Got it.

He stood, refilled his coffee, then slid a pad and pen across the table to me. I wrote everything down, then handed it back. Wire picked up and left the kitchen. I sighed, then realized I was watching his ass. Slamming my eyes shut, I turned away from the amazing view and wondered what the hell I would do with my time. I heard a door down the hall click shut and decided I'd clean up the mess I'd made first. It didn't take long to load the dishwasher and wipe down the counters. For a single guy, Wire's house was really damn clean. It was a bit puzzling, since most of the hackers and wannabes that I knew all lived in filth, too busy trying to be a badass to bother with things like hygiene. I'd even been known to grow a collection of soda cans. Of course, I promptly threw them away and did a deep clean on my house whenever I'd finished what I was working on, but the guys I knew didn't tend to follow that same logic.

Then there was Wire.

I shook my head, knowing that I'd probably never solve that puzzle. I wouldn't be here long enough. He was going to help me, then I was on my own. For the rest of my life... Now there was a depressing thought. My parents might not have won any awards for parent of the year, but they were all I'd had. Just thinking about the future was a little depressing.

I poked around the living room a bit, trying to learn as much about Wire as I could on a more personal level, even though I'd gotten a rather in-depth lesson last night. My cheeks warmed at the thought. Knowing he could be a while, I decided to get a cup of coffee and read, like he'd suggested. Pouring coffee down the front of my only clean shirt hadn't been part of the plan, but I'd never claimed to be graceful. It didn't help my hands were shaking from how much he affected me.

There was no way I was walking around with a coffee-stained shirt the rest of the day. The clothes in my backpack were dirty, so rummaging through there wouldn't do me any good. I also wasn't going to bother Wire over something so trivial. Instead, I decided to borrow a shirt from his room. I didn't think he'd mind, considering where he'd had his face less than twelve hours ago. The one he'd worn the previous day was still on the floor and I picked up, holding it to my nose and breathing in his scent. I slipped it on, grinning a little as it went all the way to my knees.

Since it was just the two of us and he was occupied. I didn't see the point in being uncomfortable. I shimmied out of my jeans and tossed them into the guest room before going in search of a book. Pants were an outside thing anyway, right? Who the hell bothered with pants around the house?

Wire had a decent collection of novels if you liked general fiction, non-fiction, and thrillers. Mysteries were my favorite, but it looked like I was out of luck. I hadn't expected him to have romances on his shelves, but those were my second obsession when it came to books. Of course, if I *had* found romances in his house, I'd have had no choice but to give him shit about it.

I selected *The Relic*, curious if the book was better than the movie. I found that was usually the case, but not always. Some writing seemed to drag on, but the condensed version in movie form was entertaining for me. It's how I'd enjoyed some storylines from the more popular authors. Their writing just hadn't been quite right for me, but I'd loved the plots and characters.

I'd only read about a chapter before there was a knock at the front door. I waited, wondering if Wire would go answer it, but he must have been in the zone because the knocking became more insistent and he didn't surface from the room he'd entered earlier. Depending what he was digging into right now, it was possible that he wasn't able to get up. Not without leaving a trail for the thief to follow.

I looked down at myself and realized everything important was covered so I decided to at least make the noise stop. It was probably just one of the other bikers. Since I was in Wire's house, I hoped that meant I was safe from unwanted attention. Only one way to find out. I was about fifty percent certain if I screamed Wire would come make sure I didn't die. If he weren't at the computer, I'd have upped the odds to about ninety percent.

Getting up, I went to open the door, and came face-to-face with a gorgeous blonde. One who was wearing little to nothing, and a rather shocked expression on her beautiful face. Huh. Either he'd lied about not being with someone, or... Yeah, I wasn't going there. I didn't want to even think about the biker sluts, or whatever they were called, hopping into his bed. Especially since I'd been in it not that long ago. This woman had biker groupie written all over her from the hip-hugging leather miniskirt to the halter top barely holding in the girls. Who the fuck wore that shit in the morning?

"May I help you?" I asked.

Her gaze scanned me from head to toe before her blue eyes locked on mine. "I'm looking for Wire. We have a date."

The way she shifted from foot to foot told me she was lying. I didn't miss the nervous way she glanced around either, as if she was worried about being found here. Did anyone realize she'd come to Wire's house? Granted, he'd had condoms in his bedside table drawer, so he evidently brought women here. I just didn't know if this one had been one of them. The pit bull in a cut at the front gate wouldn't have let her in if she weren't permitted to be here. Unless he hadn't realized where she was going. With the clubhouse not far from the gate, it would have been obvious she took a detour.

Whatever. Not my man, not my problem.

"He's busy," I said.

"Are… are you two dating?" she asked.

Seemed like something a woman would know if she had a date with a man. I just stared at her with the resting bitch face I'd learned from my mother, deeming not to answer. She nodded and heaved a sigh, backing up a few steps.

"Right, I'll just go, then."

Her skinny ass marched down the driveway to a small car parked at the end. I felt a large, warm hand settle at my hip and the heat of Wire's body press against me.

"What the fuck did Emily want?" he asked.

So he did know the skank. All right. Maybe calling her a skank, even in my head, wasn't fair. I didn't know her. What she did with her life was her business and not mine. The fact she wanted Wire -- and it made me want to bare my teeth at her like a feral wolf -- was beside the point. He wasn't mine, would never be mine. I was just an unwanted houseguest.

"She said the two of you had a date. Didn't seem too thrilled with finding me here."

He snorted. "Bet she didn't. Now I'm glad I let you answer the door. I've been trying to get my point across to that one for a while now. She's desperate to sink her claws into one of us. Wants to be an old lady."

I'd read enough biker books and watched enough shows about them to understand what he meant, and I didn't like the thought of that woman wearing his property patch. Yeah, I was getting attached too fast. I needed to put some space between us, but as the door swung shut and he nuzzled the side of my neck, I knew that all hope was lost.

Why did he have to feel so good? Smell so good? Hell. I closed my eyes, drinking in the feel of his body against mine.

"You look damn tempting in my shirt," he said.

I opened my eyes and stared at the door.

"I spilled coffee on mine. Figured if you were going to be locked in that room all day, you wouldn't mind me getting comfortable and stealing your shirt."

He murmured something I didn't catch, but the hard length of his cock rubbing against me didn't go unnoticed. Nope. He didn't mind in the least, or one part of him didn't anyway. His hand slid up my thigh, lifting the shirt high enough for him to slip his hand into my panties. A shiver ran through me at the rough touch of his skin against mine.

"Mmmm. Already wet and ready for me," he said.

Oh, God. My eyes slid shut and I leaned my forehead against the door. I'd have been embarrassed if he didn't sound so pleased over the fact I was soaking my panties. One touch from him and I'd been ready to let him do whatever he wanted. I was such a little slut. For him. The thought of any other guy doing this made me feel cold inside.

Wire worked my panties down my legs until they fell to the floor, then he nudged my legs farther apart. The way he worked my clit had me seeing stars. I panted as I leaned against the door, my ass pushing out as I silently asked for more. I wanted him. I shouldn't, but I did. Was this why the girls in college had hopped from bed to bed? Had it been this amazing every time they slept with a guy? Or was Wire unique? Maybe no one else would ever make me feel this way.

"Do you want my cock, Lavender? Want me to fuck you right here, right now?" he asked, his voice husky from need.

I wanted to beg him to fuck me, but I bit my lip to stay silent. The last thing I wanted was to sound as desperate as I felt.

His hand cracked against my ass making me yelp.

"I asked you a question."

I whimpered but still didn't answer. He spanked me twice more, and fuck if I didn't get wetter. What the hell was he doing to me?

"Yes, please. I need you, Leven."

I heard his belt clink and the rasp of his zipper. What I didn't hear? The sound of a condom wrapper being torn open. I gasped as he filled me, his cock stretching me until I'd taken all of him. His arm curled around my waist while his other hand still worked my pussy, making my legs quiver as my orgasm got closer and closer. He took his time, fucking me slow but deep.

Pleasure rolled through me, stealing the breath from my lungs. The euphoria had no sooner started to ebb than he was pounding into me, his whispers in my ear demanding that I come again. As if his voice alone had power over me, I screamed out my second release, this one coming so fast and hard that I nearly lost the ability to stand. He growled as he slammed into me again and again. I felt the hot bursts of his cum inside me. My nipples hardened even more and my pussy clenched tight around him. I was such a fucking whore when it came to this man, and I didn't understand why. So he was gorgeous. I'd seen compelling men before. But this one… he made me feel things.

His teeth scraped my neck and shock filled me when I realized he was still hard. He thrust into me again, gripping me in such a way that he slid in deeper. *Fuck me*! My toes curled as he hit just the right spot. Over and over. I was sobbing by the time I'd come again, my release running down my thighs, and yet I didn't want him to stop. It was so intense, but was the most wonderful thing I'd ever experienced. Would it be wrong to ask him to chain me to his bed and do this all day every day? Would we survive such a thing?

He came a second time, grinding against my ass as his cock twitched inside me.

"Wh-what was that?" I asked.

He chuckled. "If you aren't sure, then I did it wrong and we should start over."

Oh, Jesus. I wouldn't survive another round like that just yet. Not unless I could lie down.

"You didn't get a condom," I pointed out as he slipped from my body.

When I tried to stand fully, he pressed a hand to the middle of my back, bending me over farther.

"Fucking beautiful," he murmured.

My brain felt scrambled and I couldn't make sense of what he said.

"What is?" I asked.

"My cum sliding out of your pussy. Never gone bare before, but fuck if I don't like the sight before me right now."

He finally helped me stand and I could feel the stickiness between my legs. Our combined release had made a giant mess.

"What happened to always wrapping your dick?" I asked.

"We'll talk about it later." He pushed a wayward strand of hair back behind my ear. "I need to meet with my club first. Make yourself at home and I'll be back shortly."

He zipped up his pants, brushed a kiss against my cheek, then he was out the door. My hand went to my cheek and I rubbed the spot before I realized what I was doing. What the fuck? I felt like I'd just fallen down the rabbit hole and into Wonderland. What exactly happened in that room today? He went in there resigned to help me, and now… I shook my head, not knowing what to think or feel about the change in Wire.

What I did know was that I needed another shower.

Was it wrong I hoped I'd need more of them in the near future for the express purpose of washing his cum off my thighs?

Yep. I was a goner.

Fuck.

Chapter Four

Wire

"What's this shit Emily spouted about you having a girlfriend?" Savior asked. "Since when are you seeing someone?"

Because of course she'd come straight to the clubhouse to cry on any shoulder she could find. I fucking hated that woman. I slept with her once or twice, and now she thought I would give her more. The women who came here weren't forced, but they didn't seem to understand they were just a place to put our dicks and it didn't mean they would become an old lady.

"This have anything to do with you requesting Church be called?" Tank asked, walking up to us. "I had to leave Emmie alone with the triplets for this shit. Harlow has another ear infection, and Kasen still has that cough. They're running their mom ragged."

"It's not just about a woman," I said. And it wasn't, even though she'd brought the matter to my attention.

Torch passed us without a word and we fell in line. He didn't look pleased to be here either. Just what I needed. Everyone in the club fucking pissed at me because I'd requested Church. Shit. I'd done more than enough for these assholes for them to give me this one thing. I'd never asked for special favors. Hell, I'd signed my life away to the government to keep us safe. What the fuck more did they want?

We took our seats and waited for the others to trickle in. Once all the patched members and officers were present, Grimm shut the doors.

"I have shit to do so let's cut to the chase," Torch said. "Wire, tell us what you need."

Well, that was pretty to the point. I cleared my throat and looked around the table. Pulling my phone from my pocket, I hit the speed dial for a three-way call with Shade and Surge.

"You're on speaker," I said as the call connected to both of them. "Did you look over the info I sent."

"What the fuck is this shit?" Shade asked.

"I thought that dude was dead," said Surge. "No one's heard from Cataclysm in a decade."

"That's because I put him in jail," I said. "Or rather I sent the info to the Feds and let them handle it. Looks like he got out. Overcrowding or some shit."

Torch sighed. "All right. Back the fuck up and tell us what's going on."

"About ten years ago, a hacker by the name of Cataclysm was using his skills to erase women. No birth records, death records, nothing. All traces completely gone."

"Fucking trafficker," Wraith muttered, a dark look on his face.

"Yes and no," I said. "He was aiding a trafficking ring, for a lot of bank, but I ran across his work and started putting the clues together. It was something I did on my own and I didn't involve the club. Everything I dug up, I forwarded to the Feds since the women came from all over the country."

"And now he's out. Is he up to the same thing?" Venom asked.

"From what I can tell, he was just trying to steal money from companies. He targeted some of the larger corporations, but my ex and her husband stumbled across one of his lines of code. Got them killed."

"You know this how?" Flicker asked.

"Because their daughter came to me for help."

"Ah, the girlfriend," Savior said.

"What girlfriend?" asked Shade. "Are you holding out on us? We're supposed to know when you find someone hot and smart enough to handle you. It gives the rest of us some fucking hope."

"Shut it," I said.

"How does the girl figure into this?" Torch asked. "I'm guessing she's a fully grown woman since this is the first I've heard she's at my compound."

I winced, knowing I'd fucked up by not telling him sooner. He'd really love the next part.

"She's a grown-ass woman. And she's mine."

That earned me some stares, and a bit of laughter over the phone. Fucking assholes. They were going to make me spill my damn guts. I hated them right now.

"She's in danger, more than she knows." I ran a hand through my hair. "But that's not the reason I'm claiming her. That's between me and her."

I hadn't told her I was claiming her, or why. I knew I'd need to have that conversation with her, and soon. Right now, I just wanted to get my name on her in any way I could. Some perverse part of me wanted to see her branded with *Wire*, but deeper than that, I knew my name would lend her a certain amount of protection. She already had a fucking target on her from Cataclysm. Now I needed to protect her in any way I could. If her being mine made that easier, then I wouldn't argue. Especially after having the best sex of my fucking life. Twice. Even now I was hard just thinking about her.

"Why is Cataclysm after her?" Venom asked. "And what does this have to do with us?"

"Like I said, he's been stealing from corporations. Lavender's mom and dad found a piece of what Cataclysm is doing and they ended up dead. She tried to unravel what happened to them and now he's got her in his sights. There have been too many accidents for them to be accidental. Theft didn't seem like a good enough reason for murder, though, not even for him. Which meant something else was doing on, something that required deeper digging."

"Tell them what you found," Surge said. "Because this shit is fucked up."

I rubbed the back of my neck, knowing that all this shit was connected to me. Or more to the point, Cataclysm wanted to make me suffer.

"He's taking down every hacker I've ever called a friend, and I mean that in a permanent way. Then he's targeting any female relations, wiping their existence, and selling them through various channels. Mostly, he's been auctioning them on the dark web." I stared at the table a moment. "There are innocent girls and women, living through hell right now, all because I put that guy in jail. He knew I'd find out eventually and wanted me to suffer. I don't think he planned for me to discover him quite so soon though."

"So why kill Lavender?" Venom asked. "Shouldn't he have wanted to sell her too? And what the fuck has gone wrong with the world? We've been dealing with this type of shit since Ridley showed up at the gates. Anyone else sick of this?"

He wasn't wrong, and yeah, I was just as sick of it. There were some seriously fucked-up people in the world, and we couldn't take them all out. One problem at a time. That was all we could do. If it made the world a bit safer for women and kids, then great. We might sell drugs, guns, and had dabbled in questionable things over the years, but not once had we ever hurt women or kids. Even the drugs we sold didn't get into the hands of children. If they did, the person responsible paid the price.

"She's a hacker, and since I was friends with her parents once upon a time, he must have assumed I was a friend to her as well. Even though I hadn't spoken to her parents in over twenty years, and Cataclysm went away a decade after that."

"Because everyone knows how you felt about her mom," Shade said. "Fuck, there are those who think you're still in love with her."

"No. No fucking way am I in love with Krista. She's a two-timing bitch and can burn in hell. I've been done with her for a long time."

"We know that, but not everyone does," said Surge.

"So this Cataclysm thought he would cause you pain by killing your ex and her husband," Bull said. "Doesn't sound very smart to me. What exactly did he hope to gain? Most guys I know would pay good money for someone to off their ex."

"He's more devious than smart," said Surge. "But it doesn't make him any less dangerous. I'm also about eighty percent certain he's insane. Like a padded room type of crazy."

No, it didn't make him less dangerous. And I knew that once he realized Lavender was with me, that I'd made her mine, he'd come for her. The difference was that she was no longer fighting him on her own. She had me, my club, our extended family… and it was time for Voodoo Tracer to put the word out that Dark Labyrinth was off fucking limits. Anyone who came for her in person or through a computer would deal with me.

"How did he know your ex would find his little bug?" Grimm asked. "Seems kind of farfetched that she'd just happen upon it and he'd see her as a way to get to you."

"I've been thinking about that. When I was trying to trace him, I noticed something interesting." I leaned back in my chair. "At first glance, it looked like he'd used a botnet. Until I dug a bit more. The malware wasn't hitting random computers. Every company he stole from had agreements with either Krista and Mark's business, or with other hackers I called friends. I think he *wanted* them to find it. It honestly wasn't well-hidden, not to a professional. I just don't understand why he didn't go after them outright. Personally, if I were going to be sneaky about that type of shit, I'd plant a rootkit. They're harder to detect, and not all will be caught by programs that check for that type of thing."

"Sounds like he wanted you to know what he was up to," Shade said. "But I'm betting he didn't think you'd find him so fast. Anyone else dead?"

"I've reached out to everyone and gotten a response. Except for one. VirtualPi hasn't answered any messages. She's dead." My chest ached, knowing that Shawnie Tucker died simply because I'd considered her a friend.

I'd looked up her name and hometown, only to discover that she'd had an unfortunate accident. I knew it wasn't a fucking "accident." This asshole was going to pay when I got my hands on him. Prison hadn't taught him anything. Maybe spilling his blood would work. He might be a badass behind a computer monitor, but in real life I had the upper hand. The mug shot for Cataclysm, or rather Jeffrey Peterson, showed a middle-aged man who looked like he'd swallowed a few too many kegs. He was soft, and while prison had possibly taught him a few real life tricks, I doubted he'd made too many friends inside.

"What do you need from us?" Torch asked. "Besides a property cut for Lavender."

"You going to accept her sight unseen?" Coyote asked. "We don't need to vote?"

Torch stared him down and Coyote lifted his hands.

"No disrespect intended. I'm just saying, we don't know this woman, haven't seen her, but you're letting him put a property patch on her?" Coyote asked.

"Like we've voted on any of them," Flicker said. "Is anyone in this room going to deny a brother's claim? Not fucking likely."

"Since she's either naked or just wearing one of my shirts, you'll pardon me for not asking her to come to the clubhouse," I said.

Venom coughed to cover his laugh, and Torch just ran his hand down his face. Yeah, I was an eloquent motherfucker. It was true, though. Lavender was either still naked, or she'd put another of my shirts on. She didn't seem to have more than two sets of clothes, and they were both dirty unless she'd had some other reason for raiding my dresser. I hadn't thought to show her where the washer and dryer were located, and I damn sure needed to get more clothes for her.

Coyote opened his mouth and Torch shook his head, giving him a stern look.

"If you're about to say some smartass thing about seeing her naked, then I wouldn't," Torch said. "Not unless you want Wire to hand your ass to you, and I can promise I won't stand in his way. You'd be lucky if the damage was only physical. Don't forget he can wipe out your existence with a few keystrokes."

Well, more than a few, but Torch wasn't wrong. I could do it. Had done it.

"Me neither," said Venom. "But I might record it and have Ridley put that shit up on YouTube."

Coyote sank farther into his chair, but I could tell he was pissed. If it hadn't been the Pres and VP saying that shit to him, he'd have flipped them off. It seemed he did have a bit of common sense and remained silent. I'd have beaten the fucker's ass for saying some stupid shit like that, then fucked with his online accounts. Lavender was mine, not some club whore. She deserved respect.

"So who's the woman?" Shade asked.

I couldn't help grinning. "Dark Labyrinth."

I heard either him or Surge hacking and coughing.

"Are you shitting me?" Surge asked, gasping for breath.

"Nope. She showed up at the gates asking for Voodoo Tracer. Needless to say, the Prospect was confused as fuck. Anyway, she's mine. With or without the property patch. Anyone fucks with her, they'll answer to me."

"Jesus," Shade muttered. "The two of you are like cyber royalty. Now you'll have little genius babies to follow in your footsteps. That's scary as fuck."

"While I find this all fascinating, Church is adjourned. Get the fuck out," Torch said. "Wire, I'll have your property cut for Lavender ready in a day or two. Until then, get Zipper to ink her. Today would be good."

I nodded and looked over at the club's tattoo artist. He hung back and I waited for the room to clear.

"Any idea what you want?" he asked.

"I have a few. Give me an hour or two to figure out some clothing for Lavender and to sketch out something. You going to be here for a bit?"

"I can have a beer or four. As long as I don't touch anything stronger, I'll be fine to ink your woman." He grinned. "Take your time. But word of advice, bring her through here before the party girls arrive. For one, she'll get upset if they hit on you. And second, my woman will have my balls if I'm here around those whores, then she'll gut any of them who dares to look at me."

I snickered, but knew he was right. Delphine was the sweetest thing, until she thought someone had eyes on her man. God forbid anyone look at her son for too long either. She went all momma bear and no one was safe. Only Zipper seemed to keep her under control, and if the screams of ecstasy heard from his house several nights a week were any indication, she didn't mind it one bit.

I gave him a quick wave and made my exit, heading home to figure some shit out. The easiest thing would be to wash what Lavender had brought with her, get her inked, then take her shopping. We could get the clothes from her house at some point, but for the time being, she needed at least a week's worth of clothing. I really didn't want her, or anyone else, near the apartment she'd been renting until I was certain it was safe.

At the house, I found her curled up on the couch reading a book, her bare legs tucked under her. She was still wearing just my shirt, and I got a bit of satisfaction out of seeing her in it. It wasn't a property patch, but it was mine -- and she was mine. I should probably tell her that before someone else mentioned it. She had enough spirit that she might not agree as easily as I hoped, but I'd convince her, even if I had to tie her to the bed to do it.

"Miss me?" I asked.

She glanced up, a smile spreading across her lips. "You weren't gone all that long."

"About an hour," I said.

She looked at the book in her hands and shrugged. Obviously, she loved to read. Good to know, since it was something I enjoyed too. Maybe I needed to add a trip to the bookstore to my list for today. Something told me that the items on my shelf weren't her typical selection. She didn't come across as the thriller type.

"Why don't you gather your clothes and I'll show you were the washer and dryer are hidden? I need you to go somewhere with me in the next hour or two. And it's going to require pants," I said with a smirk, eyeing her legs again. "Not that I'm complaining about you running around pants-less."

Lavender rolled her eyes at me, but she put the book aside and stood up. "Fine. I'll get my things. For the record, I'm perfectly content staying in the house semi-naked. Or even completely naked if you'd like to drop your pants."

Tempting, but we had things to do. I smacked her ass when she walked past me, making her jump and shoot a glare at me over her shoulder. The slight smile on her lips was almost enough to make me follow her. Damn but that woman was sexy. I didn't know how I'd lucked out, but I was so fucking glad her mother had sent her my way. I had a feeling that Krista wouldn't have if she'd known that Lavender would end up in my bed. The bitch wouldn't have liked it, even though she'd never wanted to be there when she had the chance.

Lavender came back a moment later with two outfits in her arms, as well as some lacy panties and matching bra that made me wish I'd paid closer attention to what she'd been wearing last night. Unless those were from this morning. Maybe I could convince her to wear them after they were washed.

"Washer and dryer are off the kitchen," I said, tipping my head for her to follow me. The small door to the left of the stove wasn't that noticeable thanks to the room's layout. I pushed it open and waved a hand for her to step through.

"How did I not know there was a room here? I cooked not three feet from this door earlier." Lavender took in the room, her gaze scanning the cabinets over the washer and dryer, the folding table in the corner, and the shelves I used for storing the linens and extra towels.

"The door and wall are painted the same color on purpose. Makes the kitchen appear larger."

I showed her how to use the washer, which was some fancy thing I'd let Isabella pick out. I hadn't known a fucking thing about washing clothes except you put in laundry soap and turned it on. It seemed there was more to it than that. After her clothes were washing, I led her back into the living room and pulled her down onto my lap as I sank into my recliner.

"Does every man on the planet have one of these?" she asked, eyeing my chair.

"They're comfortable."

"They're ugly," she argued. "My dad had one and I think my mom threatened to burn it at least once a week."

I snorted. Yeah, sounded like something Krista would do. I eyed Lavender. "Don't even think of torching my chair, or I'll paddle your ass."

Her eyes sparkled as she leaned in closer, her lips nearly touching mine. "If that's a threat, you need to come up with a better one."

If only we had more time… I wrapped my hand around the back of her neck and tugged her closer, pressing my lips to hers. I kissed her long and deep, leaving her moaning and begging for more. As much as I'd have loved to give her a good spanking, there was no way I'd be able to get up and walk away. We'd end up spending the day in bed, and there wasn't time for that. Not until she'd been marked as mine.

Chapter Five

Lavender

I wasn't entirely certain how I'd let Wire talk me into a tattoo. Well, perhaps that wasn't the right way to phrase it. More like he'd flat out told me I was getting one. Arguing had only earned me a sore, red ass, and made his cock hard. He was still sporting wood even as Zipper finished off the design on my arm. I had to admit, it was perfect for me. While I still wasn't thrilled over getting ink, at least Wire had put some thought into it. I wasn't entirely sure how he'd known some of my favorite characters, but then again, he was Voodoo Tracer. It probably had taken him a few keystrokes to learn the basics about me.

My new ink said *Property of Wire* but around that he'd incorporated characters who were important to me, like Mokey Fraggle, Sir Didymus, Lady Amalthea, and Fizzgig. There were some scattered stars mixed in the design as well. It took up the majority of my arm, with a line of binary code down the inside of my forearm that said Forever. I was now inked from just below my elbow to my wrist. For my first tattoo, it was rather large, but I couldn't deny that I liked it. A lot. The pain on the other hand... but I knew that would lessen over the next few hours or days, and I'd be left with a gorgeous work of art once it was fully healed.

Considering the amount of agony involved, I intended for it to be my *only* tattoo. I'd heard they were addicting and once you had one you would want more. Somehow, I didn't think that would be an issue for me. For one, I wasn't into pain. Or at least, not this type. I hadn't minded that spanking too much, and had made the mistake of letting him know it.

As far as tattoos… I hadn't wanted this first one to begin with, even if I did admire the artwork now that it was on my skin. It wasn't like I could easily remove it, not that Wire would permit that. He'd explained on the way over that it was for my safety, an extra layer of protection. Since I preferred to remain breathing, I hadn't argued about getting the tattoo.

"Wire knows the drill on taking care of your new ink," Zipper said. "But if you have any questions, I'm only a phone call away. My wife is just as knowledgeable if you'd prefer to talk to a woman."

"Thank you. I might not have wanted to get it done, but your work is wonderful," I said, earning me a smile from Zipper.

"Come on, sweetheart," Wire said. "We have some other errands to run."

He'd mentioned buying more clothes for me. I didn't see the point in spending money when I had a perfectly good wardrobe back home. Or rather, my former home. I didn't think Wire would let me go back permanently, not after claiming me the way he had. I was a little fuzzy on all the details, but having his name on my arm seemed rather permanent. I'd thought I was just a passing fancy, an itch for him to scratch, but it seemed I'd been wrong. Whenever I asked what exactly it meant to be his old lady, he'd shift the conversation elsewhere. The books I'd read and shows I'd watched about bikers didn't exactly put men like him in a favorable light. When those men had an old lady, they still slept around and did whatever they pleased. Was it the same way with Wire?

He went behind the bar in the main room of the clubhouse and pulled a set of keys off a hook. Wire grabbed my hand and led me from the building, but I noticed several men staring at us. Or more accurately, they were staring at me. I didn't like being the focus of their attention and I was grateful when we stepped out into the sunlight. There were still a few men lingering outside, but they ignored me.

Wire walked over to a truck and opened the passenger door, causing me to frown in confusion. We weren't taking his bike? I'd enjoyed being on the back of it and had looked forward to a longer ride.

"Can't carry much on the bike," he said. "I want to make sure you have everything you need, so we're taking one of the club trucks."

I climbed inside and buckled. Wire still hadn't closed the door, and he leaned into the space. When I turned my head his way, his lips brushed mine. It was brief, but just enough for a tingle to start between my legs. I was such a hussy when it came to him! He grinned and winked before shutting my door.

The truck rumbled to life when he turned the key in the ignition, and he eased away from the clubhouse before heading to the front gate. The man standing there waved us through. Instead of turning toward town, Wire took the two-lane highway in the opposite direction. I didn't know where we were going, but I trusted him. Maybe I shouldn't since we barely knew one another. Letting him go all caveman and claim me hadn't been the best of ideas since he was technically a stranger, and yet... Being with Wire was overwhelming, in a good way. My mother had believed he would keep me safe, and deep in my gut I knew that he wouldn't hurt me on purpose. That was enough for now. It had certainly been enough for me to willingly strip off my clothes and let him fuck me. Or maybe lust had overridden my brain cells.

"Are you ever going to tell me exactly what it means when you call me your old lady?" I asked.

"Because it's getting really damn annoying that you won't tell me."

"Maybe I'm biding my time in hopes my charm will convince you to stick around."

I snorted. "Charm. Is that what we're calling it? More like you're hoping to fuck me into compliance."

He winked at me and my cheeks warmed. Well, at least he'd admitted it. Sort of. Not that I could really complain. I'd loved everything he'd done to me so far. If he were to pull over on the side of the road and tell me to strip, I probably would. I was already that addicted to him.

"You know, you haven't asked much about Mom and Dad other than how they got into trouble," I said. "You aren't even a little curious how things turned out?"

"Do I want to know what happened to my ex and the guy she was screwing behind my back? Not exactly."

I cast a glance his way, biting my lip. "So it doesn't bother you that you're fucking their kid and if we ever got married they'd have been your in-laws."

The truck swerved and the tires went off the road for a moment as he cast me a startled look. Yep, he hadn't even considered that, but I had. It was weird as hell, but I didn't regret the time I'd spent with Wire so far, and if he wanted me to stay, then I would.

"Please don't say shit like that ever again," he said. "I've done some fucked-up stuff in my life, but I really don't want to contemplate what it means that we're together. The dynamics are just something that we don't need to discuss again. Ever. You're a sexy woman, one I can't keep my hands off of, and you're mine. That's all that matters."

"So you don't see my mom when you look at me?" I asked.

"Fuck no! Jesus, Lavender. You're you. A separate, unique person from your parents. You may share their DNA, and their skills with a computer, but it's not like I think of them when we're together. It's just you and me." He glanced at me again before focusing on the road. "Is that why you wanted in my pants? Because you wanted to get back at your parents or something?"

"No." I glared at him. "Why would you say that?"

"Maybe the same reason you just asked if I see your parents when I look at you. I think we can agree the reason we even met is because of your mother, but that's where it ends. I didn't let you in that day because of her."

"Then why did you?"

"Because you were in trouble." He cracked his neck. "And because my dick was fucking hard just looking at you. I tried to fight the attraction but decided to embrace it. Kind of hard not to when you were trying to unfasten my pants."

"So… you fought it for all of two seconds?" My eyebrows rose. "Because you fucked me within an hour or two of letting me into your house. Great restraint you have there."

"Sweetheart, unless you want me to pull this truck over, jerk those jeans of yours down, and paddled your ass, you'd better stop while you can."

Must have hit a sore spot. I grinned, thinking about him punishing me on the side of the road. I shot my gaze over to the side view mirror and saw that there wasn't a single car behind us, and I didn't see any oncoming traffic either.

"Spank me? Does that mean I need to call you daddy? Seeing as how you're going to --" I gave a squeak as he jerked the truck to the side of the road and put it in park. Yeah, I'd thought that might get a reaction out of him.

Before I could contemplate what he was doing, Wire had jerked me over to his side of the bench seat and was working my jeans down my legs. He nearly tore my panties as he bared my ass and his hand cracked hard against my skin. I yelped, but he landed three more blows, each one harder than the last.

"I'm not your fucking father, Lavender. Don't ever call me daddy again or I swear…" I looked up to see an evil glint in his eyes. "I'll get you to the edge again and again. You'll beg for release, but I won't let you come. I'll keep you right there for days until you're mindless with need. You're my woman, not a fucking kid. That daddy shit doesn't get me off."

Oh, shit. My pussy clenched and I felt a trickle of moisture run along my cleft.

Wire rubbed his hand against my ass cheeks. I whimpered at the sting. Then his fingers were sliding along the lips of my pussy and I tried to widen my legs. My jeans kept my thighs pressed together and I squirmed.

"My, my. It seems Lavender is a naughty little minx and liked her spankings." He thrust two fingers inside me. A cry escaped my lips before I could stop it. "But was it the spanking, or the fact we're out on the open road and anyone could see what I'm doing to you?"

Fuck!

His fingers thrust hard and deep.

"Is that it, sweet girl? You want someone to see your bare ass, see how red it is and know I spanked you? Want them to see me finger-fucking your wet pussy?"

Everything started spinning and I realized I was holding my breath. I sucked in a huge lungful of air as pleasure zipped along my nerve endings. Wire groaned as he worked my pussy harder, his fingers driving into me.

I started tugging at his belt, trying to unfasten it and unzip his pants. I'd never given anyone head before, but it couldn't be that difficult, right? When I had his hot, hard cock in my hand, my mouth started to water. I gave him a tentative lick, and he hissed in a breath. Emboldened by his response, I fitted my lips around the head and sucked, slowly taking more of him into my mouth.

"Jesus fucking Christ! You're going to kill me," he muttered.

He twisted his fingers on the next stroke and I saw stars I came so hard. I knew I was soaking the seat of the truck and I didn't even care. I gasped and shuddered as my release rolled through me. My pussy spasmed and Wire kept stroking. As the last of my orgasm was pulled from me, I started sucking his cock again, having forgotten about it in that moment.

Wire slipped his fingers free of me and I heard him sucking them clean. Then his hand was gripping my hair, tight enough to pull but not hard enough to hurt me. It was easy to give up control to him, letting him drag my lips down his cock, then tugging me back up his shaft.

"That's it, baby." He pushed me down again, not stopping until I'd taken all of him. I gagged and my eyes watered. He lifted me enough for me to catch my breath, then his fist tightened even more on my hair.

"Gonna fuck your mouth, sweet girl. You swallow when I come."

Oh, God. My pussy ached at the thought, and I couldn't think of anything I wanted more. I didn't know where this version of me had come from, or if it had lain dormant all this time, just waiting for the right man. I'd read some pretty filthy books over the years, but I hadn't really pictured myself doing any of it. Until now. With Wire, I wanted to try everything.

He drove into my mouth, thrusting hard and deep. I worried I'd suffocate, but I tried to calm myself with the knowledge he wouldn't hurt me. When his cum started to fill my mouth, I nearly choked as I tried to swallow it. Maybe this was more complicated than I'd thought. My eyes burned as he pulled me off and I tried to suck down air. Wire gently wiped a drop of cum from the corner of my mouth.

"You okay, sweetheart?" His voice was low and calm, and there was a tenderness in his eyes. "Was I too rough?"

"I just didn't know what to expect. I've read about it, but…" I licked my lips, still tasting him. It wasn't an unpleasant flavor, which surprised me. I'd heard horror stories from other women about the awful taste. Or more accurately, I'd overheard them at a club. It had been my only two attempts at being a sexy woman, and I'd given up. I was me and nothing else. Tight dresses weren't my thing.

"I forget that you're an innocent." He cupped my cheek and rubbed his thumb against my skin. "Sorry, baby. I'll go slower."

I shook my head. I didn't want slow. I just wanted Wire, any way I could get him. It wasn't like I was some scared woman, terrified to please her man. The things we'd shared were incredible, but I was a little worried that I wasn't going to be enough to hold his interest, not when he'd probably been with a lot of experienced women.

"Pull up your pants, Lavender. We'll run our errands, and then spend the afternoon at home. The club will want to meet you soon, but I'll try to buy us one more night."

And just that fast, he was zipping his jeans and getting us back on the road. My heart was crashing inside my chest. When his hand reached for mine, and he laced our fingers together, something inside me calmed. Wire lifted my hand to his lips and he gently kissed the back of it. Whatever fears I had were obviously one-sided. He gave my hand a squeeze and kept driving. Wire pulled off the highway into another town a half hour later. I didn't know why we'd gone so far from the compound to go shopping, but I assumed he had his reasons. I hadn't seen much of his town. Maybe the shopping left a lot to be desired.

He pulled into the lot of one of the big chain stores. When I reached for the door handle, Wire glared my way. Slowly, I released the door and waited as he got out and came around to my side. It seemed chivalry wasn't completely dead after all. I fought back a smile as he helped me out of the truck, and my stomach flipped and flopped when he didn't release my hand.

Shopping had never been fun for me. It had been a necessary evil and nothing more. With Wire, it was different. He looked so uncomfortable maneuvering the aisles, that I couldn't help but draw things out. There was a pained expression on his face as we passed the makeup area, and even though I very seldom wore any, I decided to linger a little. The look I got after only placing a lip-gloss and mascara in the cart was priceless. As we passed the perfume section, I paused and nearly burst out laughing when he gripped my arm tighter and dragged me away.

"You don't need that shit," he grumbled.

"Maybe I want to smell nice."

He stopped and held my gaze. "You smell sweet and delicious without that crap. You don't need floral perfume to tempt me, Lavender. You do that all on your own."

My eyebrows lifted, but I let him tug me away from the row of scents. I did grab a deodorant and a few hair things. I was always losing whatever scrunchie I had in my hair. I was horrible about pulling them out while I was working on something, then when I wanted to pull my hair back up, it was always missing. I probably spent thirty dollars or more on the stupid things every month, but regular ponytail holders ripped out my hair.

The store didn't really have the kind of shirts I preferred, at least not in the women's section, so I grabbed some jeans and underthings before heading to the men's department. Wire didn't say a word as I dug through the screen printed tees. I found a classic Super Mario shirt, one from *Back to the Future*, and another that had the *Labyrinth* cover image on it. Giving up after that, I grabbed a few plain shirts, since Wire insisted that I have at least five new outfits.

"I have a perfectly good wardrobe at my apartment," I said.

"And when I think it's safe, I'll send someone to pack the place up and bring everything to the house. Until then, you need things to help you get by. What about shoes?"

I looked down at my Converse. "I don't think they carry these here."

"Is that all you wear?"

"Well… I do have about six pair of them. In the summer I wear a lot of flip-flops so I have a massive collection of those. Never really needed any other type of shoes."

He shook his head. "You'll need some boots if you're going to ride on the back of my bike. We'll stop by the Harley Davidson store, and then I'll find a place where you can get more Converse."

And that's exactly what he did. By the time we were back at his house, I never wanted to see another store again. Unless food was involved.

Chapter Six

Wire

While Lavender put her new things away, I made a call to Venom's house, asking Ridley to come over. If anyone could distract my woman, it was Ridley. She had a tendency to just take shit over, and the only reason she wasn't here already was likely due to Venom not having said a word about Lavender.

"What do you mean you have a woman?" Ridley demanded.

"Inked her this morning. I thought maybe you could come get her for some girl time, introduce her to the other old ladies." I rubbed the back of my neck. I hadn't wanted to share her just yet, but the message I'd gotten on my phone during the shopping trip had changed things. "Maybe y'all could set up at the clubhouse. You know -- if Isabella asks Torch he'll let all of you take it over for a bit."

"I'll be there in fifteen minutes. If she's not ready, I'll drag her out of there barefoot."

I cringed. "Not if you're going to the clubhouse. None of you should walk barefoot in there."

Even though the Prospects scrubbed the floors, better safe than sorry. Not only was there broken glass nearly every night, and spilled alcohol, but there were way more bodily fluids spilled in that place than I cared to think about. In the heat of the moment, it didn't bother me. In the light of day, stone-cold sober? Yeah, that was different. There was a reason my house was so fucking clean. Not that I would ever let my OCD show to any of my brothers. I'd get shit about it for years.

Ridley snickered and hung up the phone. If I told Lavender to expect the old ladies, then she'd possibly guess that I set it up, then she'd want to know why. I should have told Ridley to keep quiet, but then *she'd* have wondered what was up. The last thing I needed was all the ladies sticking their nose into this mess. If any of them got hurt, my brothers would be pissed beyond belief. Cataclysm wouldn't hesitate to take out any of them. I shuddered to think what would happen to the kids, but I wasn't going to let things get that far, which is why I needed Lavender out of the house for a bit.

It was time to let the asshole taking out my friends know that I was onto him. I couldn't risk anyone else dying. If Jeffrey Peterson thought he would hide behind a keyboard, I'd show him just how wrong he was. I just needed to dig a little more and see if he was arranging the kills himself, or if he'd hired someone. Unless he'd hired someone through his prison stay, it was probable that he'd found a contract killer on the dark web. Even if he'd encrypted the messages sent, I could unravel them. It would just take time, and I wasn't sure how much I had.

The doorbell rang right before Ridley burst into my home. She squealed and ran toward me, throwing her arms around me.

"Not another one," I heard Lavender mutter from behind me.

"Ridley isn't a club whore," I said, disentangling myself. "She's the VP's old lady."

Ridley rushed Lavender, and my poor woman looked about two seconds from running as she was squeezed tight. Jesus. Was it really that fucking surprising that I'd found someone? It made me wonder exactly what my brothers, and their women, said about me behind my back. It wasn't like I didn't enjoy women. Just because I hadn't wanted to settle down didn't mean shit.

"We're so glad Wire found someone," Ridley said. "I'm kidnapping you for a few hours. Maybe longer."

Lavender's mouth opened and shut a few times as she glanced my way, looking both startled and pleading. I pressed my lips together so I wouldn't laugh at her predicament. I could tell the last thing she wanted was to go anywhere, especially since Ridley was acting like she'd downed about four Red Bulls.

"Where are all the kids?" I asked.

Ridley gave me a downright devious grin. "With Savior and Tempest."

Shit. "Are you trying to ensure they never reproduce?"

"Are you calling my little angels troublesome?"

I just stared, waiting. Ridley cracked up a few seconds later. Yeah, even she couldn't keep a straight face and say that. She might love her kids, we all did, but the girls were hellions and she knew it. And then there was her youngest, Dawson. The kid was four years old, but hardly ever said a word. He just watched and observed everything around him, which was a fuckton scarier than the shit the girls got up to. It was like he was biding his time.

"You know, Saint and Sofia had little Tate this past year. He'll need someone close in age to play with. You should get on that," Ridley said.

Lavender squeaked and turned to run, but Ridley grabbed a handful of her shirt to halt her retreat. The thought of getting Lavender pregnant didn't exactly terrify me, and I'd already taken her bare. Several times. The responsible thing would be to wait until this shit with Cataclysm was over, but now that I'd felt her wrapped around me, watched my cum slide out of her? Yeah, I wasn't going to be able to stop myself. Besides, there was a chance she was pregnant already. Fucking hell. I glowered at Ridley, hoping she hadn't just jinxed us.

"Time to meet the others." Ridley began dragging Lavender to the front door.

I stepped back out of reach, earning me a look from my woman that promised retribution. Little did she realize that she could do her worst and it would still pale compared to some of the shit I'd already faced. But it was cute that she thought she was so scary and fierce. Like a hissing kitten. All fluff with the teensiest of claws. I winked at her, making her shriek in outrage right before the door shut behind her and Ridley.

She'd be fun to handle later. At least I knew she was safe, and that's all that mattered. I'd deal with the fact she was pissed at me, but I had a feeling she'd like Ridley and the others. She'd need friends, and those ladies loved and supported each other regardless of the circumstances. When I'd joined the Dixie Reapers, I hadn't been looking for a family, but that's what I'd gotten. It had grown over the years as my brothers settled down and started raising families. Even though things weren't as crazy here as they were over a decade ago, we still did what was necessary to protect our family, and we'd never turned away a woman in need. I was damn proud to be a Dixie Reaper, and I'd gladly give my life for any of them.

Over the years our family had expanded beyond our club. We now considered Devil's Boneyard and Hades Abyss family as well. The VP of Devil's Boneyard had a daughter married to one of my brothers. Ryker, the son of the Hades Abyss President, claimed Flicker's sister as his old lady. By extension, through Devil's Boneyard, we also had ties with Devil's Fury, thanks to the Sergeant at Arms claiming the sister of a Devil's Fury patched member, even though Jordan's brother had just been a Prospect at the time. Saint's daughter was the product of an affair he'd had with the sister of a Hades Abyss patched member. So we were one huge family, even though we still wore our individual club colors.

I'd be a Reaper until the day I died, but it was nice to know that we had allies we could call on when trouble came knocking. It hadn't always been the case, and we'd lost some brothers because of it. Cowboy had left, even though he was back now, and two others had gone to prison. We'd lost some brothers in a more permanent way over the years as well. Walking a slightly less dangerous path wasn't necessarily a bad thing.

My phone beeped with an incoming text. I glanced at the screen and saw I had several missed texts. One from Shade, another from Surge, and the most surprising were the ones from Outlaw and Shield. It seems word was out that I needed help and the cavalry was on the way. I shot of a quick message to Torch to let him know we had incoming assistance with this clusterfuck. The fact Cataclysm had been released without my knowledge pissed me off. I'd had my head buried for too long working on a project for dear Uncle Sam. Then again, if I'd stopped long enough to look around, a lot of people could have ended up dead. While my current files for the government didn't have as big an impact globally, the shit I'd just wrapped up a few weeks back could have had a serious ripple effect. When military leaders went corrupt, lots of lives were forfeit... at least, they would have been if I hadn't intervened.

On the off chance we used my room as headquarters for any computer needs, I went in there to make sure I didn't have anything lying around they shouldn't see. Like the files I had on a certain senator, who would be taking a fall before long. I just needed a little more. Honestly, I thought the shit I'd found was enough to convince him to go away quietly, but my handler disagreed. Fucktard. I think he just liked pissing me off and pushing my buttons. It had to stick in his craw that the government came to me, a known lawbreaker, to solve the problems he couldn't. Not everyone could be a genius.

If any of the shit my club got into ended up making me breathe my last, I'd been working with Surge and Shade, trying to get them up to speed. They were good, but they weren't me. I wasn't being conceited, thinking I was hot shit. The government hadn't placed me at the top of their watch list for nothing, and that had been at the age of ten. Yeah, I'd done shit I shouldn't have, gotten busted, but it hadn't stopped me. I'd only gotten smarter about it. Technically, I wasn't permitted to own a computer, but there were ways around that. I'd used every trick in the book to keep doing what I loved. When I'd made my home here with the Reapers, Torch had seen to it that I had everything I needed and I'd used my talents for the better of the club. Until I landed back on the government's list. Instead of jail time, they'd had a different proposition.

After I stashed the file on the senator, I gathered the data I'd compiled on a certain Supreme Court judge. The shit I had for the CIA job was so disjointed I wasn't too worried, but I did drop it into a drawer, then locked everything up. It wasn't that I didn't trust the men coming here, but I didn't want them involved in any of this shit. I was already a puppet on a string for our country, and I didn't need them getting sucked in too. Teaching them some new tricks to advance their skills was one thing, but getting them mixed up with the crap I'd been focused on the last six months was another matter.

There was no point sitting around waiting, so I made a pot of coffee, then settled at the computer to look over everything I'd discovered about Cataclysm's destruction to date. At least, the things I'd uncovered. I drank two cups of coffee while I tried to form a plan. I needed him to know that I was aware of what he was up to, but I wanted to keep him away from Lavender if I could. The moment he knew she was mine, the target on her would get bigger and she'd be next on his list. Which begged the question... who was next in line as of right now?

From what I'd pieced together, he'd gone after VirtualPi first, but why go from her to Krista and Mark? It didn't make sense. Everyone else had checked in, so what had I missed? There was something, a vague feeling of unease, at the back of my mind. I was missing someone. I'd made a list of everyone I'd interacted with when Cataclysm knew me. Was the list incomplete? Or... what if he wasn't going after *only* hackers and their families? If he'd done any research on me, then he had to know that while I still kept one foot in that world, it wasn't entirely who I was anymore.

Think, dammit!

The women. He was selling women through the dark web. I'd personally helped relocate two women rescued from Colombia, but I'd had at least a small part in helping all of them. Icy fear crept down my spine as I picked up my phone and tried calling the first one. The hitch in her breath and the sob that followed was answer enough. He was coming for everyone I'd ever connected with, on any level.

"Larissa, what's wrong?" I asked.

"Ember. She's gone."

Fuck. God fucking dammit!

"How do you know she's gone?" I asked.

"I found her purse dumped everywhere outside her apartment. We meet up once a week for coffee and she didn't show."

"Is her phone there? Did you call it?"

"It's been smashed," she said.

I knew it was a long shot, but I needed something. Anything.

"Larissa, was she wearing her pendant?"

"The one you gave her?" she asked, sniffling and hiccupping from the force of her tears.

"Yes, that one. Are you wearing yours?"

"We never take them off. You said it was safe to get them wet and they made us feel special."

Thank fucking Christ.

"Larissa, don't ever take that damn thing off. It has a tracker in it. I didn't tell you because I worried you'd feel like we were spying and keeping tabs on you. I'm going to activate Ember's and see if I can get a lock on her. Find the other women, make sure they're all accounted for, and get to the nearest clubhouse."

"Ember and I moved to Tennessee a few weeks ago. We were having trouble finding work and thought a change might be nice, so we got apartments a half hour from each other."

"Then find the Reckless Kings. I'll let their President, Beast, know that you're heading that way.

Tell the others to get to safety. Someone could be coming for all of you, and I know you don't want to go right back into the hell you were living in before."

"Just find her, Wire."

I promised I would and hung up the phone. The motherfucker had gone too damn far. Those women were recovering, had learned to lead normal lives, and now he was screwing shit up for them. They were innocent in all this. It only took a moment to activate Ember's tracker, and it looked like she was on the move, rapidly heading out west. I didn't know when she'd been snatched, but she was already several states away.

I sent a text to Torch and Spider.

Cataclysm has Ember. He's coming for the girls. Heading West.

Spider answered almost immediately.

Calling Destroyer.

Well, shit. If the Mayhem Riders were getting involved, it would make it a lot easier to find Ember and get her out of there. They had chapters across the western part of the US, and even in a few states out east. My phone went off several more times, but it seemed Torch and Spider didn't need me. Not yet anyway. The ringer on my phone went off and I saw an unknown number on the screen.

"Who is this?" I said as I answered.

There was a rusty sounding chuckle, like the man never laughed.

"Untwist your panties. This is Malice, Secretary for the Mayhem Riders, original charter. Send me the info on the girl."

"And how do I know you're telling the truth?"

"Don't piss me off, kid. Just fucking do it."

Kid? I snorted. I was nearly forty years old, hardly a kid. I was still trying to determine if and how I should send the information when I received an email. Except it went to an account very few people knew about. My interest was piqued when I saw it was from Malice, which meant he was more than he let on. I sent the requested information and hoped like hell he could get Ember away from whatever asshole Cataclysm had hired.

I had no doubt that Torch and Spider would reach out to all the other women that Devil's Boneyard had brought home from Colombia. Spider's crew had taken in one or two and helped them start new lives, just as my club had done. I knew a few had gone with the Devil's Fury as well. They were scattered, but I hoped like hell everyone else was safe. I felt like I'd failed Ember, even though I hadn't even realized he knew about those women. It wasn't an excuse. But it did bother me... *how* had he known? I'd been careful. Really fucking careful. I sent Beast a quick update, and hoped it wasn't too late.

Very few people knew what I'd done. My club, the other clubs involved, and... I couldn't think of anyone other than our dear US government. I didn't see them handing the women over to a man fresh out of prison. Then again, I trusted my club completely, as well as the others who knew about the women. It wouldn't be the first time someone had betrayed one of us, but I hoped like hell that hadn't happened this time. Regardless, it was obvious that Cataclysm had found the information somewhere, and I wanted to know who his source was. No way that second-rate hack had been able to track me online.

More time passed than I'd realized when I had another text from Surge.

You didn't say your woman was hot and could sing.

What the hell? I didn't have a clue what he was talking about, but it seemed that Surge had arrived. I made sure I had my keys, then walked out to my bike. If Surge was here, then it was possible others had arrived. I revved the engine and took off toward the clubhouse. When I pulled up outside, I saw a little over a half dozen bikes that didn't belong to Reapers. It seemed I would have more help than I'd realized. Music pulsed from inside the clubhouse and I shut off the bike, then went inside to check it out. I'd no sooner cleared the door than I froze in place.

Lavender was on top of the bar, belting out the lyrics to "A Million Dreams." It sounded like the version by P!nk, and if anyone asked, I'd never admit I knew that shit. My brothers would revoke my man card in a heartbeat. More surprising was the fact she was good. Like really fucking good. Slowly, I moved closer to the bar and stared up at my woman. The way she swayed, I could tell she'd had a few drinks, and the bottles of rum, tequila, and vodka left out told me she might have had more than a few. I didn't know why Ridley had decided to pull out the booze, but I hoped like hell Lavender wasn't pregnant. I knew if she'd even thought it could be a possibility she never would have had alcohol. Even though we were still learning about each other, she was too sweet and caring to have done something like that on purpose.

The song ended and I saw Ridley in the corner with the karaoke machine the club had given Hellion one, also known as Farrah, for her birthday. Ridley immediately started another P!nk song, this one something new I wasn't very familiar with, but Lavender seemed to know it. I wasn't the only one transfixed by her. The visiting club members, as well as my brothers who were present, were all staring at her with their mouths open. The second song ended and I moved fast as Lavender started to tip sideways off the bar top. I caught her and held her against my chest.

She smiled up at me broadly. "Hey! You came!"

I snorted. "If I'd known you were entertaining everyone, I'd have been here sooner. How much alcohol was required for you to get up there and sing?"

"A fuckton," Ridley said as she joined us. "But damn can your girl sing!"

She wasn't wrong about that.

"And if she's pregnant and you just drowned her in booze?" I asked.

Ridley blinked several times, and I realized she was just as sloshed and didn't even process the words coming out of my mouth. Fan-fucking-tastic. I'd let Venom deal with her. Something told me he wouldn't be too pleased to see his wife three sheets to the wind. Not that it was the first time any of us had seen Ridley drunk. She didn't cut loose like this often, but when she did, she went all out. As much as I hated that she'd gotten Lavender drunk too, I had to admit it was nice to see my woman so relaxed and having fun. After everything she'd been through lately, it must feel nice to just… breathe.

Surge's lips tipped up on one corner as I carried Lavender closer to him.

"So this is the infamous Dark Labyrinth. Have to say, I thought she'd be bigger… and a he."

"Don't let her hear you say that when she's sober."

His eyebrows shot up and Lavender giggled in my arms.

"Why?" he asked. "She going to attack me? Little bitty her?"

"More like fuck with your accounts and hijack your email," she said, then hiccupped.

Surge held up his hands and took a step back, knowing better than to tempt her into doing exactly as she'd said. Lavender had a reputation and anyone who had ever heard of Dark Labyrinth would know that she could do that and so much more. Pissing her off wasn't the best idea. I was a bit surprised she'd even needed to come to me for help. Now that I thought about it, it was more than slightly odd. She should have been able to determine it was Cataclysm just as easily as I had.

She reached up and poked my forehead. "You'll get wrinkles. Stop frowning."

"I'm nearly forty, Lavender. I already have wrinkles."

She shook her head, then groaned and closed her eyes. "Make it stop."

"Make what stop?" Surge asked.

"The room. It's spinning."

"And that's my cue to get you home, although I doubt you can sit on the back of my bike."

"I'll get a Prospect to take her home in a truck," Hammer called out from a few feet away, trying to be heard over the next song Ridley had selected, and the "vocal stylings" of Darian. I wouldn't say it sounded like a cat when you step on its tail, but… it totally did.

I gave him a nod and went outside with Surge on my heels. It wasn't long before Shade, Outlaw, and Shield joined us. I didn't know how they'd all made it here so fast, and I didn't think I really wanted to know. It took nearly eight hours to reach the Hades Abyss compound, which meant Surge had to have been flying. Unless he'd been on his way here already.

Lavender sighed and I looked down at her, smiling at the sweet look on her face as she stared up at me.

"Love you, Voodoo. Have since I was little."

What? I opened my mouth to ask what she meant, but then she went completely lax and a soft snore erupted from her lips. Well, fuck. Looked like I would have to wait until tomorrow and hope she came clean with how she'd even known me. I'd certainly never met her before.

"Something you should know," Surge said.

"What's that?"

"I sent someone undercover into your girl's apartment. Far as anyone knows, a cleaning crew went in. Found something interesting."

"Like what? Is she hiding bodies in there?"

Surge pulled his phone from his pocket and then showed me an image. It was a wall. With pictures of me.

"What the hell is that?"

"From what I can tell? Lavender either took every picture her parents had of you, or had them copied, and put them on her wall. She's been fascinated with you for a while would be my guess. Her laptop wasn't there, which means she has it with her. There was, however, a desktop. She's studied everything you've ever done as Voodoo Tracer. I think our girl here has a serious case of hero worship. For you."

I didn't know what to think of that, or how to feel. She'd said her parents had mentioned me, that her mom had talked about our breakup, or her version of it. Not one time had she mentioned anything else. I'd have remembered her saying she had a shrine on her wall. Maybe I should have freaked a little, but honestly, I was flattered. Back then, when those pictures had been taken, I was a geeky high school kid. I'd been thrilled that Krista had given me the time of day, had gladly waited for her to be ready for the next step. It wasn't until I'd become a Dixie Reaper that the ladies had started to flock to me. Deep down, I was still that geeky boy. I just hid it really well behind leather and a bike.

But Lavender had seen that version of me... the boy who had been awkward around girls. It hadn't scared her off. Might make me crazy, but to me, that just proved that we were meant to be together. I wasn't claiming her just to keep her safe. I wanted her. No one had ever made me as hard as she did, and I'd sure as fuck never stayed hard for hours with anyone besides her. I'd heard that some animals could sense when their perfect mate was nearby. Perhaps part of me had recognized something in Lavender, had known that she was it for me.

Lief, one of our newer Prospects, opened the door to the nearest truck and I eased Lavender down onto the seat. I followed behind on my bike, with Surge, Shade, Outlaw, and Shield keeping pace. It seemed I would be getting them up to speed immediately. Probably for the best anyway. The sooner we handled this shit, the better. I didn't like the thought of women I knew being in danger, and I sure as hell didn't like Lavender being on that list.

Once I had her comfortable in our bed, I sat at the kitchen table with the others and went over everything I'd discovered. It was time to come up with a plan. One that prevented Cataclysm from hurting anyone else.

Chapter Seven

Lavender

I groaned as tiny hammers beat the inside of my skull. It felt like my tongue was glued to the roof of my mouth, and I didn't even want to think about the horrid taste. Gah! I tried to roll out of bed gracefully and ended up sprawled across the floor. I shoved my hair out of my face and squinted around the overly bright room, then slammed my eyelids shut again. No fucking way. I didn't need to see. I crawled my way into the bathroom, hoping like hell no one was watching this indignity, then used the bathroom counter to pull myself up.

I managed to open my eyes enough to find my toothbrush, then scrubbed my teeth and tongue three times. Getting a brush through my hair wasn't going to happen, so I just pulled it up, then took it back down right away. Fuck! It felt like each individual hair was trying to rip my scalp apart. What the hell happened?

"Does this mean you won't be drinking again anytime soon?"

I screamed and whirled to face Wire, then nearly threw up as the room started spinning, the pounding in my head intensified, and the floor felt like it was tilting.

He chuckled softly, his hands gripping my arms to hold me upright. "Easy, sweetheart. I think you and the girls had a bit too much fun, but I did like seeing you so carefree."

What exactly had I done? I didn't remember anything after the fifth drink. At least, I thought it was the fifth. Ridley kept sliding drinks in front of me and I hadn't really kept track. I'd never been a big drinker, but then I'd never had girlfriends either. Not in person anyway. I'd talked to some online, but that wasn't quite the same as hanging out with Ridley and the others. It had been nice getting to know the old ladies. I seriously hoped I hadn't embarrassed myself. Now that Wire had inked me, I was one of them. It would truly suck if they didn't want anything to do with me.

Wire rubbed between my eyebrows. "That's far too serious an expression. Come on. I'll make something to help with your hangover."

I clamped a hand over my mouth, the thought of food nearly enough to make me throw up again. Wire chuckled and gently tugged me out of the bedroom. I heard voices down the hall and froze.

"It's fine, Lavender. Just a few friends who are going to help with your problem."

"I can't meet your friends looking like this!" I tried to pull free and go back to the bedroom, but Wire merely lifted me into his arms and carried me to the kitchen anyway.

I hid my face against him.

"Looks like he really did claim a woman," one of them said.

I looked over at the kitchen table long enough to glare at the men there. I noticed every single one had on a cut, each with a different club name. What the hell? He'd brought in a bunch of bikers to help me? How was that going to solve anything? I didn't need brute strength. I needed wizards with keyboards.

"Never realized Dark Labyrinth would be so adorable," another of them said.

Wait. What? How did they know me by that name? I looked up at Wire again and he winked at me.

"Lavender, this is Surge, Shield, Outlaw, and Shade. They aren't as talented with a computer as you are, but they can hold their own. When I told them what was going on, they offered their assistance. And they brought some of their brothers in case we need a more physical presence to get the point across."

"You mean you're all…" My mind went blank a moment.

"Keyboard cowboys?" the one called Surge asked, with a slight smirk. "Yeah, darlin'. We're all good with our hands."

Wire growled and Surge snickered.

"He meant his hands are good with a keyboard," Wire said. "You don't need to know where else his hands have been, nor do you want to."

Surge flipped him off, but I could tell it wasn't maliciously. It seemed Wire had his club, then he had this select group of men he considered his brothers as well, even if they wore different colors. I tapped his arm and Wire gently set me on my feet. The room spun again and my eyes slid shut as I groaned. Fucking hell. The last thing I wanted to do was puke in front of these men, but it was a distinct possibility.

"Hangover," Wire said.

"I'm on it," said one of the men. I cracked my eyes open and saw that it was Shield. While he pulled things out of the fridge and cabinets, Wire led me over to a chair and I sat before I fell down.

Surge, who appeared to be the youngest of them all, kept staring at me. I was starting to worry I had drool on my face or something. I smoothed my hair down the best I could, but I knew it was in complete chaos. The way he watched me made me squirm in my seat.

"What?" I finally demanded. "You're staring and it's creepy as fuck."

Surge blinked, then smiled. "Sorry. Just wondering if you have any friends who might be single. Bonus points if they're half as talented as you."

Was he serious right now? It felt like someone was pounding on my skull and he wanted me to hook him up with someone? I felt Wire's hand press down on my shoulder, and it was only then I realized I was partway out of my seat, ready to flee. I wasn't up to all this attention, especially of the male variety.

"I'd hate to kick your ass the first full day you're here," Wire said. "She's not a matchmaking service, Surge. Find your own damn woman."

Shield set a plate down in front of me. The breakfast sandwich looked both amazing and horrible. I worried that after one bite, I'd be rushing to the bathroom. I picked up and nibbled at it, not wanting to offend the guy yet terrified that I wouldn't be able to hold it down. Surprisingly, I was able to finish the entire sandwich, and I actually felt a little better.

The guys were talking, but I didn't know any of the people they were mentioning. It seemed they just wanted to catch up, which was fine, but my presence wasn't needed for that. I did, however, need to take a shower. Without a word, I slipped from the room and closed myself in the bedroom. I stripped off my clothes and went to take a shower, setting the water to the hottest temperature I could stand. I'd inherited my mother's curls, but the texture of my hair was all Dad. Well, mostly Dad. I'd learned that using what my mother always called "white girl" hair products didn't exactly tame the wild mess on my head. I also didn't dare use a hairdryer, unless I wanted to look like an electrocuted poodle.

I'd just rinsed the conditioner from my hair and quickly washed my body when large hands slid around my waist. I jolted, then felt Wire's beard scrape against my shoulder and his hard cock press against my ass. Was he seriously in here hoping to get some while his friends were in the kitchen?

"Wire…" He bit down.

"They went to the clubhouse, and it's just the two of us. You don't have to call me Wire if you don't want to. Not when the others aren't around."

"It's who you are now, isn't it?"

I tipped my head back, giving him better access. The feel of his beard against my neck made my nipples harden and I clenched my thighs tight. The man was downright lethal. I had no doubt that panties had dropped for him at the crook of a finger. And now he was mine. I reached back and slid my hands up and down his thighs, the crisp hair scraping against my palms.

Wire shifted, rubbing his cock against me as his hands went from my waist up to my breasts, giving them a squeeze before he flicked my nipples. I gasped and arched into his touch, needing more. He twisted and tugged at the sensitive tips, and I found myself pushing my ass back against him. His hips flexed and his cock slid up and down, nudging a little farther between my cheeks with every stroke. I felt the head press against the tight ring of muscle and I tensed a moment. Wire chuckled and gave my breasts a squeeze.

"Easy, sweetheart. I'm not taking you there. Not right now anyway."

Not now? But someday? I had to admit I was intrigued, but I was also a bit worried it would hurt.

My nipples were hard and aching as he played with them, my breasts felt heavy. I could feel my clit pulsing and I rubbed my thighs together. He bit down on my shoulder as he pinched and twisted the hard peaks and I saw stars as my eyes slid shut. My body shuddered as I came and I pressed myself tighter against him, the head of his cock nearly pushing inside that forbidden spot. I gasped and my eyes flew open. Wire didn't move, didn't try to force his way into my body. He just played with me, working me up all over again.

Abruptly he pulled away. I tried to turn, but he braced a hand on my shoulder and held me still. I heard the snick of a lid as he released me, but I remained still and facing away from him. It sounded like he was stroking his cock, then I felt fingers pressing between my ass cheeks.

"Easy. The way you're pushing back on me, I'm worried I'll end up inside you without lube."

I wanted to tell him he was crazy, that there was no way I'd impale my ass on his cock, but I'd already proven myself a liar. I'd come really damn close to doing exactly that because he'd made me feel so good. Pleasure had overridden everything else, and I'd acted on instinct. I heard him put the bottle away, then his hands were on me again, pulling me against him.

His slick fingers worked my nipples, and the way he pinched, twisted, and tugged on them, I knew I'd be sore later. At the moment, I didn't care. I just wanted more. Wanted him. He reached over my shoulder and removed the showerhead, then adjusted it, angling it so that it hit the apex of my thighs, then he twisted it until a strong pulse of water came out.

"Spread your legs."

I parted them as he commanded.

"Now hold yourself open, and hold onto this." He placed the showerhead in my hand. "Let the water hit your clit."

My hands shook as I obeyed. The steady beat of the water had me moaning. Between the thing Wire was doing to me, and now my clit getting some much needed attention, I was close to coming again. I didn't know how he'd managed to get the water to hit me just right, but I wasn't going to argue.

"That's it, baby. Just feel. Don't hold back."

He pumped his cock up and down the crack of my ass again, and I felt the heat of his pre-cum. The next pulse of water that hit me was enough to send me over. I came, pushing back against him again. I felt the pinch and burn of his cock trying to enter my ass, but I felt out of control. Wire pushed in a little farther, then retreated, only to slide in again. A little deeper with every stroke.

"I had planned to save this for another few weeks," he murmured. "But fuck! You feel incredible, Lavender."

I whimpered and shifted.

"Jesus. Bend over a little, sweetheart."

I bent enough to give him better access. The burn of his cock stroking in and out of me, combined with the water pulses hitting my clit and his hands working my nipples, was almost more than I could handle. I didn't know if I wanted to beg him to stop, or ask for more.

I came a third time, and it seemed to be all he'd been waiting for. Wire shoved me over farther, then gripped my hips tight and drove deep and hard into my ass. I cried out from both pleasure and pain as he claimed me. He growled with every slam of his hips against me, and I felt his cock getting harder. Soon he was coming, filling me up, and still my body begged for more. I reached between my legs to play with my clit. My ass hurt, but riding that edge of pain seemed to do something incredible. I needed it, wanted it. As Wire held still, his cock buried inside me, I felt him panting for breath.

"I didn't mean to take you like that," he murmured and started to withdraw.

I reached back and grabbed his ass, holding tight until he got the hint.

"Baby, I didn't stretch you or anything before I fucked your ass. I know you have to be hurting."

My fingers worked my clit faster until I was coming a fourth time. I'd never had so many orgasms at one time before and my head was spinning. I gasped and everything started to go black. I felt Wire's arm band around my waist to keep me upright and heard the showerhead bang against the wall when I dropped it. When I opened my eyes again, I was facing him and he looked worried.

"I think you passed out," he said. "I need to get Dr. Myron to see you."

"I'm fine," I assured him. "I think it was just too intense."

I shifted my stance and winced, then whimpered. Yeah, my ass hurt. Quite a bit. Maybe it hadn't been the best of ideas to try that just yet. Sitting wouldn't be fun for the rest of the day. Wire put the showerhead back in place on the wall and gently washed me before cleaning himself, then helped dry me off. The way he kept gazing at me, as if waiting for some sort of reaction, was both sweet and annoying. I was fine. More than fine.

"I know you're a tough girl and you can handle anything," he said. "But please let Dr. Myron have a look just to make sure."

"Fine. Call the doctor."

He kissed me gently. "Why don't you get dressed and relax a bit? You can put a movie on or read. There's a gaming console if you'd rather get your frustration out that way."

I reached up and ran my fingers through his beard. He was being so sweet to me. I hadn't known what to expect when I came here, but Wire was different than I'd thought he would be. In a good way, but still different. Even though I'd had something of a crush on him forever, I'd thought maybe he'd pale in comparison in real life. Instead, he was so much hotter. I only hoped he never found out about my room back home. If he ever saw my apartment, I'd die of embarrassment. I'd had a slight obsession with him growing up, and it had only gotten worse over the years. Meeting him in person was the best thing to ever happen to me, and not just because he was sleeping with me. Although, that was definitely mind-blowing.

It was on the tip of my tongue to tell him I loved him, but I knew it was entirely too soon for that. I'd probably just scare him off. Instead, I pressed a kiss to his lips, quickly put on some clothes, and went to the living room. I browsed his game selection, but they were typical macho bullshit games and I decided I'd pass until I could get my own. I didn't have a console at the apartment, but I played enough online games with my laptop I could possibly hold my own. Getting out the computer wasn't something I was ready to do just yet. I didn't know if the maniac who had killed my parents would find a way to trace me or not. I'd been careful and yet he'd still come after me.

I didn't know what Wire was doing to keep me safe, other than keeping me at the compound, but I hoped he didn't get hurt in the process. I hated not knowing what was going on. Maybe I should have asked where things stood, but part of me didn't really want to know. If he wasn't any closer to stopping the guy, then I'd be twice as scared as I was now. At the moment, I was trusting him to keep me safe and alive. Since he'd inked me, said I was his, I had to believe he didn't want anything to happen to me.

Wire came in and paused in the doorway. "The doctor had an opening in two hours. I'll be busy with the guys trying to solve your little problem, so I asked Ridley to go with you. You'll have at least one Prospect with you, and possibly Savior. I don't want to take a chance with Cataclysm still running around out there."

I nodded, then froze. Cataclysm. I knew that name. How did I know it? Wire slipped out of the room, but the wheels in my head kept turning, until I remembered. Wire had helped put that man away. My mother and father had spoken about it once, even though they hadn't known I'd overheard. If he was responsible for everything happening, then he must be out of prison. I just didn't know why he'd killed my parents or come after me. It couldn't be revenge on Wire because he hadn't been a part of our lives. Was it all just a coincidence? Or was something else going on?

I didn't dare get my laptop and boot it up, even though I was curious to learn everything I could about Cataclysm. This was a battle I would gladly sit out. Besides, I might be good, but no one could beat Voodoo Tracer. If anyone could put an end to the craziness, it would be Wire.

I only hoped I wasn't wrong for putting my faith in him.

Chapter Eight

Wire

"What have we got?" I asked Shield. We'd holed up in my room at the house, each of us tackling the problem from a different angle.

"I already shut down his accounts. As of right now, he doesn't have a cent to his name. At least, nothing he can access. I diverted the funds, bounced them around a few places, and they're now in an account in the Caymans."

Well, at least he wouldn't be able to pay anyone to do his dirty work. That would possibly make him desperate, but I hoped it meant he'd get sloppy.

"I've put the word out that anyone who helps Cataclysm will be on your hit list," Surge said. "I made sure that meant that not only would you fuck with their lives, but they would have several clubs coming for them too."

Outlaw leaned back in his chair, putting his hands behind his head. "As of right now, no one will pick up any jobs he has out there. Destroyer already picked up your girl and he didn't leave much to identify of the man who'd taken her. Why the fucker had to send me that shit I don't know, but I used it as a scare tactic. Any bids on Cataclysm's jobs just vanished."

"What other jobs?" I asked.

"He was sending someone after a few other women you've helped in the past. A Gracie Wilcox, Serena Bartle, and Elsa Monroe. Any of those names ring a bell?" Outlaw asked.

Gracie, Serena, and Elsa. The names were vaguely familiar, but I couldn't place them right off. I looked at Outlaw and could tell he knew exactly who they were. He'd just wanted to see if I did.

"All right, fucker. Who are they?" I asked.

"You helped Gracie about seventeen years ago. Her boyfriend beat her and left her on the side of the road. You hacked his accounts, siphoned the money into an account for her, then helped her relocate several hundred miles out of his reach."

Now that he mentioned it, I did remember Gracie. And the others…"Serena was the waitress at the diner off the highway. A guy was holding a gun to her head when I walked in."

Outlaw nodded. "And you not only made sure she made it out alive, but once you realized he was a serial rapist, you made sure he was never seen again. Do I want to know where he is?"

"Here and there." Literally. I made sure there were no fingerprints or teeth to identify him, then buried the pieces across two states. That had been over a decade ago.

"Elsa Monroe was an unwilling captive of a pimp who was working the Florida coast. He made the mistake of crossing the Alabama state line and offering her services to you. Not only did you help set her up somewhere safe, the pimp disappeared and the other girls in his stable were freed," Outlaw said.

I nodded. "He thought he was a badass, so I showed him a bigger predator."

Outlaw raised his eyebrows.

"Shark bait," I said.

He smirked. "Well, it seems Cataclysm somehow found the same trail I did and put them on his list. I've made sure they're safe. Elsa still lives in Florida, so the Devil's Boneyard are going to take her in until things settle down. I've got Devil's Fury going after Serena, and Hades Abyss is picking up Gracie. All the little birds will be safe by nightfall."

"There's something you should know," Shade said. "He knows you have Lavender here. I don't think he'll hide in the shadows for much longer. Now that he's crippled financially, we wiped out his little bits of code, and taken all the players off the board... Well, that leaves you and Lavender. He'll be coming here. Soon would be my guess."

"Then I guess it's a good thing we have plenty of people here to welcome him," I said.

"You have Lavender safe behind the gate, right?" Surge asked.

Everything in me froze. Fucking hell. No, I didn't. I'd sent her off to the doctor, thinking Cataclysm wouldn't strike just yet, but with everything taken out of his hands, he'd be livid and running on rage. Shit. I'd placed my woman and Venom's old lady in danger.

I called Savior, hoping like hell he was with them.

"What?" Savior asked, his tone clipped.

"Tell me you're with Lavender and Ridley."

"Well, I could but it would be a lie. Torch asked me to make a run right after you called. I think he put Diego in the SUV with them, and Bats was supposed to ride along."

Fucking hell. I didn't bother saying bye and just hung up, calling Bats immediately. When his phone kept ringing and he didn't answer, I felt panic claw at my gut. If anything had happened to Lavender, Cataclysm wouldn't just die. He'd suffer in agony for weeks before I finally let him feel the relief of death. And that's if Venom didn't beat me to it. Everyone knew that the only people who could bring that man to his knees were his woman and kids. Anything happened to Ridley, and he'd come unglued.

I tried Diego next and same thing. No answer. Ridley was the one to finally pick up.

"Where are you?" I asked.

"The doctor. Did you forget already?" she asked.

"Diego and Bats aren't answering their phones."

She sighed. "The office has a new no cell phone policy. They probably turned the ringers off and haven't realized they have any missed calls. What's so urgent?"

"I think Cataclysm will be coming for Lavender. I need her back here as soon as possible. I don't know where he's holed up so it could take him minutes, hours, or days to reach the compound. He no longer has the financial resources to play his games. He only has one move left."

"Well, shit. Your girl hasn't had a chance to speak with the doc yet, but we'll head back. I'm sure she can reschedule. I'll just tell them we have an emergency at home."

"Thanks, Ridley. Make sure Diego and Bats know what's up and to be extra vigilant. If anything happens to you and Lavender…"

She snickered. "Venom would paint the world red if that man fucks with me. But I hear you. I'll make sure they know to be more cautious than usual, although I already feel like they're breathing down our necks. They're both in the hall right outside the door."

"Just get home. Safely."

I hung up and hoped like hell they made it. I didn't have a clue where Cataclysm was hiding. Even though it had been easy enough for us to fuck with him, his trail was all over the damn place. He could have been anywhere from down the fucking street to all the way out in California. None of us had gotten a lock on him, which was surprising. Either he'd improved, or he'd had help. And if someone had those kind of skills, then I wanted to know who the fuck they were.

"Who would know your every move?" Shield asked. "Is it possible for someone to be tracking your system?"

"No." Unless… My eyes narrowed as I stared at my computer. I didn't trust the government even a little, but they wouldn't have been that stupid, would they? And even if they were tracking everything I did, why would they share that with Cataclysm?

The damn spyware was so well-hidden I would have missed it if I hadn't been looking for it. Had in fact missed it repeatedly. I had various scans I ran on a daily if not hourly basis, but this little shit had managed to design something that didn't appear to be malicious and got overlooked if you weren't trying to find it. I had to grudgingly admit it had worked, but it pissed me the fuck off. How long had it been there? I dug deeper, trying to find the attribution. Someone had planted this damn thing on my system, and I wanted to know who. When I realized it had been embedded in software provided to me by Uncle Sam, I was fucking livid.

"Who is it?" Surge asked.

"Marvin Henshaw. My handler. I don't think he created it, though. He's not anywhere near good enough, but there's a chance whoever did design it didn't know how it would be used."

"What now?" Outlaw asked.

"Now it's time to play with this asshole," I said. I had a botnet in place and used it to send every virus I had at my disposal to Marvin Henshaw. Not just his work computer, but every electronic device he had that was attached to an email account. By the time my little army was finished, he wouldn't be able to access his phone or even his fucking smart watch. "Mr. Marvin Henshaw, when you fuck with the --"

Shade covered my mouth. "Don't even quote *Hackers* right now."

I shoved his hand away and grinned. "What? It's true."

"Way to stay humble," Shade muttered.

I flipped him off, then bolted out of my seat when I heard the front door open and shut. Lavender looked a little confused, and a bit scared, as she rushed toward me. Her arms closed around my waist and I held her tight, thankful she'd made it home in one piece. Part of me had wanted to go after her, but that would have meant leaving and if I hadn't been here, then I wouldn't have discovered Henshaw's treachery.

I wondered if anyone else knew about it. Had he acted alone, or had the government allowed him to do it? There was only one way to find out. While Henshaw might have been my handler, I knew the people who presided over him. They didn't like getting their hands dirty with the type of work I did, but it didn't mean they were ignorant of the things I discovered. In fact, I knew it was the higher-ups pulling the strings and not Henshaw at all. He was merely a puppet.

Tugging my phone from my pocket, I unlocked the screen and scrolled for the number I wanted. It wasn't one that I had used often, but I'd kept it on hand just in case. Now I was thankful I had. I pressed "Send" and waited while the phone rang. Better to tackle this shit now and hit it head on.

"Who is this and how did you get this number?" the voice on the other end said.

"Now, Marsha. I'm hurt that you don't remember me."

She inhaled sharply. "Wire. Why are you calling me? You have a handler. And furthermore, why the fuck don't I know this number?"

I wasn't about to divulge all my secrets. Had to keep her and everyone else on their toes.

"Yeah, about that... It seems dear Marvin is working with his own agenda and end game, and I don't think the outcome is in my favor." I told her what he'd done, and who he was helping. To say she was pissed was an understatement.

"Don't make me do damage control down there too," she said before disconnecting the call.

I didn't know what the fate of Henshaw would be, and I didn't really care. I had a feeling his new décor would involve bars. He'd assisted Cataclysm, a man who had arranged for a woman to be abducted and taken across state lines, not to mention the murders he'd implemented. Yeah, good ol' Marvin was about to have a really tough life. Even more so if I ever found out where he was imprisoned. One phone call and his life would be a living hell.

"What's going on?" Lavender asked. "Who is Marsha? And who's Marvin Henshaw?"

"We'll talk about it later. Right now, I need to figure out the best way to put an end to all this mess."

The ground rumbled and a loud explosion took out the windows in my house. I tossed Lavender to the ground and covered her with my body. She gripped me tight as I sheltered her, not knowing what the fuck was going on. I heard the pipes of half a dozen bikes heading to the front of the compound and I knew I needed to join them.

Shield, Shade, Surge, and Outlaw came out of my sanctuary and looked pissed as hell. Shield gave a chin nudge to the front door.

"Go. We'll keep an eye on your woman."

I stared down at Lavender, my heart slamming against my ribs. I kissed her hard and fast. "Love you, sweetheart. Don't do anything foolish while I'm gone."

Before she had a chance to reply, I was up and running to my bike in the driveway. When I neared the gates, I came to a stop and stared in stunned horror. Someone had blown the damn gate completely off. It was lying on the roof of the clubhouse, and the bikes out front were lying on the ground. Smoke filled the air. I scanned the area, checking on my brothers. It looked like Diego had been on the gate, and he was down but moving. There was a lot of blood, but the fact he was conscious was a good sign.

A man came into the compound, walking through the smoke like a phantom.

"You took my life from me," Cataclysm said. "So now I'm going to take yours."

He held up his hand and I saw he held a detonator. Before I could stop him, he pressed the button. Half the fence was taken out, and I saw figures emerging from the other side. I barely registered the fact my gun was in my hand and pointed directly at Jeffrey Peterson. I pulled the trigger. Not once, not twice. I unloaded the fucking clip, reloaded, and started shooting again. The fucker went down, a bloody smile on his lips.

"Too late," he said. "I was just a distraction."

Distraction… I turned and raced for my bike, then hauled ass back to my house. The front door stood wide open. A splatter of blood on the front step caught my attention. A glance inside made my heart stall and nearly stop all together. I rushed to Surge's side, hoping like hell he wasn't dead. I found a steady pulse, then checked the others. Except one. Outlaw was missing. And so was Lavender.

Torch and Venom rode toward me like the hounds of hell were nipping at their heels. When they came to a stop, I realized the Pres was bleeding and Venom looked a little ragged as well.

"We tried to stop them," Torch said.

"Who was it? Who has her?"

"I don't know," he said. "But we'll find out, and we'll get her back."

"Outlaw is missing," I said.

"No, he's not. He's with Lavender. For whatever reason, they tied the both of them and took off," Venom said.

"And he wasn't wearing his cut," Torch said.

I racked my brain. I knew that Outlaw had it on when the windows were blown out. Why would he remove it? I looked around and saw a bit of black leather in the bushes under the front window. I walked over and jerked it out, seeing it was his Devil's Fury cut.

"Why would he take it off?" I asked.

"I don't know, but I just hope he's able to keep both himself and Lavender safe," Torch said. "Grizzly will be pissed if his man dies."

"Then why are we standing here? Let's go after them!"

Venom shook his head. "Can't. They set off smoke bombs. A fuckton. We couldn't see which way they went. I made it one step toward the truck where they'd tossed your woman and Outlaw before they set that shit off."

Dammit. God fucking dammit.

I'd get them back. I didn't know how or when, but it would happen. If those assholes hurt so much as one hair on Lavender's head, then I'd kill every fucking one of them. And I'd make damn sure they didn't see it coming. I wanted to see the look of surprise, of shock, as they realized they were about to breathe their last.

Chapter Nine

Lavender

"Why did you tell them you're Wire? Won't they know you're lying?" I asked, as I tugged against the ropes securing my wrists and ankles.

"To buy him some time. It's obvious these men don't have any idea who Wire really is or what he looks like. Once he locates you, he'll come in here guns blazing. No way he'll just sit around and wait to see if he gets a ransom note. You're his old lady, Lavender. He won't take this shit sitting down."

"Why did you do it?" I asked. "You could have hidden or something."

The four large men had burst into Wire's home. Surge had gotten off a shot, hitting one of them in the arm, then everything had happened so fast I didn't know if anyone had survived. Somehow, Outlaw had managed to toss his cut before the men came for us. I didn't know why he'd done it or how he'd known they were coming. Outlaw and I had been shoved into the back of a truck, and Surge, Shield, and Shade were lying on the floor, looking lifeless.

"And leave you defenseless with these assholes? Not happening. At least if I'm here and they think we're together, then they hopefully won't touch you."

I shivered. The idea had crossed my mind. The men who had snatched me looked like ruthless killers. I doubted raping a woman would keep them from a good night's sleep. Maybe it was how they passed every Tuesday and today was just another day for them.

Outlaw brushed his shoulder against mind, drawing my attention to him.

"We'll get through this."

I nodded, but I wasn't certain I was as confident as he seemed. I'd heard the blasts, as well as gunfire. What if Wire couldn't come for me? What if he'd been shot or killed? What if… I swallowed the knot in my throat. I couldn't think about a world without Wire in it. The idea of never seeing him again was too painful. Tears blurred my vision and Outlaw bumped me again. I glanced over him. He gave a slight nudge with his chin and I leaned against him.

"Be strong, Lavender. He'll come, you'll see. And until then, you're not in this alone."

"How are you going to protect me when you're tied up just like me?" I asked.

He grinned, then winked. A moment later, he pulled his arms from behind his back, then tossed the rope across the room. He worked his ankles free, then unbound my wrists and ankles too. I sagged against him, grateful that I wasn't here alone. The place they'd thrown us was cold and dark. A sliver of light allowed me to see him, but it didn't give me much hope for our future. The window was too narrow, and too high up. Even if Outlaw gave me a boost, I'd never fit through it.

"There's something you should know about most men," Outlaw said as he released me and reached for his belt.

I squeaked and skittered away, but he merely arched an eyebrow at me.

I stared at his hands, terrified that maybe I needed to worry more about the man caged in here with me than the ones outside. He unbuckled his belt, then unzipped his jeans. Fear clawed at me as he reached into his underwear and pulled out… a phone? My gaze locked on his and he winked. The fucker.

"No need to worry, Lavender. I don't want Wire to kill me. But like I was saying, most men won't feel up another man's junk. Unless they swing that way."

I watched as he powered on the device, activated the GPS, then sent a message.

"I'll keep it on silent just in case." Without another word, he stuffed it back into his underwear and fastened his pants and belt back. "Won't take Wire long to trace that and come for you."

I hoped he was right, especially since I heard booted steps coming our way. If those men came in here, I didn't know what I'd do. No way I'd ever go with them willingly. I'd fight every step of the way.

Outlaw must have read my emotions and thoughts on my face.

"Whatever happens, you survive. Hear me, girl? You stay alive. For him."

I nodded and tried not to cry.

The assholes who snatched us came into our little cell, their focus on Outlaw.

"Should have known you'd get free, but it didn't do you any fucking good. You're still locked in a cage," one of them said.

Two of them hauled him to his feet and started dragging him from the room. I clamped a hand over my mouth as another came toward me. My eyes went wide as he hunkered down in front of me. He reached out, winding my hair around his finger.

"Plenty of time for us to play later, pretty little thing. Don't worry. When we're done with your man, he won't much care what I do to you. Might even volunteer to hold you down for me." He gave me a sadistic smile that made the blood in my veins go cold.

My gaze shot to Outlaw, but his jaw was firmed and his expression shuttered. He'd expected this. Even knowing there was a chance he'd get hurt, he'd made sure they took the two of us together. And because of the phone he'd stashed… oh God. What if they found the phone? I shot to my feet and rushed to Outlaw.

"Aww, look. The little thing wants to give her man a proper goodbye." The men laughed. "Go ahead, sweet thing. Give him something good to think about."

I could hear my heart pounding in my ears as I leaned up and pressed my lips to Outlaw's, and tried to subtly reach into his pants, shoving my hand past his belt and into his underwear. He sucked in a breath and jerked free of the men to wrap his arms around me. The way he hunched his shoulders, I knew he was doing his best to shield me from their view. I withdrew the phone and tucked it under my shirt before backing away. Outlaw gave me a quick smile as I scurried into the corner of the room, trying to hide in the shadows.

The man who had touched me leered. "Back for you soon enough. Make it easier on yourself and be wet and ready. Doesn't matter to me if you aren't. I like hearing 'em scream."

Bile rose in my throat as they shoved Outlaw from the little cell and slammed the door shut. I huddled, facing the wall, trying to hide the fact I was using the phone. I pulled up the last text Outlaw had sent and let the person on the other end know that he'd been taken, and that they were coming for me next. I hoped like hell it was Wire that got the message, and that help really was coming. I didn't know if Outlaw had long enough to wait. He'd told me to do whatever it took to survive, and I hoped he did the same. It had been sweet of him to try and help me. I didn't want him to pay a steep price for being a nice guy.

I put the phone to sleep and tried to hide it in the room. I knew if I kept it on me and they found it, I'd be in even more trouble. It was the only reason I'd been brave enough to take it from Outlaw. Since I hadn't really kissed him, and I'd done my best not to cop a feel while my hand was in his pants, I didn't think Wire would be too upset. It seemed like hours passed before the door opened and one of the men came in again.

"Get up." His voice was dark and gruff.

I stood on shaky legs and moved toward him. He jerked me out of the cell and shoved me ahead of him down a long hall. When we stepped into a large room and I saw what they'd done to Outlaw, I couldn't stop the tears that streaked my cheeks. His chest rose and fell, so I knew he was still alive, but I didn't know how. There was blood, so much blood. Outlaw coughed and blood bubbled from his mouth.

"Please," I begged. "He needs help."

"Not my problem," the man said as he shoved me again.

"Don't... don't hurt her," Outlaw said, his voice soft, as if it just speaking caused him pain.

Even now, he was worried about me. I hoped he pulled through. The thought of Outlaw dying because he'd tried to save me, to give me hope and comfort, was almost enough to make me throw up. The man shoved me again, hard enough I fell to my knees, but he only laughed.

"You want to see your precious Wire one last time? Crawl to him, bitch."

I didn't even hesitate. I scurried across the floor on my hands and knees until I was next to Outlaw. His eyes were swollen shut, his nose looked broken, and blood matted his hair and beard. They'd taken a knife to his face and I couldn't help but cry. As gently as I could, I reached down to take his hand, then gasped in horror.

"Asshole won't be doing shit with a computer now," the man said from behind me. "Busted his hands good."

"I'm sorry," I said. "So, so sorry."

"Live," he said.

I nodded. I knew what he meant. Someone would be coming for us, and I needed to stay alive until they got here. It didn't matter what these men did to me. I had to fight, to stay strong. If there was even a chance that Wire was still alive, that he would come save me, then I had to make sure he had something to save. If I let them break me, then the men who had been hurt or died today would have suffered in vain.

"Sorry, pretty thing."

It was the nasty man from before. He hauled me to my feet and spun me to face him.

"Your dear Wire there can't give you what you want anymore. I doubt he'll ever get hard again. But you and me can have some fun. You'd like that, wouldn't you? Want to spread your legs for me?"

I tried not to flinch, not to show my fear and revulsion. It's what he wanted. I wouldn't cower, wouldn't react to his words.

"Has the pansy ass over there given you a good, hard fucking?" the man asked, his breath fanning across my face. "Bent you over, shoved his dick in you, and made you take it?"

I didn't answer, which only seemed to make him angry. He sneered at me, then backhanded me across the face. Even though the copper taste of my blood filled my mouth, I merely spat it on the ground and faced him again. Wire needed me to be strong, so did Outlaw. I wouldn't break, no matter what.

The man grabbed my arm, tightening his grip as he stared at my tattoo. "You let him brand you like fucking cattle. Is that what you are? You just his good little heifer who takes it whenever he gives it to you?"

I pressed my lips together and stared up at him defiantly.

The man chuckled. "It's cute, you thinking that you can beat me. The silent treatment doesn't matter to me one bit, little girl. I'll have you, and you *will* scream before I'm done. I'll fuck every hole you've got, then let my men have a turn. Or maybe that turns you on." He reached between my legs and squeezed. "Is this cunt nice and wet for me?"

Something inside me snapped and before I could stop myself, I spat in his face. His laughter died and his eyes turned even colder. He shoved me backward and I'd have fallen if one of the other men hadn't caught me. He pulled out a gun and shot Outlaw in the leg. I bit my tongue so hard I bled in order not to cry out. It's what he wanted. My fear, my pain. I wouldn't give it to him. Giving him that much, would give him power over me, and I refused to let him have that.

"Cut the bitch's clothes off," he ordered.

The other two approached, knives gleaming in their hands. They made quick work of my clothes, leaving me naked and vulnerable. Still, I tipped my chin up and stared them down. Wire wouldn't have claimed a weak woman. I wouldn't cower or cry, wouldn't beg for mercy.

"Decent tits," one of knife wielders said as he reached up to fondle me.

I didn't so much as blink. The man I was starting to think was their leader started to unfasten his pants. He'd just shoved them down his hips when I heard what sounded like a metal door slam somewhere in the building. The man stopped and looked at the one who had grabbed my breast.

"Go see what the fuck that was."

"Probably rats knocking over those metal oil drums," said the one holding me still. "Told you this placed was infested."

The leader stroked himself as he eyed my body. Inside, I was a wreck, but outwardly I was calm and cool. I held his gaze, refusing to back down. The fact his man hadn't come back told me enough. We weren't alone anymore. Another bang and the man stopped jerking on his dick long enough to glare at the other man who had cut off my clothes.

"Go see what that fuck-up is doing."

Yes, please go see. One at a time, Wire would take them out. They were all gonna die. I smiled, a slow, genuine smile as I thought about these men dying, them being unable to hurt anyone ever again. I'd live through the indignity of them stripping me, touching me. None of them would get anywhere near close enough to rape me. A prickle along my nape was enough to tell me Wire was close. Really close.

An enraged roar rang out across the large room. I could hear several sets of boots charging in my direction. The man pinning my arms released me to reach for his weapon, but it was too late. A blade protruded from his throat, his eyes wide, as he sank to the floor. I smiled at Wire, but fury ignited his eyes.

"Who? Who touched you?"

"You killed the two who stripped me, as well as the one who grabbed my breast."

"And him?" Wire asked, jerking his head toward the one trying to pull up his pants.

"He wanted to have some fun with me but never got around to it."

"He was going to rape you." Wire's eyes went such a dark green they were nearly black. His gaze locked on the leader of the now very dead men. "You like putting your dick where it doesn't belong?"

"Who the fuck are you?" the man asked.

"The one who is going to make you wish you'd never been born. I'm going to fucking end you, but first I want to hear you beg."

Wire's gaze slid over to me. "Leave, Lavender. I don't want you to see this. It won't be pretty."

I looked over at Outlaw and saw that several Dixie Reapers and Devil's Fury were carefully lifting him. I was torn. Part of me wanted to ensure that Outlaw would be all right. He'd risked his life to give me a better chance at surviving. But I also wanted to make sure the man who'd intended to hurt me would never be able to do that again.

"I'm staying," I told him.

"Did you just defy a direct order?" Wire said, his voice deceptively soft.

I lifted my chin and stared at him. A slight smirk graced his lips.

"Very well, beautiful. Remember this act of defiance later when your ass hurts too much for you to sit."

I seriously hoped he didn't mean a repeat of the shower. Not unless he planned to use lots of lube and take his time, because I was honestly still sore. I folded my arms and refused to move. Wire shook his head and faced off against the man who had tormented me. I watched as his gaze lowered and took in the name on Wire's cut.

"Wait. If you're Wire, who the fuck was that other guy? Because your girl kissed him and put her hand down his pants."

Wired pinned me with his gaze.

"I'll explain later," I said. Then decided I'd better explain now. "I couldn't have sent that second message if I hadn't pulled the phone out of his underwear. It wasn't like I was trying to grab his dick."

Wire closed his eyes a moment and shook his head before focusing on the other man again.

"The man you thought was me is called Outlaw and he's part of a different club. One who would very much like to get their hands on you, but you and I are going to have some fun first. I never wanted my woman to see this side of me, but so be it."

What side of him? I knew he was a biker, but the cold look in his eyes didn't match the guy I'd been getting to know. My Wire was sweet and tender. This one was… a killer. Was that who he was? For that matter, if he was going to take out this piece of trash, I wasn't exactly upset over that, but it was the thought he could do it without remorse that bothered me a little. Did that make him one of the bad guys?

No. This was still my Wire. No matter what happened, I knew he was trying to protect me, to keep me safe. He didn't want this man to come hurt me again, or to be able to hurt anyone else. It didn't matter if I thought he should turn the guy over to the police. When I'd arrived at the Dixie Reapers' compound, I'd known they weren't exactly law-abiding men.

"What's a computer geek like you going to do?" Taunting Wire probably wasn't in the man's best interest.

Wire drew a wicked-looking blade from somewhere and I stifled my gasp. Gently, I reached out to grab his arm.

"He needs to pay," Wire said.

"I know. I know he does, but..." I licked my lips. "There has to be another way. Hasn't enough blood been shed already?"

"So I just let it all go? He nearly killed Outlaw, was going to rape you, and I just walk away?" he demanded.

"No." I released my hold on him. "Do whatever you have to."

The guy must have been dumber than I thought since he started spouting off shit that was guaranteed to piss off Wire.

"Your girl there was going to have lots of dick in her cunt and ass. I had first dibs, but we were all getting a turn. Multiple turns."

Wire growled and advanced a step.

"Bent over. Tied down. Spread open. I was going to take her every way I could. Make her scream. Gag her with my cock, then start over."

It was then I realized what the guy was doing.

"He wants you to attack," I said. "He's goading you."

I wasn't afraid anymore. He couldn't hurt me. Even though he'd told me what he'd planned, had cut my clothes off, it could have ended much worse. I felt like I needed to scrub myself clean, but I'd deal with that later. Right now, my focus was on Wire.

"They didn't do anything, Wire. Yes, I'm naked. Yes, one of them grabbed my breast. But I'm okay. You got here before he could do anything else." I placed my hand in the center of his back. "You stopped him before anything else happened."

He turned to face me and I saw two other Dixie Reapers move in to detain the man who had threatened me.

"You swear to me right here and now that none of them raped you? They didn't..." His throat worked and I saw the anguish in his eyes. "They didn't put their fingers inside you? Or any other parts of themselves?"

I let my arms curl around his neck. "I'm fine, Wire. Honest. I just want you to take me home, help me get clean, and help me forget being here. That's all I need. Let the others handle him. Please. There's been enough violence today."

"We've got it, man," said one of the Reapers. "She's right. You need to get her out of here, help her forget everything. We'll keep him breathing in case you need a piece of him later, but for now, get your woman out of here."

Another Dixie Reaper came up and removed his cut, then his shirt, handing it over.

"She needs to cover up. I know this is fucking with your head, but pull yourself together."

Wire nodded and took the shirt, then helped me into it. "Thanks, Grimm. You're right. I need time to cool off, need to take care of Lavender. That's what's most important right now."

I reached up and tugged on his beard until he lowered his head and I could kiss him. It meant the world to me that he would let go of revenge, at least for now, in order to take care of me. His fellow club members dragged the man away and Wire curved an arm around my waist. When we got outside, I slammed my eyes shut against the bright sun. I'd honestly thought it would be night by now. Did the sun never set in the south? I knew it was hotter than fuck compared to back home.

He lifted me and I felt the cool leather of a seat under me. I opened my eyes enough to see I was on the passenger seat of a truck. Wire ran his hand down my hair, and looked like he was scared to let me go. I could see his bike behind him, and I knew he'd be taking it home. I just didn't know who would be driving me back to the compound.

A groan had me turning and I gasped when I saw Outlaw stretched across the backseat. He looked even worse in the daylight than he had inside. I had to bite my lip to stop myself from crying. Even though I didn't know him that well, he didn't seem like the type who would want me to cry over him. He'd done what he felt was necessary to give me a chance to get out of there and back to Wire, and I would be forever grateful to him.

"One of the Devil's Fury is going to drive the two of you back to the compound," Wire said.

"He needs a hospital," I whispered. There was no way he could recover from all that without the proper equipment. "His hands, Wire. He needs x-rays and top notch medical care."

Wire was already shaking his head, but I wouldn't let this go. Outlaw had nearly died trying to give me a fighting chance, and I wouldn't repay him by letting him die, or being permanently crippled. It wasn't fair. I knew that life was often not fair, but this time I had a chance to do something and I would, even if Wire didn't like it.

When the Devil's Fury VP, Slash, slid behind the wheel, I knew I'd have to talk fast after Wire left. There was one chance to save Outlaw, and I would do whatever it took. It was the least I could do after everything.

The bikes pulled out ahead of us, with three more taking up the rear. The highway wasn't far and soon we were traveling at high speed back toward the

Dixie Reapers' compound. I didn't know exactly where we were, but when I saw the sign for the Alabama state line, I knew the men had taken us farther than I'd realized.

"If you want to save him, he needs a hospital," I said, keeping my voice low.

"They ask too many questions."

"Then I'll answer them," I said. "I'll tell the police I was kidnapped and Outlaw tried to save me, that they nearly killed him before you found us."

"And the men who took you? What are you going say about them? Because they're dead, sweetheart. And that last one will be soon enough. Your club doesn't need that kind of heat. Outlaw knew what he was doing. He wouldn't want the Reapers getting into trouble with the law over this."

I reached and grasped his arm. "Please, Slash. I'll come up with something. Tell them the men got scared when they heard a bunch of motorcycles and they ran. I'll do anything it takes to convince them. Just get him some help. I don't want him to die."

He glanced my way twice before giving a sharp nod. When we saw the sign for a hospital, he veered off the highway and didn't stop until we reached the ER doors. I slid out of the truck, not caring that I only had on someone's T-shirt. I opened the back door as two nurses came out. I quickly explained what happened and they managed to get Outlaw out of the truck and whisked away before the first motorcycle pulled up.

Wire looked pissed. Seriously pissed. I didn't care. I knew this was the right thing to do. I wouldn't repay Outlaw's kindness by letting him die. It was stupid and pointless. An officer pulled up right behind the truck and got out, eyeing the bikers heading our way before zeroing in on my lack of clothing.

"Miss, are you all right?" he asked.

"I'm fine. Now. I was kidnapped by men dressed all in black and taken to what looked like an abandoned building."

He glanced at the ink on my arm and I inwardly winced. I'd forgotten about it and now he'd know I belonged to one of them. That wouldn't help me pretend that all this was just a coincidence and they happened by.

"Which one do you belong to?" he asked.

Wire stepped forward. "Me."

The officer eyed him up and down before nodding. "All right. So what exactly happened?"

I gave the condensed version, but explained that the men had tried to blow up the compound and snatched me from our home. I played dumb when it came to the location of the warehouse I'd mentioned, and of course, the guys couldn't seem to remember where it was either, just gave the officer a vague direction. Not knowing if any bodies had been left behind, I wasn't about to lead the cops directly there. They could search for it, give the guys time to hide any evidence if necessary. However that worked. When I was finished, the officer made some notes and went inside.

"I think that actually worked," Slash said. "Your woman has a good head on her shoulders. Thanks to her, Outlaw just might survive this, and none of this shit will come back on our clubs."

Had they thought I would just throw them under the bus? These men were my family now. When Wire claimed me, he made me part of the Dixie Reapers. I wouldn't do anything to jeopardize their safety. When the officer stepped back out of the hospital, he paused in front of me.

"Your story matches what the local police are saying in your hometown. I can't talk to the man you brought in since he's in surgery, but I'll be checking back soon. Stay out of trouble, young lady."

I watched as he got into his car and drove away, then I sagged against Wire. Whatever strength I'd had left was now gone. I'd used up my last bit of fight just trying to get here and jumping through that last hurdle. Now I just wanted a shower and some sleep.

Chapter Ten

Wire

Getting Lavender home had been my top priority, but she'd refused to leave until she knew Outlaw would be all right. The hospital staff had given her some scrub bottoms, and once Outlaw was out of surgery and in recovery, I'd made arrangements to borrow the Devil's Boneyard truck with the promise a Prospect would return it. As for my bike, I'd get King to return the truck and bring home my Harley. I hated letting anyone else handle her, but Lavender was more important. I'd worried I'd never get her out of there, not when we'd learned Outlaw had flatlined twice, but the staff assured her he was doing well. I think they could see that she was seconds away from collapsing.

She'd slept part of the way home, but had woken just as we'd reached the outskirts of town. It was almost as if she'd sensed that we were nearly there. She still had shadows under her eyes, and I noticed her hands trembled from time to time. After what she'd been through, she was allowed to fall apart. I was waiting for her to really let loose and cry, but she hadn't yet.

Passing the downed fence and then pulling through where the gate was missing didn't exactly make me feel like she was very safe here. Torch already had men working on it, but it would take time to repair the damage. Lavender looked at everything, her face pale and her features pinched. It looked like war had come to the compound, and in a sense, it had.

"Is everyone all right?" she asked.

"Torch was shot in the arm, but he's okay. A few others were injured, but no one is dead. Not on our side anyway. The man responsible for all this isn't breathing anymore. For that matter, anyone we could reach who helped him isn't among the living either." I hesitated a moment, glancing at her as we pulled to a stop in front of the house. "I didn't want you to see me like that."

"I knew you were protecting me, Wire."

The house was a mess. The door wouldn't shut all the way from where it had been kicked in, and the windows were still busted out. Blood stained the floor in the entry. Why the hell had I brought her here?

"Stay here, sweetheart."

I got out and shot off a text to King. *Come get the Boneyard truck and bring me an SUV. Getting Lavender out of here.*

Heading inside, I gathered a few changes of clothes for each of us, collected the bathroom items we'd need, shoved everything into a duffle, then made my way back out to my woman. She was still sitting in the truck, staring at everything with a bleakness I didn't like. King pulled up in the SUV and hopped out. I dug the keys to my bike from my pocket and tossed them over.

"Return the truck and pick up my Harley from the hospital. Just park it here for now."

"Where are you taking her?" he asked. He hadn't looked at Lavender, but I could tell he wanted to. I couldn't blame him. I probably looked as crazy as I felt. I'd never been so protective of someone before. I'd wanted that man's blood, wanted to spill every fucking drop and hear him scream while I did it, and that wasn't me. I'd never been that guy. Most of my work for the club was done at the computer. I'd taken out the trash when needed, but I'd never enjoyed it.

"I don't know. This place isn't safe, though. I need a new door, new windows. The debris needs to be cleared and the floors cleaned. I can't let her go in there."

King nodded. "I'll get started on it when I get back. I'm sure Diego will help."

Lavender's brow was furrowed when I helped her from the truck and led her over to the SUV. "We aren't staying here?"

"No, sweetheart. The place is wrecked. We'll go find a hotel or a one-week vacation rental. Preferably somewhere away from here. I think we could both use a break."

"Won't your President be angry you're leaving when there's work to be done?"

I shrugged. "Honestly, I doubt it. He'll understand my need to get you somewhere I feel is safe. You were taken, Lavender. I didn't know…" I clamped my lips shut. Not knowing if she was safe, if she'd been hurt, was agony. When I'd walked in and seen her stripped naked and that asshole with his dick out, it felt like I'd been sliced to the bone. I'd failed her.

She reached over and placed her hand on my thigh. "Take me somewhere then, Wire. Anywhere. As long as I'm with you, that's all that matters."

I nodded and pulled out of the driveway. As we cleared the compound, I turned left. If I'd gone right, it would have taken us back the way we'd come and I wanted to forget the last twelve hours or so. The sun had fallen and it was dark now, but the headlights cut through the murky country roads until the interstate was in front of us. I got on and headed east. It was after midnight when I stopped, but we definitely had a change of scenery.

I stopped out front of a beachfront cottage with a rental sign hanging on the side. Even though it was late and I'd probably piss someone off, I dialed the number and hoped the person would answer. This place was perfect for the rest Lavender needed. I cracked the window and could hear the ocean waves and smell the salty air.

"Do you have any idea what time it is?" a gruff man asked.

"I'm sorry, sir, but I'm stopped in front of your property that's for rent." I rattled off the address. "I know it's last minute and really late, but my wife…"

My throat tightened. I didn't want to share all the details, but I did tell the man I'd just found her after she'd been kidnapped and I thought she needed a vacation away from home and our family. I told him I'd pay whatever he wanted if we could have the place for a week. He not only agreed, and sounded much nicer after hearing about Lavender, but said he'd be over in ten minutes with the keys.

I hadn't planned this and didn't have a lot of money on me. I pulled out the few hundred in my wallet and hoped he'd take it with the promise to pay the rest of the amount in full, and in cash, after we'd gotten some sleep. I'd passed several banks along the way and could stop by an ATM once I knew Lavender was settled. She'd need a swimsuit, and so would I, since I fully intended for us to take advantage of the beach.

A Hummer pulled up next to me and a large man got out. He didn't look like the type you'd want to meet in a dark alley, but I was far from worried. I got out, checking to see if Lavender was still asleep. She was out. I eased the door shut and went to greet our temporary landlord.

I handed him the cash I'd had in my wallet. "I'll get the rest in the morning, but that's all I have on me."

He took the money, then handed me a key. "You've got it for the week. If your wife needs more time, just let me know. I don't have this place booked for the entire month right now. I'll hold off on accepting any rentals on it until I know for certain you'll be leaving in seven days."

"Thanks."

He eyed my cut. "That have anything to do with her kidnapping? You going to bring trouble here?"

"No, sir. The incident was due to someone from my past, and not club-related. A man I'd put in jail decided to get even when he was released."

He held out his hand to shake and I noticed the frog holding a trident on the inside of his wrist. Judging by his age, which I figured was early fifties, it seemed our landlord was retired and most likely an Ex-SEAL. My gaze lifted and held his.

"You need any help while you're here, you let me know," he said, then looked over at the SUV. His face went soft as he gazed at Lavender. "Got a girl about her age. My Maisy is too bookish for her own good, though. Probably won't ever make me a grandpa."

I waited for the comment about Lavender being too young for me, but it never came. The man got back into his vehicle and left with a slight wave. I unlocked the house, then went back to get our things. Once I'd checked the place out and turned on a few lights, I woke Lavender and lifted her into my arms. She nuzzled her face against me.

"Come on, sweetheart. Let's check out the house."

She blinked at me several times, then looked around. When she saw we were on the beach, she gasped and her eyes went wide. "Is that the ocean?"

"Yep."

"I've never seen it before."

"We can explore the beach all you like, but first you mentioned wanting a shower."

The light dimmed in her eyes and she nodded, making me feel like an ass for bringing it up. I should have let her be. I showed her the master bedroom and while she looked out the window at the beach, I unpacked our things. Our clothes went into the dresser, our shoes on the floor next to it, and I put our bathroom things next to the sink and in the shower.

I turned on the water, running it as hot as I thought she could stand it, then went to get Lavender. She let me undress her and nudge her under the spray. I removed my clothes and got in with her, pulling her into my arms and pressing kisses to her cheek, her neck, her shoulder.

She clung to me and that's when she finally let the tears fall. The sobs wracked her small frame and I held her as she let it all out. I ran my hand down her hair and murmured words of comfort. When she hiccupped and looked up at me, the heartbreak I saw in her eyes nearly took me to my knees.

"I'm so sorry. It's my fault, baby. He was after me and targeted you."

She shook her head. "It's no one's fault but his. He made that choice, not you. When you had him arrested, you did the right thing. That man was evil and twisted."

"I've never been scared of much, but when you were gone, when I saw what they'd done…" She reached up and placed her fingers over my lips. I kissed them and reached up to take her hand, holding onto it. "I love you, Lavender."

Her eyes teared up again but she smiled. "I love you too."

I winked. "I know. You told me when you were drunk."

Her mouth dropped open. "I did not!"

"Oh, yeah. You certainly did." I smiled at the outrage stamped on her face, then kissed her. "Best moment of my life, sweetheart."

I took my time washing her hair and her body, trying to ignore the fact my cock was hard as a fucking steel post. When her nipples hardened against my palms, I had to fight back a groan. I'd had no intention of making this about sex, thinking it was the last thing she would want or need. The way she pressed closer told me I'd been wrong.

"What do you need from me, baby?"

"I need you to touch me."

I pinched her nipple. "Already am."

She moaned and her eyes slid shut a moment. "I... I need..."

"You need what?"

Her eyes were unfocused, but she was looking up at me. "I need you to use me. Fuck me. Make me scream for you."

I took a small step back. "Lavender, this isn't you talking."

She reached out and grabbed my dick, her hand sliding up and down. "Remind me I'm yours, Wire."

"Club whores call me that. Not the woman I've claimed."

"If a club whore had you by the cock right now, would you be backing away?"

No. I wouldn't. I'd have bent her over, shoved my dick into her, and fucked her until I came. But Lavender wasn't a club whore, and she'd been through a trauma. She wasn't acting right, and I didn't like it. This wasn't my sweet, sassy woman.

I moved in closer again, reaching for her. I curved my arm around her waist, holding her still, as I used my other hand to part her thighs and stroke her pussy. Her body nearly went limp as I rubbed her clit. She was already slick and ready, but this wasn't about me. I didn't care if I came or not. I wanted to replace the horrors she'd recently faced with good memories, and me treating her like a whore wouldn't accomplish that.

I brought her to the edge twice before sliding my fingers into her tight channel. I pumped them in and out, feeling her pussy clench and unclench. She was close, so fucking close. I needed her to come.

"That's it, sweetheart. Give me that cream. Come for me, Lavender. Come right the fuck now!"

She cried out and her nails bit into my shoulders as she obeyed, giving me her release.

"Good girl. Such a good girl," I murmured, kissing her jaw and her neck. I kept working her pussy until the last of her aftershocks had stopped.

"That… I…" She stopped and licked her lips. "I need you to tell me what to do. I want to please you. Leven."

Her gaze held mine.

"On your knees," I told her. She sank onto the shower floor, her hands braced on my thighs. I shook my head and tapped her fingers. "Behind your back. No touching unless I say so."

She crossed her wrists at the small of her back, and I gripped a handful of her hair. Her lips parted and a flare of excitement lit her eyes.

"I'm going to feed you my cock, pretty girl, and you're going to take all of it. When I come, you swallow. Got it?"

"Yes, Leven."

"Open."

Her lips parted and I thrust inside. I used the grip I had on her hair to drag her down my length, not stopping until she'd taken every fucking inch. I fucked her mouth with long, slow strokes. She gagged a little once or twice, but I didn't stop. For whatever reason, she needed this, and I would give it to her. I pumped my hips faster, driving deeper until my balls drew up and I was spilling down her throat. She swallowed it all, then panted for breath when I pulled free.

"That's my baby," I murmured, rubbing my thumb across her lip.

I reached down and tugged on her nipples, making her cry and beg for more. I pinched and twisted the hard tips, loving the flush that covered her chest, up her neck, and settled in her cheeks. She panted and squirmed. I worked those hard tips until I could tell she was close to coming.

Sinking to my knees, I helped her stand, then lifted her.

"Legs over my shoulders, sweetheart. Open that pussy up for me."

She leaned against the shower wall as I positioned her right where I wanted her. Gripping her ass, I lifted her up so that my lips could devour her pussy. I nibbled at her clit before plunging my tongue inside her. I licked, sucked, nipped. My teeth scraped her bundle of nerves and she twisted in my grasp, making the sexiest sounds. No matter how much she pleaded, I didn't let her come. She was nearly in tears from frustration when I finally released her, positioning her on her knees.

I leaned over her back and bit down on her shoulder as I thrust deep and hard into her tight pussy. She felt like heaven! I couldn't hold back no matter how much I wanted to and I fucked her like a man possessed. I wrapped my arm around her waist, holding her still as I slammed into her again and again.

"Yes! Yes, please! Leven, I need it! Need you!"

I took her even harder.

"Yes!" she screamed. "Fuck me! Make me yours! Mark me!"

It was like every bit of control I had evaporated. I barely even remember biting her harder, fucking her deeper. I shot my cum into her, not stopping even after every last drop had drained from my balls. I released her waist and reached for one of her nipples, giving it a slight twist and pinch. Lavender screamed out again, coming so hard it felt like she might squeeze my dick off. More cum burst from me, leaving me shaken and wondering what the fuck had just happened.

"Damn, baby."

I withdrew from her pussy, or tried to. I only got so far before she slammed back against me, taking me deep again. Even though I'd come twice, I was still hard. I'd never had this kind of reaction to a woman before, but I felt addicted to her sweet pussy. It was like I was eighteen and could go again and again.

"What's come over you?" I asked, leaning down to kiss her shoulder where I'd left my teeth marks.

"I felt completely out of control of my life earlier," she said, her voice so soft I nearly didn't hear her over the water. "I hated it, hated feeling weak and helpless. I fought any way I could, and I tried not to give them power over me."

I ran my hand down her spine, trying to understand what she meant.

She turned her head and held my gaze. "I want to give you control, Leven. I'm yours, in every way possible. I needed you to take what you wanted from me, to show me who was in charge. I needed you to be in charge of your pleasure and mine, because it's safe to give that control to you. I know that you'll never hurt me."

I pulled free of her and turned her. Lavender lay on her back on the tiled shower floor, staring up at me with complete trust and love.

"Did they tie you up?" I asked, rubbing at the slight marks on her wrists.

She nodded.

If this was what she needed, I'd give it to her. I stood up and shut off the water, then helped her to her feet. I dried the both of us, then led her over to the bathroom counter, I bent her over and held her hands to the marbled top.

"Don't move, Lavender. Do you understand? If you move, you'll be punished."

Heat flared in her eyes and she nodded.

"Look in the mirror. Watch what I do to you."

I pressed against her ass, then reached around to cup her breasts. They were the perfect size, and I kneaded the soft mounds. Her eyes were dark with passion as I rubbed my roughened palms over her nipples. They were darker from the abuse they'd taken in the shower, but she seemed to love it. My sweet girl liked it at least a little bit rough. I tugged on the tips and she pressed her breasts closer to my hands, her back arching. Her hands slid a bit across the counter and I released her.

"Naughty girl. I told you not to move."

I stepped back and brought my hand down on her ass with a loud *crack*. A handprint was left on her right ass cheek and I decided to do the same to the left. I landed blow after blow, and watched as her pussy got so wet her thighs were getting shiny from her juices. I kicked her legs farther apart and the next swat landed on her pussy.

She gasped and tensed, then moaned. I spread her pussy lips and felt her swollen clit, then gave her another smack. Lavender cried out as she came, but the way she twisted and squirmed told me she still wanted more. She might have orgasmed, but it wasn't enough.

"Need you," she said. "Need your cock."

I smacked her again. "You get my dick when I say you can have it."

I turned her over and set her up on the counter, shoving her legs wide.

"Hold your pussy open."

Her hand shook as she reached between her legs and parted the lips of her pussy. I gathered her cream on my fingers and used it to stroke my cock. She couldn't sit still, her hips rocking and shifting as she watched me jack off. I coated her pussy with my cum, then used my fingers to smear it across her soft skin.

"Leven…"

"No, you were a bad girl. Only good girls can come on my cock. Only good girls get stuffed with my cum."

She whimpered.

"How are you going to make it up to me?" I asked.

"You could fuck my ass. You liked it before."

My cock twitched, already rising to the occasion yet again. Fucking hell. At this rate, I'd rub my dick raw.

I reached out and gripped her hair, pulling her head back. "Your ass is mine, isn't it? Just like your pussy and your mouth. All of you belongs to me, right?"

"Y-yes, Leven."

"Then I'll fuck your ass if I want to. Offer me something else."

Her eyes went soft and dreamy a moment. "A baby?"

Everything in me went still. She wanted a baby? *My* baby? Hell, yeah! I could get behind that idea. I leaned down and pressed my mouth to hers in a hard kiss.

"You want me to fuck a baby into you?" I asked.

"Yes. That's what I want. I want a family with you, Leven. A little girl or boy who is part of us. I want forever with you."

I loosened my hold on her and helped her off the counter. Gathering her gently in my arms, I kissed her the way I'd been dying to. I took my time tasting her, savoring the feel of her lips on mine. I poured every ounce of love I felt into that kiss.

"Come on, sweetheart. Let's head to bed and we'll work on that baby. We have all week. Maybe when we go home, I'll have knocked you up."

I spent the rest of the night, well into the daylight, making love to the only woman I could never live without. The next week passed too quickly, with lazy afternoons on the beach, and most of our days spent fucking anywhere and in any way that we could. By the time we left to return home, we'd both healed from the ordeal of her being kidnapped and nearly raped. Or as healed as we were going to get anytime soon.

Epilogue

Lavender
Two Months Later

I ran a hand over my stomach and smiled, wondering if Wire had even noticed the changes in my body. My breasts were larger than usual and my nipples were always super sensitive. It had been that way for weeks. When my period never came, I went to see Doctor Myron, and he confirmed my suspicions. I was pregnant. Doctor Myron had cautioned that it was still early in the pregnancy and to try to tone down my excitement. But since I was young and healthy, he didn't see a reason I wouldn't carry the baby to term.

Even more exciting, several of the clubs were coming today. Devil's Fury was here, and I hoped that meant I'd get to see Outlaw. The compound was back to normal. The fence was back up, the gate in working order, and the little damage the clubhouse had sustained was also repaired as well as new windows installed. It was a celebration of sorts. Even the damaged bikes from the blast were back up and running, and looking better than ever.

The sun nearly blinded me as I stood on the front stoop and waited for Wire. He'd gone to welcome everyone while I finished getting ready. I hadn't told him about the baby yet, but since I'd heard we were having a party today, I'd decided to wait and share the news with all our family and friends. It seemed like the right thing to do. After all the bad that had happened, everyone could use a bit of light in their lives.

Minutes passed and my feet started to ache. Still no sign of Wire. Something was wrong. I could feel it. Determined, I started walking in the direction of the clubhouse. Wire had sent some Prospects after my belongings, but my car hadn't fared so well. It seemed Cataclysm had done so much damage that it was deemed totaled. I hadn't seen the need for another one just yet, but soon I'd need a way to transport the baby.

Music poured from the clubhouse, so loud I could hear it through the closed doors. I frowned and looked around, seeing Ridley a few feet away with her arms crossed and fury stamped on her face.

"What's going on?"

"They're having a party without us. The kind we aren't welcome at," she snapped.

What type was that? I decided I would just find out on my own. I marched up the steps and shoved the door open, then nearly gagged on the cigarette smoke and... was that weed? Awesome. I covered my mouth and nose and went inside. The woman who had come to Wire's house that first day sauntered by in nothing but a pair of panties, and as I looked around, I saw several more scantily clad women, and a few who had ditched their clothes completely.

Wire was kicked back at a table near the bar, laughing as he drank a beer with Venom, Bull, and Flicker. Oh. Hell. No.

I didn't stop moving again until I was barely a foot from them, then I screamed for all I was worth.

"Are you fucking kidding me?"

Wire's eyes went wide and Venom stood so fast his chair fell over.

"What the fuck are you doing here?" Venom demanded. "I told Ridley no old ladies allowed in here."

My gaze zeroed in on Wire. "And you agree with this? That it's perfectly fine to sit here with whores spreading their legs all over the place?"

Wire just stared at me.

"Fine. You want it that way? I'll just find someone else to help me raise this baby."

I didn't give him time to even respond. I turned and stormed off, slamming the clubhouse door open as I stomped out onto the porch and down the stairs. Outlaw was coming up at the same time and I nearly plowed into him. He reached out to steady me and I got a good look at him. He'd shaved his beard off and scars marked his face, as well as the rest of him.

"Outlaw," I said softly. Then I hugged him tight. "I'm so glad you're okay."

He hugged me back. "I'm fine, but you seem to be in a right snit."

"Wire's an asshole. They're all fucking assholes."

"Fuck this shit," Ridley muttered as she marched past me and entered the clubhouse. Not two minutes later, all the naked women came running out, not even bothering to dress first. Venom followed behind them with a screaming Ridley tossed over his shoulder. The thunderous look on his face didn't bode well for her, but I figured she could handle herself.

When Wire stepped out, I ignored him.

"I didn't touch any of them," he said. "You know you're the only one I want."

Outlaw raised his eyebrows at me and I just shook my head. I didn't need his help with this one.

"Are you really pregnant?" Wire asked, coming so close I could feel the heat of his body.

"What the fuck do you care? You'd rather be in there drinking beer and staring at other women's tits than spending time with me. I thought it was a family party, that all of us were welcome."

Wire brushed my hair to the side and kissed my neck. I hated when he did that. It made my knees all weak and made my heart flutter.

"Love you, Lavender. And I didn't look at any of them. Why would I when I had the perfect woman at home?"

I turned on him them. "Exactly. If you have the perfect woman at home, why not leave when you saw that shit and come home to me?"

He just stared.

"Fine. Go back to your whores. I'm going home. And don't even think of getting into the same bed as me tonight. You probably caught something in there."

Outlaw chuckled as I stepped around him and started walking back to the house. It didn't take Wire but a moment to catch up to me, taking my hand and pulling me to a stop. I didn't want to look at him. I was so... hurt. How could he have wanted to be there with all those women wandering around without clothes? Was I not enough for him anymore?

The cell phone in my pocket rang and I pulled it out, seeing it was Ridley.

"Are you grounded?" I asked.

She snorted. "More like his dick will shrivel up and fall off because he won't get any if he goes all caveman like that again. He spanked me!"

I snickered because I knew damn well she'd liked it. I could hear it in her voice.

"Anyway, I called Darian, Isabella, and the others. We're meeting in town at the little Italian place. Isabella is going to ride with me, but the others haven't decided if they're taking their own cars. If the men are going to whore around, then we're going out to lunch. At the club's expense. Isabella snatched the card Torch uses for club business."

I heard Isabella muttering in the background.

"I didn't see Torch at the clubhouse," I said.

"He wasn't there," said Wire.

"Maybe not, but he knew what was happening," Ridley said. "And she's pissed as hell at him. So Torch is watching all the kids, with some help from Sarge who was the only other man not at the clubhouse other than Prospects. It's girl time!"

"Um. I'll need a ride."

Wire took the phone from me. "Ridley, she's pregnant. No drinking, and nothing dangerous. And you need to take protection with you." He slid his gaze over to me again. "In fact, I'm coming too. I'll sit elsewhere, but I'm keeping an eye on all of you."

He hung up the phone and gave it back.

"You don't get to do that," I said.

"What?"

"Act all concerned. You didn't care when you were in the clubhouse, didn't even give me another thought. Are they prettier than me?"

I hated that my voice sounded so small on that last part. I hadn't even meant to ask. Wire softened and pulled me into his arms.

"Baby, there is no one more beautiful than you. I'm sorry. I was an ass and should have left the second I saw what was going on. You're my one and only. I can't tell you how thrilled I am that we're having a kid together."

Two SUVs pulled to a stop next to us and Ridley rolled down one of the windows. "Get in."

I heard the pipes of several bikes and saw Venom, Bull, and several others coming to a stop behind the vehicles. It seemed the women had made their displeasure known, and I had a feeling quite a few Reapers would have blue balls tonight if they didn't do some groveling.

When I opened the SUV door and tried to get in, Wire stopped me, sliding in first, then drawing me down onto his lap.

"What are you doing?" I asked.

He shifted his hips and I felt the bulge of his hard cock press against me. My eyes went wide and I felt my cheeks get warm.

"Making sure you know you're the only one I want," he said.

"Awww," Mara said. "That's so sweet. But if you're going to hump her leg or piss on her to mark your territory, get out of the car first."

The women cracked up and my cheeks got even hotter. Wire winked at me and I hid my face against him. I couldn't stay mad at him. How could I? Just one look and he had me ready to rip off my clothes and offer myself to him. I was such a hussy. When we reached the restaurant, the ladies went off to a large set of tables that were pushed together for us. Before I could head in that direction, Wire dragged me toward the back, then shoved me into the women's restroom.

"What are you doing?" I asked.

He twisted the lock on the door and raised his eyebrows, then pointed at the counter.

"Drop your pants and bend over, baby girl. You disrespected me in front of my brothers and now you need to pay the price."

Oh, God! I squeezed my thighs together as my panties grew wet.

My fingers trembled as I unfastened my pants and shoved them down my hips, along with my panties. I leaned over the counter and pressed my hands to the surface, my gaze holding his in the mirror. My heart was racing as I thought about the amazing week we'd spent in Florida.

His hand came down on my ass several times, making the cheeks burn and sting, but I just got wetter. When he shoved his fingers inside my pussy, I nearly came, my eyes crossing from the pleasure. I heard his buckle and zipper, then his fingers were replaced with his cock. He set something on the counter and I tried not to freak over the fact he'd had lube in his pocket. Where the hell had it come from? We hadn't been home before coming here. Did he just walk around with that now?

"You're going to come on my cock, and then I'm going to fuck your ass."

My heart rate tripled. He'd bought me a few butt plugs and I'd been working my way up in the sizes, but I wasn't wearing one right now. As he drove his cock into me, he opened the lube and worked his fingers into my ass.

"Pull your shirt up," he said.

I gripped the hem with one hand and pulled it over my breasts. The way he stared at them in the mirror, I knew what he wanted. I popped the front clasp and let my breasts swing free. He lifted his hand off my hip and reached up to play with my nipple. It hardened to the point of pain as he tugged on it.

"Oh, God, Wire."

He pulled his fingers from my ass long enough to spank me twice more.

"Leven." I moaned. "Fuck me. Please."

He took me hard and fast until I was crying out my release. My pussy was still fluttering around his cock when he pulled free and pressed between my ass cheeks. He slowly sank into me, his fingers working my nipple even more. As he rode me, driving in deep and taking what he wanted, I knew I was seconds from coming again.

"Beg me, sweetheart."

"Please, Leven. I want your cum. Give it to me."

"Want my cum in your ass?" he asked, pounding into me.

"Yes! Yes!"

"Come for me, Lavender. Come now!"

I cried out again as I came, my ass squeezing his dick. He groaned and I felt the hot spurts of his cum. He pressed his chest to my back as he panted for breath, still playing with my nipple and cupping my breast.

"You're going to pull up your pants and go out there with my cum sliding out of you," he said. "Your panties will be drenched, but I want you to remember what happens when you're bad."

If this was my punishment, I'd do my best to be bad as often as possible. He stroked in and out of my ass a few more times, making me whine and want to ask for more. My hormones were already out of control and it was like I just wanted to come over and over. I was such a little whore when it came to him.

"What was that?" he asked, slipping free of my body.

"N-Nothing."

He turned me and lifted me onto the counter, and I knew what was coming. He jerked my pants and panties to my ankles, then shoved my knees apart so that my pussy was exposed to him. My clit pulsed as I watched him jack off, spraying me with his cum. It coated my clit and the lips of my pussy. As he rubbed it into me, brushing against my clit, I nearly came again.

"I don't think I'm all that hungry," I said, my eyes heavy as I tried to focus on him.

"Oh no, sweetheart. You'll go out there and have fun with your friends. Then when we get home, you'll get on your knees like a good girl and worship this cock."

"Leven." His name came out more like a sigh.

He stepped closer and kissed me hard and deep. "Love you, sweetheart. So fucking much."

He helped me off the counter and put my clothes back in order. Then he washed his cock and his hands at the sink before zipping his own pants. With a wink, he took my hand and led me out of the bathroom. A line of wide-eyed young women were waiting, one of them staring at my man.

"Can I be next?" she asked.

"Sorry, ladies. I'm a one-woman man."

I tried not to snicker at her crestfallen expression as he led me to the table, where Ridley and Isabella gave me knowing looks. I knew my cheeks had to be flaming hot as I settled at the table.

"I know that look," Darian said. "She's so far gone. Ass over teakettle in love."

I couldn't deny it.

"Good. Well, now that he's fucked you into submission, let's order some food," Ridley said.

I choked on the water I'd just sipped and the ladies burst out laughing. And so went the rest of lunch, with them taking shots at me for getting fucked in the bathroom, then telling me about all the times their men had done something similar over the years. I'd never felt so close to other women before, and for the first time in my life, I truly belonged somewhere.

Wire hadn't just saved my life, he'd *given* me life. I'd just been existing before now. Thanks to him, I had the love of an amazing man, and more family and friends than I knew what to do with. And a baby on the way… Life couldn't have been more perfect.

Well, unless there was a way to ban naked women at the clubhouse. I doubted that would ever happen, but with these ladies helping to lead the charge anything was possible.

Harley Wylde

Harley Wylde is the International Bestselling Author of the Dixie Reapers MC, Devil's Boneyard MC, and Hades Abyss MC series.

When Harley's writing, her motto is the hotter the better -- off the charts sex, commanding men, and the women who can't deny them. If you want men who talk dirty, are sexy as hell, and take what they want, then you've come to the right place. She doesn't shy away from the dangers and nastiness in the world, bringing those realities to the pages of her books, but always gives her characters a happily-ever-after and makes sure the bad guys get what they deserve.

The times Harley isn't writing, she's thinking up naughty things to do to her husband, drinking copious amounts of Starbucks, and reading. She loves to read and devours a book a day, sometimes more. She's also fond of TV shows and movies from the 1980s, as well as paranormal shows from the 1990s to today, even though she'd much rather be reading or writing.

Harley at Changeling: changelingpress.com/harley-wylde-a-196

Changeling Press E-Books

More Sci-Fi, Fantasy, Paranormal, and BDSM adventures available in e-book format for immediate download at ChangelingPress.com -- Werewolves, Vampires, Dragons, Shapeshifters and more -- Erotic Tales from the edge of your imagination.

What are E-Books?

E-books, or electronic books, are books designed to be read in digital format -- on your desktop or laptop computer, notebook, tablet, Smart Phone, or any electronic e-book reader.

Where can I get Changeling Press E-Books?

Changeling Press e-books are available at ChangelingPress.com, Amazon, Apple Books, Barnes & Noble, and Kobo/Walmart.

ChangelingPress.com

Printed in Great Britain
by Amazon